taking mine

rachel schneider

Shivaun,
Not all habits are bad...like buying books. RSchneider

Copyright © 2015 by Rachel Schneider
All Rights Reserved.

ISBN-13:978-1522950967
ISBN-10:1522950966

This book may not be reproduced, scanned or distributed in any printed or electronic form without permission from the author. Please do not participate in or encourage piracy of copyrighted materials in violation of the author's rights. All characters and storylines are the property of the author and your support and respect is appreciated. The characters and events portrayed in this book are fictitious. Any similarity to real persons, living or dead is coincidental and not intended by the author.

The following story contains mature themes, strong language and sexual situations. It is intended for adult readers.

Cover Design: Murphy Rae with Indie Solutions
www.murphyrae.net

Editor: Murphy Rae with Indie Solutions
www.murphyrae.net

Interior Formatting: Elaine York
Allusion Graphics, LLC/Publishing & Book Formatting
www.allusiongraphics.com

dedication

To Alicia, for forcing me to continue when I had doubt, and doing so through the toughest year of your existence. There's truly no one more selfless than you.

chapter 1

EVERYONE COMES TO A POINT in their life when, if desperate enough, scared enough, they'll do anything to protect the people they love. I'm not sure whether I've reached that point or if I've lived it my entire life. I've never known any different. It's easy to see the different. It's not so easy to be the different.

Thunder rumbles from a distance and a car honks a few blocks away. This side of the city doesn't get much traffic at this time of the morning. It's an unwritten understanding that if you're not from the west bank, you don't venture in unless the sun is out. During summer months the crime rate is surprisingly low. It's during winter when people start to get desperate. I suppose it's because the effort it takes to commit any sort of crime in this heat isn't damn worth it. The weight of my hair coats the back of my neck in sweat, and I pull it to the side, tucking it away in the process.

It's my lack of funds that has propelled me to such desperate measures. I received a letter from the university a few weeks ago stating my withdrawal from the P.B. Scholarship. My GPA slipped and I couldn't get it back up. I was warned the semester before that I would lose my entire funding. And I did.

I busted my ass for weeks, studying, pleading with professors, almost resorting to groveling to get extra credit. Some helped, but not all. I didn't have a really good excuse. Saying it's just too hard doesn't cut it. The thought of my brother, Kip, finding out makes my chest hurt. If I think about it too long, about how disappointed he'd be, all the air in my chest seems to work against me. Kip has worked his entire life to guarantee I could do or be whatever I want, putting himself on the back burner to do so.

I keep my eyes out for any car that may look like a real commodity. Most on this street wear more rust than actual paint, bordering along the lines of scrap metal, but when you're in as big of a bind as I am, you'll take what you can get. I haven't lifted a car in two years. I'm not proud of it. I'm lucky I've never gotten caught. Some close calls, but nothing ever came of them. But here, now, about to do what I vowed to my brother I'd never do again, my heart feels like it's imploding.

It takes me by surprise, the spark in my chest. I remember all the times I've chased this spark, pushed for it, looking for a trigger. Nothing I have ever tried has given me a thrill like taking something that isn't mine does. The feeling of getting away with it is enough to set me on a high for days. I haven't felt it in months, years, it feels like. Haven't felt much of anything lately. Hence my propensity to steal. Could be worse, I suppose. I could do drugs. Or men. I could do men.

Obviously I feel my heart beating, my chest expanding, the occasional rumble of my belly reminding me to eat. Stress is a common occurrence; school and money tend to do that to me. But the only thing that has instigated a reaction in me in a very long time is the thought of getting away with what I'm about to do. I'm disappointed, but it's easier to be mad at myself than ashamed, so that's what I do.

A distinctive rumble of an exhaust breaks me from my mood. A black Chevy Chevelle is pulling to a stop a few cars down. A robust man, twice the size of a small Fiat, unfolds from the driver's side. He's wearing name brand clothing and enough gold chains to feed a small third world country. The bag in his hand gives him away. He's a dealer. It makes what I'm about to do all the easier. I stay away from family vehicles or anything that puts a damper on my conscience. Drug dealers, on the other hand, have it coming for them. Karma and all.

I wait until the man disappears into one of the dilapidated townhomes. Dealers are tricky. They don't stay long. They're in and out as quickly as possible. I can't hesitate if this is the one.

rachel schneider

I move across the street quickly, my steps assured and posture relaxed, like I've got somewhere to go but nowhere to be. I don't look left or right, checking for witnesses. It only draws suspicion. It wouldn't matter much in this neighborhood regardless. Call time for police here is slow in the very unlikely event someone reports something. This neighborhood isn't a tattle-tale kind of place.

I slide the slim jim out of my waistband. The older model cars are easiest to pick, with a simple latch mechanism that pops up easily. The second I have the car door open and I slouch in, the smell hits me. I cough through a gag. What the actual fuck creates an odor so pungent? Did he eat straight methane gas this morning? Pushing past the urge to keel over and die from asphyxiation, I pop off the bottom of the steering column to find the wires to the ignition system.

I've been lifting cars since I was seventeen, and each and every time since the first, I recall Taylor teaching me how to distinguish wire colors. Kip has always refused to acknowledge that I picked up where he left off. Taylor, my brother's best friend and my personal grand-theft tutor, taught me everything I know. It's not that Kip doesn't know; it's just unspoken. It's hard for him to tell me I can't do something when it's the very same thing he did. Hypocrisy at its finest.

After a few failed starts, the car rumbles to life. I quickly tap the gas to keep the engine purring. The door the man disappeared into opens as I get the seat adjusted and window down. I take one good whiff of fresh air as I accelerate and give a two-finger salute to the bellowing man. A trail of obscenities follows me down the road before I hang a right onto the interstate.

Don't judge me.

THE GARAGE IS BUSY when I pull the Chevelle into the shop a little past one in the morning. Toby's Car and Auto is a run-of-the-mill auto shop: oil changes and tire rotations. But sometimes, half the time, it's a little iffy. A chop-shop.

taking mine

Taylor's dad died when Taylor turned eighteen, leaving Toby's to him. It never was a clean business, but Taylor and Kip banded together to venture as close to legit as possible. They've amassed a large clientele. A buyer will give an order for a certain amount of parts that they want, and we deliver. Mostly classic cars that are harder to find, sometimes a mass quantity of a certain brand. In the between time, we lift and break down automobiles and sell the parts on the black market. The sum of a vehicle is worth more in pieces than whole. It's how Taylor and Kip met.

They'd been lifting cars together since high school under Taylor's dad's watch, Todd Moore. He wasn't an honest man, per se, but he was a decent man in the eyes of the three of us. When Kip and I were struggling after our mom left, Todd took us under his wing. He didn't want to see us go into foster care, so he gave us what he could, taught us what he couldn't, and left us with backbone.

My ears ring after I cut the engine, the sound echoing off the metal walls. The shop doors open from both sides of the warehouse, giving access to the alley and the main street. Dan slides the overhead door down behind me.

"Lilly," he says, smiling down at me through the window. "You always preferred rust buckets."

I roll my eyes. "I take what I can get."

"Oh, yeah. I forgot about your moral compass. Still afraid to boost minivans?"

Dan's ribbing rolls off my shoulders. He acts like a hard-ass, but I remember when he returned a car after he found an infant car seat in the trunk. Becoming a father kind of does that to a man.

"Is yours still parked out back?"

He laughs and steps away from the door, letting me out. "Melanie took the kids to her mom's for the week. I'm stuck taking the bus."

"A carjacker who takes the bus to work. Comical. Is Taylor in?"

"In his office." Dan closes the driver door behind me and peeks his head in. I laugh when I hear him gag. "Jesus Christ, what the fuck is that smell?"

"Was your mom riding bitch?" Ethan asks, laughing as Dan covers his nose with the neck of his shirt.

Dan punches him in the shoulder and they tussle for a moment before returning to work, removing an engine from a Thunderbird. Totally a Dan steal.

There's a thin slice of light coming from the door to Taylor's office. The blinds are drawn over the window he uses to keep watch over productivity. I know he had to hear me enter, so I tap lightly on the door as I open it.

"Working late…" My words trail off as I scan his empty office. His usually tidy desk is littered with activity logs and inventory sheets. A few balls of scrunched up paper are tossed around the wastebasket next to the door.

"It looks like you're the one working late." A small shriek flies from my lips as I jump away from the voice behind me. Taylor's smirk gives away that he was trying to sneak up on me.

I slap the back of my hand against his chest. "Stop being a creeper."

"What about you? You're the one snooping in my office." He peaks through the blinds, looking into the shop. "I don't remember an order for a Chevelle."

"There's not one," I say, leaning against the glass partition. Taylor holds the keys in his fist as he awaits my explanation. "I was hoping you'd let me sell it."

"You're in need of some cash?"

There's no way in hell I'm telling him about my suspension from the scholarship program. Taylor has always been pretty good at keeping things between the two of us, but I'm not taking the slim chance he might tell Kip. "I need a new computer for school."

He walks around his desk. "Why didn't you tell me? You know I'll always help you out." His eyes rake over my face, trying to gauge my honesty.

"I know we haven't been getting in any large orders lately."

"Toby's is doing fine. We've got a couple of jobs lined up." He swivels slightly in his chair, still watching me.

taking mine

If Taylor decides not to sell the car, I'm royally screwed, in more ways than one. It leaves me being the one to ditch it, and that's always risky if there's a dispatch out. We eye each other over the length of his tiny office. Taylor's dirty-blond hair looks two-toned under the fluorescent lights. His Italian heritage reflects in his skin and eye color, both close to a honey-brown hue. His features are strong, giving him the all-American look.

"I don't have anyone here to dismantle it. Workers are going to be here in…" He eyes an imaginary watch on his wrist. "Six hours or so, and we can't have an undocumented vehicle sitting in the shop. What exactly were you hoping I'd do with it?"

"What about Dan and Ethan? It'll take them a couple hours, max three, to dismantle the Thunderbird."

He thinks for a moment and then taps his knuckles against the desk. "Tell you what, I'll break it down tonight, personally, but you're on inventory duty for the next month."

I scan the inventory logs heaped across his desk. "Something tells me this isn't much of a hardship on your end."

Taylor's smirk tells me that I'm right. "Come on, I haven't broken a car down in years. I'm drawing the short stick here."

"What if I help?"

"You can help by getting started on these check-in sheets." He picks up a stack of papers almost a foot high and drops them on the desk in front of me.

"I don't get an option, do I?"

"None," he says, standing. "I'll take care of the car for you tonight, given I get fifty percent of the profit for half the work."

"Fifty percent? No way. Thirty-five."

"Are you trying to negotiate dropping a car on me last minute? You're lucky I don't make you dump it."

I inwardly cringe. "I'll have to stay late at least twice a week to organize the mess in inventory. Work with me here."

He clicks his tongue as he thinks. "Forty percent and maybe next time you'll think about just coming to me for money when you need it."

"You had to add a little chastisement to harden the blow, didn't you?"

His shrug is halfhearted. "Kip would kick my ass otherwise. Speaking of which, I'm guessing you need me to cover for you tonight, too?" I give him a cheeky smile. "Thought so. Okay, fine. You start working on the stockroom tonight, so when Kip double-checks the time tomorrow you'll have a legit alibi."

Not really what I wanted to hear, considering I've got class in the morning, but I'll take what I can get. "Thanks, Taylor," I say, kissing him on the cheek as he leaves me with a mountain of paperwork.

I PLACE MY THIRD CUP of coffee on my desk and it knocks my phone to the floor. Too tired to pick it up, I leave it. A few students non-discreetly side-eye me.

"Making new friends on the first day of the semester, hmm?" Kaley picks up my phone and hands it to me.

"You know me, always the people person."

"Be careful, that glorious attitude of yours is going to ward off hopeful prospects."

The thought of any male coming within ten feet of me this morning pisses me off. I blame Taylor. "I can only hope."

"Come on, Lilly. It's the start of a new school year."

Kaley is the closest thing I could ever call a best friend, but days like today I want to duct tape her mouth shut. I swear she wakes up every morning with the sun shining out of her ass. She's too damn happy. I didn't get home until four and my earliest class is at eight. Three hours of sleep isn't conducive for me to pretend to like people. It's really not.

"This year is going to suck balls," I say, copying the important notes Professor Whitticker is highlighting on the syllabus.

"That doesn't really deviate from normal, but why is that?" she asks, lounging against her armrest, braiding her long brown hair. Some may think Kaley's the stereotypical rich girl from uptown with her high-end designer handbags—which she is—but she's also ridiculously smart. We met in high school and she still ceases to amaze me. She never takes notes, barely pays attention, and passes each class with ease. I, on the other hand, bust my ass for a couple of mediocre test scores.

"I'm on academic probation."

She uncrosses her legs and sits forward. "I'm sorry, it just sounded like you said academic probation."

"Since when do you have hearing problems? You can hear gossip four rows down while the slides play."

"Just because I hear you doesn't mean I'm listening. Now repeat that for me."

I finish off my note reminding me to bring back the syllabus signed next class period. God forbid I lose five points. No, seriously, I hope God forbids it.

"Technically I'm suspended from the scholarship program. I get zero moolah until I bring up my GPA."

"My ears are protesting as you speak."

"Tell your ears they need to take advice from your legs and open up."

"It's the same scenario. My legs don't open for just anyone they see." She recrosses her legs and smiles at the boy one row down.

I roll my eyes. "Does that include Knee-Slapper Tommy?"

She quits smiling and groans. "I can't escape the horror."

I tsk. "You should have known the same guy who sings show tunes as he—"

"Okay! Okay," she whisper-yells for me to stop. After a few moments of silence, Kaley leans into me. "I know a study group that gets together a few times a week. Might be able to help."

I hate study groups. They're equivalent to group assignments. Plus, with doing overtime to clean up inventory, I'm going to have zero time for anything else. "Maybe," I answer noncommittally.

I asked Kaley to tutor me one time and it was an epic fail. Kaley trying to explain anything is like trying to take directions from a drunk. They know what they're saying, but the other person trying to listen is confused as fuck. Only she makes sense to herself.

Professor Whitticker ends the class early. Even with enough caffeine in my system to send a rocket to the moon, I'm slow to pack up.

"Lunch," Kaley says, already leading the way.

"As long as they have more coffee."

We end up at the cafe right off campus. With free Wi-Fi and hours until midnight or later, it's a popular student destination.

As I sip my fourth cup of the day, I question whether or not I should have gotten that extra shot of espresso. "How many classes are you taking this semester?" I ask.

Kaley keeps eying the carrot top in the corner in cut-off jeans. I snap my fingers to direct her attention back to me.

She blinks. "I'm sorry, what?"

"Classes? How many are you taking?"

She ignores my question and muses, "Since when do hipsters think blue jean shorts work?"

"Jorts," our waitress chimes in, refilling our cups.

Sometimes I feel like the people around me are talking in a foreign language and failed to notify me.

A boy with bright blond hair and tall enough to touch the ceiling waltzes up to our table. Kaley's back is to him as he holds a finger up to his lips, signaling for me to keep my mouth shut. He places his hands on the back of her chair and tips it backward. Kaley screams, trying to grip the table in front of her. He catches her right as she's about to hit the ground.

"What the fuck, asshole?" Kaley yells, not bothering to suppress her outburst.

He laughs and eases her back upright. "Sounds like you're just as uptight as you were last semester."

I eye Kaley. The last word I'd use to describe her is uptight, and I'm confused as to why this boy seems familiar enough with her to think she is. He pulls the chair next to us and settles down, lounging with his legs spread apart.

"And you still have a problem with boundaries, I see." She smiles at him. "Lilly, this is Lance. He's in the study group I was telling you about."

He blows me a kiss. "Nice to meet you, Lilly."

"Charming," I say. "Can we go?"

Lance nods in approval as if he was the one I was speaking to. "This place in general gives me the creeps. I bet there's a checklist somewhere that says crazy, stalker ex-boyfriends must visit here on a regular basis. The free Internet is a major turn-on. Helps with the online stalking."

I look at Kaley. "You have enough crazy stalker ex-boyfriends to fill this place twice."

"You're right," she says, holding up a finger to signal our waitress.

Lance stays put, swinging his knees back and forth as he watches us pay our checks. I'm uneasy with how comfortable he is. In some ways, he reminds me of Kaley. She can feign casualness better than anyone I know. Except, Lance's isn't false. It's a real sense of familiarity he carries with him, and he watches Kaley with zero interest in hiding it.

"Catch you later?" Lance asks, standing with us.

"Unfortunately," Kaley says. "The group still meets at five?"

His smile grows as he shoves his hands in his pockets. "Finally going to hit up a study session this year, Kaley? Maybe you're more flexible than I thought."

"Um, no," she says, applying a layer of lip gloss. "But Lilly might."

"I never said that."

"You said maybe, still counts."

Lance rocks forward on his toes. "Hey, if you change your mind, we meet here Monday, Tuesday, and Thursday," he says.

Just for the sake of not arguing, I concede, "Okay, I'll think about it."

"Sure." He kicks a smile up on one side, winking at Kaley before approaching the drink counter. He leans on his forearms and smiles at the barista, making the girl blush as she takes his order.

Kaley smiles over at him, a touch of interest lingering. She catches me watching her and wipes the smirk off her face. I raise an eyebrow in return. She doesn't speak as I follow her out the door.

I'm crossing the threshold when the door slams back into me. My face hits the glass and my to-go cup of coffee trails down the front of my t-shirt and jeans. I can't decide whether I want to hold my nose or pull the shirt drenched in piping hot coffee away from my chest. I'm trying to do both when I feel two hands holding both of my shoulders, keeping me steady.

"Are you alright?" a deep voice asks from above me. I look up into deep eyes rimmed in the most perfect set of lashes I've ever seen. He releases me once I'm steady and runs a hand over his crew cut. "I'm so sorry. I wasn't watching where I was going."

My mind is too jumbled to process everything all at once. I can still feel the sting of coffee on my chest and my nose definitely hurts. Yet all I can focus on is how incredibly good looking he is. I can imagine the love drunk look cartoons get when struck by cupid. Or maybe I've been hit harder than I think and it's the tiny blue birds that circle when an anvil drops on a cartoon's head. That's what it is.

I run through all of this before I realize I've been standing in silence with my mouth hanging open. I snap it shut, giving him a tight-lipped smile. "I fucking hate two-way doors."

Yeah, that didn't sound deranged at all.

He cocks his head a little, looking at me sideways. "I didn't hit you too hard, did I?"

There's not one thing about him that can be pinpointed as to what makes him so attractive. His nose is slightly crooked and a scar runs through the top of his lip. Hit in the face by something, most likely. His five-o'clock shadow tells me he's a habitual shaver.

I shake off my adoration and attempt to talk like a normal human again. "What restaurant has swinging doors?"

"Yeah, all I know is they make decent coffee." His eyes scan my wardrobe. "Which you're wearing. Let me buy you another, make up for it?"

I briefly catch a glimpse of Kaley throwing me two thumbs up behind him. "Umm."

"Oh, I'm sorry. I'm Justin." He smiles, holding his hand out for me to shake.

I feel like my brain isn't wired to take in so much sensory input. Concentration on one thought at a time takes too much effort. Ignoring

Kaley, I shake my head and take Justin's hand. "Lilly. And I appreciate the offer, really, but I'm fine. I was pushing my caffeine intake for the day. I'll take it as a sign to rein it in."

Kaley begins jumping up and down behind him, silently reprimanding. Justin follows my gaze over his shoulder and Kaley stops, demurely tucking an imaginary hair behind her ear. "Kaley," she says, introducing herself. Justin gives a small head nod and looks back toward me.

"She's weird," I answer. Kaley flips me off and I tamp down the desire to smile.

A couple of students squeeze by us, pushing Justin and me aside to make room. "Okay," he says. "I guess I'll see you around."

"Sure."

He smiles when I don't make an effort to move. "Okay," he repeats. Turning around, he gives Kaley a short wave. "Nice to meet you, Kaley."

She hums a response around her straw.

"And you, Lilly," he says, passing by me to get through the door. His body hovers over mine as his arm braces the door open above my head, my back to the glass. He slowly lets it close behind him, never breaking eye contact.

"Hot damn," Kaley says once he's out of earshot.

I watch as Justin looks up at the order board and retrieves a wallet from his back pocket. He must feel my gaze on him because he looks back over his shoulder and a smile spreads across his face. It holds a hint of cockiness, just enough to let me know he *knows* I'm dumbstruck. He probably gets this all the time.

And someone is more than welcome to come shoot me in the face.

I force a smile back and can see his chest give with a hint of laughter. If I thought he was good looking before, I was mistaken. His smile when laughing changes everything. Hot damn was right. For once, Kaley's nonsense makes sense.

taking mine

I CUSS AS I DRIVE UP to the house. Kip's old Chevy pickup is parked out front, leaving the carport open for me. He's used this tactic since I first got my license. He'll leave the parking spot open for me so when he makes up a reason to leave later, he can pull in behind me when he returns, forever blocking my car in for the night. He thinks he's slick, but it's a joke. One that's getting really old. No doubt my overnight stay at the shop is his reason for using his signature trick.

He's sitting at the kitchen table when I deposit my books on the couch. "Hey, Lil. How'd school go today?" He eyes my coffee-stained apparel and I shrug. A beer and a pile of bills sit in front of him. I can't count how many times I've come home to this very same scenario.

"Same old, same old. How was work?"

"Steady. Taylor said he had you working on inventory last night?"

"Yup," I say, popping the top off another beer and switching out his empty one.

He sips it, grateful. "He's been struggling since the last shop guy left. Can't keep anything in order."

I take the seat across from him. "And what does he have you for?"

"I've been on the floor. We're changing six to eight air compressors a day, and that's on top of routine oil changes and tire rotations. It's just that time of the year again."

Kip wears a bandana around his forehead when he works on engines. Right now he has the red fabric pulled around his neck, the majority of his face and neck covered in grease except for the white patch of skin that was protected from the elements around his hairline.

"Plan on hiring another hand?"

"Can't find anyone qualified. You know how Taylor is, uses his dad's old tactics when hiring someone."

Meaning he interrogates them until they either leave or cry. Or they never show up for work. I've witnessed both.

I know it's a wasted effort, but I offer. "I could cover a few oil changes if need be."

"No," he says, pinching his lips together. "I'm still pissed at Taylor for making you work a full night before the first day of class. Focus on school, I'll take care of the shop."

"Taylor didn't make me work. I chose to. I wanted to try to knock out what I could before I got caught up in a mountain of homework. I have almost all the paperwork done. It's really only grunt work left."

Kip runs his hand through his shoulder-length hair. Our hair is the same shade of soft blond, but his turns darker when it dries in sweat. The strands fall back against his shoulders. "I've got a few more applicants to run through. I'm going to cut your hours as soon as we get someone in."

My eyes stray to the red words blazing from the papers in front of him. Final notices, late fees. Kip's spent his entire life taking care of me, and heck, sometimes Taylor, who tends to be a loose cannon sometimes. But he never complains, takes on the responsibility as if he was born to be second. Always second.

"How about I make chicken fajitas for dinner."

He looks up from the papers and gives me a grateful smile. "That sounds amazing. I'll just run to the store and pick up some groceries."

Of course he will.

I OVERSLEPT. If there's one thing Whitticker hates, it's his class being interrupted. He's notorious for kicking students out for being disruptive. I hastily redo my bun, tucking away stray tendrils that escaped during my mad dash across campus. I attempt to school my breathing as I open the door to the auditorium. Apparently, I misjudged the amount of strength it takes to open a fucking door. The metal ricochets off the concrete wall, effectively halting all activity.

Professor Whitticker stands with his marker poised to write on the board, eyes narrowed into thin slits in my direction. "Mrs..."

"Foster," I answer for him.

"Yes, you. Why are you late?"

The auditorium's silence descends on my nerves as everyone's eyes train on me. I open my mouth to lie, but I get the impression he's too good of a bullshitter to believe a dog-ate-my-homework story. Hoping he gives credit for honesty, I tell him the truth. "I forgot my syllabus. I had to run back home and grab it." This was in spite of Kaley's reminder text she sent me last night.

"All assignments are picked up within the first five minutes of class and you're bordering closer to ten. Your effort was futile." And then he chuckles. Fucking *chuckles*. As if my entire future isn't hanging by a thread, and he helped whittle it away a little bit more. "Take a seat so I can continue my class, Mrs. Foster."

I clench my teeth, looking to where Kaley and I sat last class period. In my seat sits the guy who was a row below us, the one who Kaley spent the entire time smiling at rather than taking notes. I narrow my eyes at her and she shoots me an apologetic look. Sighing, I avoid eye contact as I shift to the middle aisle, mumbling apologies the whole way down.

The entire class is silent, the only sound being Whitticker's dry erase marker squeaking across the board. I flop into my seat, my breathing barely starting to level out from sprinting. My embarrassment grows tenfold as I fumble to find a pencil. The farther I dig in my book sack, the more irritated I get.

A finger taps me on the shoulder and I angrily drop my backpack, giving up on doing anything productive for the day.

"What," I huff out.

"Need a pen?" The voice smoothes over my nerves enough to draw my attention to the person sitting next to me. My mouth falls open the moment I recognize the deep set of brown eyes.

"You're in this class?" My voice is a few octaves higher than I mean for it to be.

Both of his eyebrows shoot up. "You make me really question how hard I ran into you the other day."

"Sorry," I say, quieter. Gently, I take the pen from his outstretched hand. "It's been a rough morning."

"Can't be any worse than wearing coffee for the rest of the day."

I can't help but smile. This, in turn, makes him smile. "I'd rather wear coffee any day of the week than be put on Whitticker's shit list."

A shush from the front of the room pulls Justin and me apart. Professor Whitticker's angry eye is directly pinpointed on us, once again drawing the attention of the entire class. I cower slightly, wishing I could become invisible.

Justin tears off a piece of paper and passes it to me.

I'm bad luck.

His handwriting isn't too bad. Okay, it's bad. But it's legible enough for me to read. I look down at the torn paper and back to him. Passing notes back and forth in class makes me feel like we're in high school—the difference being no boys in high school would have been able to compete with him. What am I saying? Boys in college can't compete with him.

taking mine

I turn the paper over and scribble on the back.

You must be imaginary. I don't believe in luck.

His chuckle sends a pack of butterflies straight through my body—considering they have a lot of room to fly, banging off the walls and whatnot. I took Anatomy and Physiology my second semester of college, so logically I know there's not space for butterflies to even be—let alone fly—but that's what it feels like.

He rips off a larger piece and tosses it over.

I'm flattered you conjured me up. Am I everything you dreamed I'd be?

It's my turn to laugh, getting us into more trouble. This time, I care a little less.

I bet that's why people keep shushing me. Talking to myself and all.

His eyes dart to me and then around the room. He jots down one last note before standing up. I quickly read it.

Let's find out.

In the middle of Mr. Whitticker's lecture, in the middle of a sentence about how important lobbyists are to our democratic system, Justin reaches across his back and strips off his t-shirt. My gasp echoes along with those of the girls around us. His lean body mesmerizes me as he toes off his shoes. Whitticker still has his back to the class, unaware of the striptease of my life happening. Justin's sinewy arms begin undoing the fly of his pants when he catches me checking out the dimples right above his ass. His eyebrows sweep up as he drops trou, smirking when the girls surrounding us bust into giggles. A couple of guys give a few laughs.

He hooks his thumbs into the waistband of his boxer briefs and a catcall from the back of the room follows a round of whistles. I yelp, covering my eyes. He open-mouth laughs when he sees me peak between my fingers.

"Excuse me!" Professor Whitticker's booming voice reverberates around the entire room. "What do you think you're doing?"

The entire classroom flies into an uproar of laughter.

"Making sure I'm real, sir." The seriousness of Justin's answer doesn't deter Whitticker's wrath. But it does garner even more laughs, including mine.

"Get your stuff and get out of my classroom. Meet me after class."

Justin bends over and pulls his jeans back up. He winks, passing my desk and holding his t-shirt and shoes in one hand. "I think we can confirm that you didn't concoct me after all."

I raise my eyebrows. "Disappointed?"

"Are you?" he challenges back.

"Now, Mr. Townsend." Whitticker waits with a hand on his hip.

Justin leisurely strolls down the steps. With the lecture on pause, every student watches him walk out of the door. It's like everyone gets a reality check when the door snaps in place. A loud rush of whispers, accompanied by glances in my direction, immediately follows. My phone buzzes on the edge of my desk, one silent vibration after another. Kaley's name with an increasing number of text messages pop-up on the screen.

Mr. Whitticker calls the class back to order, threatening point deductions, and I quickly turn my phone on silent, shoving it under my notebook. I attempt to gather myself and focus on Whitticker's squeaking marker again, but nothing can wipe the smile off my face. I bite my lip, seriously trying to rein it in. I keep replaying every detail. The way he pulled his shirt over his head, his muscles stretching when—

A quick ruckus of sound snaps me from daydreaming. People are packing up—class is already over. I palm my cheeks, feeling the heat still radiating from them. The entire class period flew by without me taking one single note.

Kaley skips down the stairs, sliding into the seat next to me. "Oh my God! What was that?"

I shake my head, in my own state of disbelief. "I have no idea."

My face probably looks as flush as hers does. "Yes, you do. Tell me everything."

There's a few people lingering, trying to overhear our conversation. I saddle up my stuff and stand. "Let's get lunch and I'll fill you in."

taking mine

KALEY SWIRLS HER TEA AROUND and sniffs it. Deeming it worthy, she takes a sip. "Do you think he's in a lot of trouble?"

"Probably. Whitticker's one of those teachers that gets off on power trips."

"True," she says.

"Excuse me," a man passing behind Kaley says, forcing her to scoot up.

Kaley smiles up at him. "No problem at all."

Both of their smiles linger longer than they should.

I give her a disapproving look. "He's twice our age, Kaley."

"He's not that old."

We look over at him at the same time and he catches us staring. "He has gray hair and crow's feet."

She rolls her eyes. "It's just flirting. It's not like I'm going to fuck him in the bathroom."

I bite my tongue to keep from responding. I can't judge. She's got her vices and I've got mine.

I've wondered if I got lucky having no dad. Kaley has one, but he might as well be dead considering he's gone half the time. Her parents travel, I don't know what for. I'm not sure Kaley even knows why. But it's a whole new level of loneliness in a mansion with only fish as pets. At the very least, I've always known someone loves me—Kip.

"You could be leading him on," I say.

She shrugs like it's no new news to her.

"Leading who on?" a voice says behind me. I already know it's him. If I couldn't tell by his voice, Kaley's reaction would have given it away.

I carefully cool my features.

Justin pulls a chair up beside us and straddles it, folding his arms along the back.

Kaley jumps on the opportunity for a distraction and shifts the attention to him. "How much trouble are you in?"

"Withdrawal from the class," he says. "Not too bad."

"He flunked you?" I ask, astounding. "How is that not bad?"

"He could have had me expelled."

The waitress comes by again, refilling my coffee and taking Justin's order.

"What are you majoring in?" I ask, blowing into my cup, attempting to cool the scalding hot liquid.

After a moment of not receiving an answer, I look up to find Justin staring at my mouth. I don't catch on until I open it to take a sip and his eyes follow the movement. Pausing mid sip, I wait for his attention to shift back into focus. I can see him pull himself together, like gaining traction after slipping.

Kaley hides a smirk behind her cup.

"Um, English. And you?"

"Undecided."

Kaley taps out a response on her phone before shoving it into her purse. Justin and I watch her stand with her tea. "I've got to meet a friend about some Biology notes."

I start to stand with her. "Okay, let me get the check—"

"Stay," she says. "I'm probably going to be a while. I'll call you before we go out tonight."

She doesn't wait for a reply and saunters to the door, waving at the gray-haired man along the way.

"She's..." Justin trails off.

"She doesn't take Biology."

He looks at me questioningly.

"She's not meeting someone about Biology notes. Nor were we planning on going out tonight."

It dawns on him. "Oh," he draws out. "She's dropping hints."

"More like atomic bombs and trying to disguise them as balloons."

The waitress comes by again, handing Justin his coffee, her top few shirt buttons undone.

Classy.

taking mine

Justin waits for her to leave before picking up the conversation again. It's the first time I can take a leisurely drink of my coffee without feeling like he's watching my every move.

"Are you two close?" he asks, rolling his cup between his hands.

I shrug. "Depends on how you look at it. Closest thing either one of us has to a best friend."

He bends to take a cautious sip, and now it's my turn to be mesmerized by his mouth. My eyes trail the stubble along his face, down to his neck as he swallows. I have a quick image of running my lips over his Adam's apple.

I like to torture myself, apparently.

"So, where do you go when you go out?"

I smile. "Oh, I'm not going out."

"No?" he asks. "Why not?"

"I don't drink, I don't dance, and I have no interest in being hit on by guys who wear polos and drink cheap beer. It leaves a lot to the imagination."

He tilts his head to the side. It adds just the right amount of boyish charm to be cute. "What if I fight the guys off for you? I'll be your designated bodyguard for the night."

"You forgot about the drinking and dancing."

"I'll buy you endless non-alcoholic beverages, and dancing is optional—fun, but not mandatory."

"Look," I say, trying to let him down nicely. "You make a compelling argument, but I really can't. I need to get a jump-start on my schoolwork. No room for dilly-dallying this year."

"Dilly-dallying," he repeats.

I nod.

"Okay," he says, resigned. "Education is first priority."

I snort. "Says the guy who got kicked out of a class on the second day of the semester."

His smile grows. "But it was worth it."

"You have a thing for public nudity?"

"It looked like *you* did."

He's flirting with me. *Holy shit*. I'm not a blusher. In fact, I can't recall a single time I've been uncomfortable enough, but he oddly makes me self-conscious.

"I'm sorry," he says. "I didn't mean to embarrass you."

"You're worried about embarrassing me now." I laugh. "How about when you were stripping in class?"

He shakes his head, smiling at the table and then back at me. "I wasn't trying to draw the attention to you. I was trying to draw it away. You were worried about Professor Whitticker. I figured I'd eclipse your minor wrongdoing with a much bigger one. A much, much bigger one. He probably doesn't even remember you."

When he puts it that way… "Then I guess I should be thanking you."

His eyes crinkle at the corners when he smiles. He looks older. Not as drastic as Kaley's infatuation a few tables down, but like maybe he's seen some shit in his time that most haven't. The kind of look that accompanies soldiers coming home from war.

"How old are you?"

"Twenty-four," he answers, caught off guard by my question. "How old are you?"

"Twenty-two." For some reason, I don't want our conversation to end, and it's a tad unsettling.

"Tell you what," I say, standing.

He leans back, looking up at me. "What?"

"Blackjack's. Tonight."

"The shady bar on the west bank that biker gangs frequent?"

"They don't frequent," I say. "Just every now and then."

He drinks the rest of his coffee, setting the empty cup down with new determination. "Blackjack's it is. I'll make sure I'm packing."

"Don't be so dramatic. You'll live." I keep a straight face as I add, "Maybe."

He breathes out a laugh. "Looking forward to it."

taking mine

WHEN I GET HOME, I find Kaley occupying my bed, wearing nothing but her bra and underwear, lying belly down and flipping through a car magazine from my nightstand.

"It should be a testament to our friendship that I don't find this weirder than I do."

She jumps at the sound of my voice. "Don't do that to me," she breathes out, letting her body relax.

"You're the one half naked in my bed; technically, you shouldn't be doing this to me."

"I thought you were Kip again."

"Another testament," I lilt, plopping down next to her. Kip's seen Kaley naked more than anyone else in his life. Most likely, anyway.

"So, how'd it go?"

"We're going out tonight," I say.

"Shut up," she says, sitting up.

"To Blackjacks's."

Her excitement dissipates. "You are the lamest college student I know."

"Do you want to go or not?"

She kicks off the bed. "I'm going. This is the first time I've seen you take a liking to anyone since high school. I'm absolutely going."

"It's not like that. We're just hanging out, one time, as friends. Nothing more. Don't make this something it isn't."

"I'm not." Her smile tells me otherwise. "I'm making it what it is. The boy basically made a public declaration that he's into you. There's no way he wants to be just friends. Not unless it's the benefits kind."

"Kaley." I say her name in warning.

She gives me a devilish smile, backing toward my closet. "We're going to go out tonight and you're going to let Justin buy you a drink and give him the benefit of the doubt."

"Kaley," I repeat in the same tone.

"Here," she says, throwing me the sequined dress she bought me last Christmas.

"Nope," I say, tossing it back.

We do this a few more times before she gives in. "You're so stubborn."

"I'm consistent."

"You're going to dress like a hobo, aren't you?"

"You're going to dress like a whore, aren't you?"

I duck just as my car magazine flies past my head. "I'm approachable," she says.

"I don't want to be approachable."

"Couldn't tell," she deadpans.

A HEAVY WEIGHT SITS at the bottom of my stomach as we walk up to Blackjack's downtown. Kaley's heels echo, bouncing off the vacant buildings. The bar sits right on the edge of town, bordering the west and east banks. Blackjack's gets business from both sides, college students and working class, sometimes people of a darker nature. The warehouses surrounding the bar have been vacant for years. Wearing heels is equivalent to painting a flashing beacon on your back saying, *I'm over here, one set of footsteps, so I'm alone. Come and get me. Oh, and I can't run.*

The bar's front door is solid black. The only indication it's an open establishment is a small neon sign shaped like playing cards. Rock music thumps through my chest as we enter. Two men in security t-shirts check our IDs and usher us through. Considering it's a weeknight, the bar is decently packed, the dance floor occupied with people jumping around to the music.

We squeeze our way through the crowd, trying to get to the bar. Kaley takes the initiative, parting the crowd before her. Kaley dresses to the nines wherever she goes. It's not that she's wearing anything outlandish, but her clothes scream designer, expensive. We're an odd match, me in the skinnies I've had since high school and worn-out Chucks.

The bar is overrun with patrons, and the two female bartenders tend to gravitate only to the male customers. The petite bartender stops in front of us, looking over our heads to the person behind us. "I'll take two beers and whatever these two ladies want." An arm stretches out beside me, gripping the bar next to my hip. Trapped in, I swivel my head, following the arm back to its owner. Justin's eyes lock onto mine and my chest constricts.

In this lighting his eyes are cast in shadow, highlighting his cheekbones and jaw. There's something carnal about being so attracted to someone, something that makes me want to leap out of my skin because I can't handle what my body is telling me. And it's weirding me out how he keeps popping up everywhere.

"Lilly," Kaley shouts in my ear, snapping my gaze away from Justin. "What do you want to drink?"

"Soda is fine."

I pull a twenty from my back pocket, bumping into Justin behind me. I clench my teeth. I can acknowledge the fact that the back of my hand just grazed the front of his jeans or I can ignore it. I feel Justin's chuckle more than hear it. Shooting him a glare, I push a finger into his chest, trying to put distance between us.

"Where would you like for me to go?" He laughs.

The crowd has us blocked in and it gives no room for adjustment. People push past us, trying to escape with their drinks in hand, so Justin grips my hip, guiding me away from the traffic and putting himself even closer. I smell him and I'm sure he can smell me. His breaths fan my shoulder where my shirt stops. I don't know what prompts me to do it, but I look up to find him watching me. Or not me, but my neck. Self-consciously, I place a hand against my pulse point, blocking his view of my racing heart.

Kaley passes the drinks back to us, breaking us apart. Justin grips my drink along with his two beers in one hand, pulling me along with the other.

"I have a friend holding a pool table," he says over the music. I can't play pool. Granted, it's better than dancing, but asking would have been nice. Kaley shrugs her shoulders, skipping behind us.

The pool tables are nestled above the dance floor, on the opposite side of the band, and Justin takes the time to help Kaley up the few stairs in her heels.

"This is us," Justin says, pointing to the farthest table. I immediately recognize the tall blond-haired boy leaning against the railing.

"You sneaky bastard." Kaley points at him. "Did you know I was going to be here?"

Lance smirks. "Contrary to your beliefs, I have a life."

Justin looks between the two of them and then to me. "They know each other?"

"Apparently," I say.

"Do you know how to play?" Lance asks, a slight northern accent rolling off his tongue.

"Don't be condescending," she snarls.

He smirks.

Kaley pulls the cue stick from his hand. "I'll break first."

Lance holds up his hands in surrender. "Ladies first?"

"Teams? Boys versus girls?" Justin asks.

"No," I say. "Kaley and Lance and me and you."

Now it's my turn to be under the wrath of Kaley's glare. She wants to meddle in my business, I'll meddle in hers. And it's also what she gets for lying in my bed with no clothes on. Lance wastes zero time racking, also avoiding her.

I lean close to Justin. "I don't know how to play."

"It's alright, I'll help you."

Kaley breaks, scattering the table and dropping a stripe into a side pocket. She shoots Lance a look, eyebrow raised, challenging.

"Don't get too cocky. Beginner's luck. Statistically, breaking gives you the best odds to sink a ball."

taking mine

I can see Kaley's teeth clench from fifteen feet away. Something about Lance irks her in just the right way. I kind of love it. She makes another bank shot before missing and it's our turn. Justin scopes out the best position, aiming for a solid in a corner pocket. He makes the first shot, but misses the second. Would nice be too weird to describe his forearms? Because they are.

Justin and I laugh as Kaley prances around Lance, directing him on how to shoot. He bends over, lining up his shot, and she leans over him, using her hands to demonstrate the right angle. Lance looks up from his position, listening to Kaley drone on, and shakes his head. I now have a better understanding of why he thinks of her as a stick in the mud.

The bad thing about going last is that all of the easy shots are taken, leaving me with only complicated combination shots. Justin lets me scope out the table myself, figuring out which position I feel comfortable with. I see nothing I can successfully pull off. I give him a look, asking for guidance, and he shakes his head, motioning for me to shoot.

Feeling frustrated, I line up my cue stick and shoot. Not only do I fail, but I completely miss the cue ball. The cue stick slips from my grasp and scratches the felt on the table.

I look at Justin. "Don't laugh. You said you'd help."

He tries to tamp down his laughter, failing. "You're right," he says. "I just wanted to see what you could do first. Good news is you have a general idea where the ball needs to go and what you need to do to get it there. Bad news, you don't know how to hold a cue stick, let alone shoot straight."

"Well, it would be great if my partner would help me."

"Okay," Justin says, taking a sip of his beer and setting it on a stool. "Come here." He waves me toward him.

Timidly, I walk toward him, trying to deflect my nervousness. He takes the stick from my hands and turns me around so my back is facing him. "You're not holding the stick right. Here." He picks up my hand and leans it on the side of the table. "Create a bridge with your pointer finger and thumb." He positions my fingers for me. "Now hold it at hip level. You want it to be angled as close to horizontal as possible, so when you shoot, you don't miss its mark. Try."

I line the cue ball back in its original position and lean over. I have my cue stick ready to aim when Justin's hand clasps over mine. "Loosen your grip. You're not trying to stab the ball. Relax. Imagine you're trying to push the ball forward, not murder it."

Taking a deep breath, I line up my shot. On my exhale, I push the stick forward. The cue ball hits a solid with a clack, and the ball rolls to the side pocket and drops in...followed shortly by the cue ball.

"Scratch."

"But it was much better this time. You'll figure out the amount of force the more you play."

Lance and Kaley still beat us, but we hold our own for the greater part of the game. A couple of people wait on the outskirts of the table, vying to play the winner. Sweat runs down the nape of my neck and I hold my hair up, fanning myself. Justin shifts his head toward the exit and I nod. We escape into the back parking lot, the air balmy against my damp skin.

"Do you think they'll keep our spot?"

"Hard to say. Depends on Lance's sobriety." He pulls a cigarette pack from his pocket, slipping one between his lips.

"Didn't know you smoked."

He lights it, inhaling and exhaling, before answering me. "Bad habit, I know."

"Everyone has a vice, right?"

He eyes me over the ember and smoke. "What's yours?"

For a split second, I think of just saying, *I steal cars for a living.* Sometimes I get so tired of feeling like I have a deeply hidden secret the world would look down upon if they knew. There is only a handful of people in my life who know what I do, but they do the same thing, so I've never had an objective point of view. Is it a vice if it's not born of habit?

"Procrastination."

He smiles around his cigarette. "That's all you've got? You get lazy every once in a while?"

"When my scholarship is on the line, yes. It's kind of what I'm doing right now."

The sound of tires squealing pulls our attention to the far side of the lot. A dark 1969 Mustang is coming in sideways, kicking up bits of gravel and pelting the side of the building. The course rumble of the engine sets my hair on end. It's the year Ford introduced the Mach 1. It's a two-door Fastback, a classic pony muscle car through and through. Sleek in all the right places and just big enough to house a V8 with the perfect amount of torque to keep it on the ground. And it sounds original. Two men step out and it's very evident that they're from the east bank. It's the polos. Stupid designer polos.

"Nice car," I say as they pass.

The driver stops, giving me a once-over. "Gets me places."

"How much horsepower?"

"Enough to go fast," he says, smiling ear to ear. "Need a ride?"

Justin takes the last drag of his cigarette and flicks the butt on the ground, keeping his eyes trained on them behind me.

"Hey, bud. This your girl?"

I'm not his girl.

"She's not my girl," Justin says.

"In that case," the driver says, grabbing his junk. "I've got plenty of horsepower to give you a ride right here."

"Go fuck yourself."

Justin kicks off the wall and stands to his full height. It's a classic intimidation tactic, but I still take a second to admire it mid rage.

"You have ten seconds to go inside or get back in your car and leave."

"Oh, a badass," the driver says, stepping forward. "Playing hero tonight?"

I place my hand on Justin's arm, shaking my head. "He's looking for a fight. Don't give it to him." He doesn't say anything as he holds his ground, but I know he'll make a move if they do.

The driver smirks. "Are you sure she's not your girl? That leash around your neck seems a little tight." He feigns a choking noise while pulling at an imaginary collar around his throat.

I give credit where credit is due, and Justin's impulse control is extraordinary considering the tension rolling off of him. The driver, not satisfied with Justin's lack of response, takes a step closer, putting himself within reaching distance. Justin noticeably bristles at my side. I tighten my grip on his arm, my fingernails digging into it. He tears his eyes from them to me, and I try to relay my calm to him. It takes him a couple of deep breaths before I see the tension fade.

He nods.

I release him, and he lets me navigate him back toward the bar when the driver barks out a laugh behind us.

"There's no way the pussy is that good."

Justin stops mid step. Now this guy is really, really asking for it. Justin shrugs out of my grip and spins back around.

"Justin," I almost beg him.

It goes through one ear and out the other as he stalks forward. His face is carefully blank as he stops inches from the driver. "It takes a big man to spew the shit coming from your mouth. Want to say it to my face?"

I've never claimed to be particularly smart. I think it's pretty evident I'm not, especially as I wedge my way in between them, placing both my hands on Justin's chest, attempting to put distance between them.

"He's baiting you. I get you're trying to fight for my honor and all, really, but I honestly don't give a shit about anything that comes out of his mouth."

"Listen to your girl. I'm not interested in white trash, anyway."

I close my eyes, losing my own sense of calm. It's not the first time I've been called that. In fact, it was a common occurrence in high school. Private school can be a bitch. And then the dumbass pulls the last string holding me together—literally, the string hanging from my shirtsleeve—and I lose all sense of self-control. I see red. A loud hum fills my ears and I've already thrown the punch before I even realize

taking mine

what I'm doing. The sound of my fist hitting the driver in the face makes me sick. The driver bends over, hand over his nose while blood drips through his fingers, and I struggle to shake the pain from my hand. Justin stands over him, still assuming a defensive position.

"Is that what you wanted?" Justin seethes through his teeth.

The driver laughs, wiping his blood-covered hands on his jeans. "Got to admit, you've got a good throw for a bitch."

"That's enough," I say, outright pulling Justin with all my might. "You made your point. Let's go."

He doesn't budge, and I smack him on his shoulder with as much force as I can. This breaks his façade and a small smirk forms at the corner of his lips. He thinks this is funny.

"Don't fucking smile at me."

"I'm not," he says, outright smiling.

I fight the urge to smile back, infuriated that I'm persuaded by his. "You're an asshole."

"Uh, oh." The driver smiles. "Lover's quarrel."

"Shut the fuck up before I show you what a hit to the face really feels like." Justin snaps at him.

This, out of everything that just happened, seems to stop the driver from continuing to provoke Justin, laughing as he and his friend enter the building.

I'm confused, I'm flustered, and I'm generally pissed off.

Growling, I spin away from Justin and march inside. I know he's following and I can practically feel his grin the entire way.

Kaley and Lance are sitting on a couple of stools, out of the way of the pool tables. Judging by the amount of shot glasses lining their table, they're well past the point of tipsy. Lance wraps an arm around her waist as she flies off the stool in our direction.

"Lilly," she draws, arms raised high above her head. "Where'd you go?"

I look at Lance. "We were barely gone for fifteen minutes. What happened?"

Kaley uses her fingers to shoot an imaginary gun at me, then Justin, laughing when he pretends to be wounded.

"We may or may not have wagered a minor drinking game with our table."

"Minor? She can barely stand." I sniff one of the glasses. "Did you give her tequila?"

Lance's face sobers. "Why? She's not allergic, is she?"

"Let's go. We're lucky she still has clothes on."

Kaley throws an arm around my shoulder, causing both of us to lose balance. "We own,"

she slurs.

Lance shakes his head. "She only had two shots. I took the brunt of the work. I swear I'd never have let her get this wasted if I had known." He replaces me, better competent to withstand her weight.

"She can't do tequila. It does something to her."

Once we're outside, Justin asks us where we parked and I point in the direction. Lance does his best to shuffle Kaley along. She's now silent, on the verge of passing out. He gets tired of her feet dragging and cradles her. There's a throb in my hand, and I clench my fist to try to relieve it. I'm focused on the sound of our feet shuffling when I hear Justin huff out a breath. I look and find him staring at my fist, smiling. He sees me and immediately straightens his features.

"Can you explain to me what the actual fuck is funny about you getting into a fight?"

Lance looks over his shoulder. "You got into a fight?"

Justin rolls his neck and side-eyes me. "Not me," he says. "Lilly did. Although, it was more like doing someone a favor. He wanted it."

"I didn't have to give in," I say.

"He wanted it, Lilly. Probably some form of self-punishment or some shit."

"And what does that say about me? Willing to be the person to dole it out?" I can't meet his eyes when I say it, feeling slightly disappointed in myself. He doesn't respond.

taking mine

I direct Lance to a stop when we reach Kaley's BMW, and she's sound asleep in his arms. I attempt to dig through her pockets, looking for the keys. Lance shifts her around, trying to help while keeping a good grip on her. I check all of her pockets twice before I conclude that they're missing. Somewhere between doing tequila shots and shooting pool, they must have slipped out.

"I'll run back and see if I can find them or if someone turned them in," Justin says.

People don't turn in lost items around here. If it's gone, it's gone, and it's not coming back. I wouldn't be surprised if someone swiped them right out of her pocket, hoping she'd ditch her nice sports car here for the night. But I let Justin go anyway. He seems to like playing the hero card. When he returns empty handed, I'm not surprised in the least.

"It's okay," I say more to myself. "Can you just give us a ride?"

"What about her car?" Lance and Justin both look around at the state of the neighborhood and abandoned buildings.

"I'll call a tow."

Lance sidles up against the car, trying to find a comfortable spot with dead weight in his arms. Justin jogs off in the direction of where he parked as I dial the first person I can think of.

"Lilly, do you know what time it is?" Dan's voice crackles through the speaker, barely a whisper.

"I'm sorry. I know it's late and you've got work in the morning, but I need a tow."

"Is everything okay? Did you get in a wreck?"

"No, no," I hurry to reassure him. "It's Kaley's car. She lost her keys and it's parked by Blackjack's."

He says my name and I can tell he really wants to say no. He's silent on the other end of the phone as I casually rethink the probability of something happening between now and morning. I'm scanning my vicinity when the '69 Mustang catches my eye. It's parked illegally. It's as if the universe is telling me to steal it. Really, the douche bag is asking for it. I double-check that Lance isn't in hearing distance when I reply.

"What if I tell you there's a Mustang Fastback sitting behind the bar?

This catches his attention. "What year?"

"Your favorite. And it's the original engine."

He cusses before responding. "No way. No one would be stupid enough to bring a car like that to the west bank."

"Well," I say. "You'd have to meet the owner to believe it."

"I almost hate having to dismantle something like that," he says, sighing. "I'd have to call Ethan in to help."

"Is that a yes?"

"Yeah, I'll be there in a few."

"I'm getting a ride home with a friend. Drop Kaley's car off in the employee parking lot at the shop."

We hang up right as Justin pulls up in a brand new Jeep Wrangler. Justin hops out and folds his driver seat forward.

"This is going to be fun," Lance says, looking at the small space he needs to fit Kaley through.

"Give me her feet," I say, climbing into the back.

Justin helps Lance, passing her feet through the door. One of her heels nearly pokes me in the eye, so he pulls off her shoes and drops them on the floorboard. Lance bumps his head trying to gently lay her down across the back seat with her feet in my lap.

"Alrighty," he says, feeling accomplished once she's in unharmed.

"Where to," Justin asks, cranking the engine and looking at me in the rearview mirror.

In all honesty, I barely know Justin or Lance. Giving them directions to where either of us lives doesn't sound like a wise idea. I'm tempted to tell him to drop us off at Toby's, but I look down at Kaley's sleeping head nestled against the door and decide against it.

"I suppose my house is closest."

I live on the outskirts of the city, close to the west bank, but it's still considered to be more rural development. Our neighborhood is scattered with nice refurbished homes, and the working class who can barely maintain the color of their shutters. Kip and I fall somewhere in the between. Our house is a small brick home with one bathroom that's a bitch to share.

The lights are on when we pull up. I cuss.

"What's wrong?" Justin asks.

"My brother's awake."

He and Lance trade glances.

"He's protective. I don't bring boys home."

Together they help me extract Kaley with as much grace as possible. I catch our door, holding it for Lance as he carries Kaley into the living room. "Just put her on the couch."

He lays her down, cradling her head as he deposits her. I position her feet on the edge and cover her with a blanket. She jerks away from my touch, sitting up so fast it scares Justin and me back a step.

She leans to the side, hands wrapped around the hem of her shirt. "I'm so hot," she says, already working the material over her head.

"Hold up," I say, straightening her body.

"We should probably get her some water," Lance suggests.

"Good idea. Glasses are in the cabinet next to the fridge." I throw him a nod in the direction of the kitchen.

I glance down the hall—Kip's bedroom light is off. He may have left the lights on for me.

"Whoa!" Justin closes his eyes, turning away from Kaley's direction.

I turn and find her standing—in nothing but her underwear. Only a strip of cloth covers her bottom.

"I feel so much better," she says, stretching her arms over her head.

It's this most opportune moment that I hear Kip come in through the kitchen door and find Lance pouring a glass of water.

"Who the fuck are you?" I hear Kip say.

"He's with me," I yell from the living room. "He's a friend."

I wrap Kaley in the blanket and usher her down the hall and into my bedroom. She throws herself belly-first onto the bed and passes out immediately. Thankful I don't have to attend to her, and I hurry back to the front of the house. Kip's face is blazing red, trained on Justin and Lance standing in the living room. Lance has a glass of water in one hand and a bottle of Tylenol in the other.

"Who are they?" Kip demands.

"Lance," I say, taking the items from his hands and setting them on the coffee table. "And Justin." I stand between them. "They're friends from school."

"Since when do friends from school come home with you in the middle of the night?"

I bristle at his tone, hating that he has the nerve to Dad-mode me in front of them. "Since Kaley got shit-faced at the bar, lost her keys, and we needed a ride home."

In proud Lance fashion, he has the ability to act like Kip's not practically foaming at the mouth in front of him. "Let me introduce myself," Lance says, taking a step forward. "I'm Lance and this is my best pal, Justin."

Justin follows through and says, "I assure you our intentions are pure, only wanting to make sure Kaley and Lilly made it home okay. Nothing more."

Kip looks to me and I raise my eyebrows in response. *Yes, you're a total asshole.* "I'll walk you out," I say, already opening the front door.

"Nice to meet you," Lance says.

Justin nods, smart enough not to push Kip too far.

"I'm sorry," I say when we reach Justin's jeep.

"Seems like a nice guy," Justin says.

Lance smiles. "No worries. Got out unscathed. Mission accomplished."

"Thanks so much for helping. I don't know what I would have done without you two."

"We take payment in beer, kisses, or anything of monetary value. We'll send you our bill." Lance blows me the same kiss he did when we first met, and I laugh.

"I'll be sure Kaley gets it. I'm all paid up on my best friend duties."

taking mine

"See you at lunch on Friday?" Justin leans his forearm against the steering wheel. "The cafe?"

"Sure," I say.

"Let's roll," Lance says, banging the roof of the Jeep. "I have a date with some ice cream and Netflix."

They leave and I'm left standing on the sidewalk, dumbfounded by the night's events. Seemingly out of nowhere, I've found that I've gained two new friends, one of whom I'm absurdly attracted to. It irritates me that I'm so mesmerized by him, especially because tonight he proved he's got as much of a temper as any other hot head out there. It was in my honor, but still.

chapter 4

TAYLOR MOTIONS FOR ME to enter his office, now back to its immaculate state, thanks to moi. He's more subdued than normal, only giving me a tentative smile as I sit across from him. I assumed he called me in for the money we made on the Cheville, but it's not looking promising.

"What's up?" I ask.

"Dan gave you a tow last night?"

"He did."

"He said you're the one who tipped him off on the Mustang."

"I did."

"It didn't occur to you that someone who drives a car like that into the west bank is up to no good?"

"I—"

"He works for Jimmy," Taylor says, cutting me off.

Oh shit.

"Jimmy? The guy we did some up class orders for a couple of years ago?"

"Yeah, the kid Dan lifted the car from works for him. I got a call this morning asking why we were attempting to sell one of his worker's cars back to him in parts."

A pinch of fear shoots through my chest. "What are we going to do?"

He leans forward and steeples his chin on top of his hands. "I managed to talk him out of retaliating."

He doesn't have to elaborate on what exactly retaliation would be for me to understand that it's not good. Kip and Taylor both have protected me from the harsher reality of the life we live. Don't get me wrong, I get the gist of it, but I'm not consumed by fear, and it's probably because I've never had to deal with the logistics.

"With conditions," Taylor continues. "He wants the car replaced. Whether we put it back together or buy a new one, it has to be replaced."

"Fantastic," I add dryly.

The thing about putting a car back together is it's just not feasible. It's possible, but it takes a lot more time and effort than it does to take it apart. Then you run the risk of not getting something quite right. Something will tick a little differently than before. Essentially, an engine could run forever if the parts are replaced periodically, but it's not that simple.

"Considering it'll be easier to sell the parts and buy a new one, we'll still come out ahead, so he wants the profit."

"That's not that bad."

Taylor sits forward quickly, placing both palms face down on the desk. "I don't think you quite understand the missile we dodged. Jimmy is fair, but even I'd unleash hell if someone did that to one of my employees. Imagine if someone did that to you, Lilly."

That's irrelevant because Kip makes me drive a piece of shit Honda, but I don't voice this. "You act like I knew the asshole worked for him. I figured he was another rich kid wanting to redeem his badass card and start a fight."

"You can't commission Dan to lift a car for you because you're pissed off at somebody, Lilly. That's not how this works."

I roll my eyes. "Because that exceeds our moral standards, but doing it for money doesn't?"

His eyes harden. He takes measured breaths before responding. "You might want to reevaluate your own morals the next time you need money for a *computer*." He spits out the last word, knowing my excuse is a farce. "Or better yet, I'll let Kip know you've resorted to old habits for kicks."

We have a stare-off, neither one of us speaking. My teeth are clenched as tight as his are, mine from sheer will to keep my mouth shut. He slowly eases the tension from his jaw and sits back. I mirror his body language and cross my arms. He digs in his desk drawer, retrieving a white envelope and setting it on his desk. It's familiar, much like the ones I used to receive on a regular basis.

"This is for the Chevelle. It didn't get much."

The excitement that had blossomed in my chest deflates. I unfold the envelope and flip through the twenties. It's enough for a down payment at the bursar's office. That's the important part—buying time.

I'm getting up to leave when Taylor says my name, stopping me. "I only took twenty-five," he says, his voice softer than before.

"Thank you."

"Do I need to be anticipating another late-night drop-off?"

I'm still hesitant to tell him, especially with frustration still simmering inside him, but I need at least two more sells to pay for this semester alone. Depending on how the meeting with my advisor goes, maybe for the rest of the year. So I need him to be on my side.

"Yeah."

He nods like he already knew my answer. "Can you give me a heads up so I can have the shop ready?"

"Sure."

He nods one last time, dismissing me.

I flip through my money again, cussing under my breath. Dan passes by, snatching the only hundreds from the stash.

"Hey," I call after him.

He turns, walking backward. "Next time you call me away from my family in the middle of the night for no reason, do your research. This is for the tow."

I PUSH THE REMAINDER of my books to the side, making room as the waitress drops off my turkey panini and coffee. I'm at the cafe. It's Friday and it's lunchtime. I agonized over whether or not to show up. Showing up would mean I care. I don't want to care. So I figured

I would do homework, at the cafe, during lunch. And if he shows, he shows. I mean, it was his suggestion. If not, I'm doing homework. Win, win. Bonus, the high-back booths are optimum study spots.

I'm shoving half a sandwich in my mouth at the exact moment he shows up, and I'm positive it's another way the universe is screwing me.

Justin taps his chin, indicating I have something there. His smile grows as I wipe off a long string of Parmesan cheese.

"Whatcha studying?" he asks, sliding in across from me.

"Quantum Physics."

He squints at the binder of my book. "Looks an awful lot like Criminal Studies."

"Close enough."

"Criminal Studies. Political Science. I thought you were undecided."

"I am."

"That's funny, because those courses are usually reserved for students interested in political science or law."

I take another bite of my sandwich, smaller this time, and hopefully more gracefully. I shrug. "I thought I was going to apply for law school. Not anymore. I had already reserved the courses. Whitticker has a two-year wait list on his class, so I felt like I shouldn't drop it."

"Was?" he asks, confused. "Not anymore?"

"Losing academic favor doesn't look very good on an application. That's beside the fact my GPA has fallen below a three-point-eight, which is almost unheard of to be accepted with. The time and money it would take to bring it up pushes me past the five-year extent law schools like to see students have their undergraduate completed by. Long story short, I made a plan B."

He raises his eyebrows. "Ready to hear it."

I pause. "I'm working on it."

He stands, reaching over the table and pulling my backpack into his lap. "Philosophy and Human Rights. Looks like there isn't a plan B, only A."

"Like I said, my classes were already scheduled."

He digs through my bag, making me self-conscious. He picks up little scraps of paper I've written reminder notes on, only to never look at them again once they reached the endless pit that is my backpack. He finishes his perusal and stuffs everything back in.

"With the classes you're taking, with the credits, you could bring up your GPA two or three points by next semester."

He makes it sound easy. "I could, but I won't."

"Why not?"

There are plenty of things in my life that should make me feel ashamed that I won't. As a matter of fact, there are a lot of things I've been kind of unrepentant about. But right now, sitting in front of Justin with him watching me so intently, I'm embarrassed to say I'm struggling. I'm struggling so hard. I've always been a straight-A student through high school and the start of college. If there's one thing Kip did not waver on, it was my education. He paid for the best, drilling me with note cards and studying way into the night with me. It's the one thing I felt pride in, that I made him proud, too.

Somehow Justin can sense all of my frustrations without me voicing them. "Hey," he says slowly, brows cinched. "What's wrong?"

I run my hands over my hair, pulling my ponytail back and trying to gather my emotions. "It's the second week of school and I already feel swamped."

Justin relaxes a little, partly relieved that I'm not going to break down right in front of him. "What do you need help with? If I can help, I will. And Lance is pre-law. I bet his study group might help."

I laugh. "That damn study group. Since when is Lance pre-law? I can't see him being a lawyer."

"He swears there's a million strippers who are ready to file a sexual harassment suit somewhere."

"That actually makes sense."

"So, will you think about it?" After a moment of silence from me, he says, "Don't think of it as a study group. Think of it as a group of people who study…together."

"Oh, thanks for the wonderful insight. Since you put it that way…"

taking mine

At this point, what can it hurt?

Justin's looking at me with such sincerity that I want to turn away. His brown eyes are so dark. Depending on the shadows, his pupils almost bleed into his irises. It reminds me of the deepest parts of the oceans, the dark pools of water where no one really knows what's waiting at the bottom. It's alluring. And just like those deep pools, I'll probably never know what's in them.

The stubble on his cheeks is a little bit longer today, possibly due to a missed day of shaving. It only accentuates the definition along his neck. He swallows, and I watch his throat bob with the motion. He clears his throat and I snap my eyes back to his. There's an intensity in them that floors me. I suck in air, trying to ground my senses. The only thing I can focus on is the look in his eyes. It's like he wants to reach over the table and kiss me. Self-consciously, I bite the inside of my bottom lip. His eyes move from my eyes to my mouth and back again. And yet, at the same time, it looks like he's uncomfortable.

Justin runs his thumb over his bottom lip, at a loss for words. I haven't seen this Justin before. I've watched him strip in front of hundreds of students, I've watched him stand his ground and punch someone in the face, and I've watched him hold his own in front of my brother, but I haven't seen cautiousness in him until now. And damn it all to hell it if it doesn't intrigue me more.

SO WHEN I FIND MYSELF sitting in one of the café's bright orange armchairs at nine at night, unable to study because of the person sitting next to me, I blame no one but him. I'm beyond fucking irritable. I've watched him bite the stupid cap on his pen for the past hour straight, and the only thing I can tell you about Criminal Justice is that it's not flipping fair how he is so casually good looking.

Study group, they said. *It'll be good for you*, they said. This is not good for me. If anything, this is very, very bad for me.

Want to know what the weirdest part of my attraction is? We're going to call it an attraction even though at this point it's bordering along the lines of something else—my desire to yank that pen out of his mouth and stab him in the eye with it. My reaction to him is uncontrollable, and it drives me to want to do something about it, but I don't know what. I'm mad at him for making me like him, even though it's not really his fault.

Twisted, I know.

Lance has spent the past two hours on his phone, randomly smiling at a text here and there. The only people actually doing anything productive are Courtney and Blake sitting across from me. They're both Psychology majors, so they've been trading notes all night. Justin shifts in his chair, pulling the pen out of his mouth to jot something down in the margin of his textbook. I look down at the chapter in front of me and let out a deep breath. I am so screwed.

"Ha!" Lance rapidly sits forward, eyes glued to his phone.

"What?" Courtney asks, derision in her voice. She handles Lance about as well as Kaley does.

"Ashley is mocking up pop quizzes for Whitticker. She thinks it's going to be distributed on Monday."

Blake drops his pen into the binder of his notebook and Courtney mumbles something akin to a curse on Whitticker's children. I, on the other hand, am absolutely baffled as to who Ashley is.

"Lance has been dating Whitticker's student teacher," Justin says. "This is why study group is important."

If someone had told me straight that study group is code for insider knowledge on pop quizzes, I wouldn't have protested so much. Knowing the day a pop quiz is going to land on my desk is a catch twenty-two, though. I can walk into class knowing I'm not going to be ambushed, great, but I also have no idea what to study. We cover a chapter a day, and since our first quiz, we've covered two more. A new anxiety takes root in my chest.

"I'll finish today's chapter and draw up a mock test. Basics and key points. I'll email them to everyone tomorrow," Blake says.

taking mine

"I don't want to put more work on you," Courtney says.

"I'm already going to do it for myself so I might as well share," he says. "And I think it might help Lilly, who looks like she's about to pass out."

I don't argue a good point because I do feel a little light-headed. "I don't see why Lance can't con his way into grabbing the answer key," I say.

Blake smirks. "The answer key isn't in Ashley's pants. That's why."

"Isn't he in her pants for academic purposes?"

He gives me a condescending look. "He's a guy. He's in her pants because he wants to be."

"I feel like that's not a wise use of time."

Justin smiles, amused. "You don't think sex is a wise use of time?"

I can feel the heat crawling up my neck and into my cheeks. This is the second time he's made me blush, and I hate it even more than the first time. I fumble for words. "No, I mean, yes." I pause, taking in a breath. "What I meant to say is that if I had the opportunity to squeeze some test answers out of Ashley's pants, I'd do it."

Blake smiles. "Girl-on-girl action."

I barely get a chance to roll my eyes before Lance chimes in. "Trust me when I say nothing else is going to fit inside Ashley's pants. I can guarantee you the test answers aren't in there."

I drop my forehead into the palm of my hand. "I'm not saying anything else."

Justin laughs, pulling my hand away from my face. "Guys, quit teasing her.

I puff out a breath. "You'd think I'd be used to it. Kaley has zero filter."

"I've gathered that," Justin says. "Last week she told me satin underwear feels like slipping into soft butter."

"Imagine my brother and her in the same room for longer than ten minutes."

After a few minutes, everyone turns back to their own musings. The café is busy. There's a mixture of patrons, half of them studying and the other half waiting until it's socially acceptable to venture out into one of the surrounding bars. It's loud and crowded and grating.

The book in my lap snaps shut, and Justin pulls it away and shoves it in my bag.

"What are you doing?"

"You haven't studied all night," he says.

The butterflies in my chest reawaken and fly into my throat. Does he know I've pretty much reached creeper status? His focus is on gathering our stuff, face turned down. He's not giving anything away as I look at him. He looks up, a backpack on each shoulder, motioning for me to follow.

"Where are you going?"

When I don't move, he tips my chair forward, leaving me to either stand or face-plant; I stand. "We're going to get some food."

"I really need to study."

"You will, but stressing out isn't helping. You need a night off from thinking about school or grades or any other bullshit you're worried about."

"I wouldn't call it bullshit," I mutter, aware that he may or may not fall under that category.

He takes the lead and saunters toward the exit. Left without many options, or wanting one, considering I really haven't studied, I follow him outside. It's still a little early for bar hopping, but people are already milling about, getting ready for a night out. The bars surrounding the café are already playing music, chalkboard signs put up with their drink specials.

"Where do you want to eat?"

Isn't the worst fate in the world being asked where you want to eat? I look left and right down the street, already knowing it's only lined with college bars and greasy pizza places. "If you're up for a little walk, there's a burger place about eight blocks west of here."

"As long as the burgers are good."

He's quiet, hands shoved in his pockets as we walk, neither one of us forcing conversation. The farther west we make it, the less crowded the streets become, leaving the bars and college life behind us. Chuck's is in the middle of the urban side of the city, more commonly frequented by families. It's quieter, less seedy. The restaurant sits between a gas station and a townhome, its wood exterior reflecting its history.

It's a seat-yourself type of establishment, and Justin and I pick a booth in the corner with a view of the street. Justin lets me order for the both of us, and I swirl the straw around in my drink, watching the bubbles float to the top.

Justin looks out the window. "This place is what, a mile from your house?"

"Yeah, Kip and I eat here at least once a week."

He opens his mouth and then shuts it.

"What?" I implore. He shakes his head. "You were about to say something."

"I don't..." Sighing, he finally looks at me. "It's only you and Kip?"

I nod, already understanding where this conversation is going.

He waits a minute and says, "Where are your parents?"

The only person I've ever told is Kaley, and even then it's the watered down version, not the real life version. I'm hesitant because it can bring pity. And already seeing Justin's hesitance to ask, I can only imagine how sorry he's going to feel for me. That's the last thing I need.

"Well," I begin. "My dad died when I was a little over two—I don't remember him—and my mom left when I started my first year of middle school. Kip had just started as a freshman in high school, but really, it was just the two of us for long before that."

He nods. "Makes sense. He's very protective."

"He's very annoying," I repeat in the same tone.

He quirks his mouth into a smile, returning his attention to me. "I'm sure it's mutual."

I narrow my eyes at him. "Aren't you supposed to be on my side?"

He shrugs. "I imagine it's hard to protect a little sister when she looks like you."

I'm stuck between the little sister part and the looks like me part.

The waitress comes by and deposits our food. Justin's eyes widen at the sight of the large burgers stacked on our plates with a healthy dose of fries in red baskets.

"Squish it down. It makes it easier."

I demonstrate, smashing the top bun down, letting grease and condiments seep from the sides. I pick it up, past the point of embarrassment since the turkey panini incident at lunch, and take a bite. Justin repeats my movements, biting into his much more successfully than I did and somehow making it look tasteful. He chews, tilting his head, contemplating.

"So," I say, impatient. "Good, right?"

"It's really good." He smiles, laughing a little. "Actually, it's the best burger I've eaten in a while. It's so juicy," he says, lifting the burger for another bite.

"It's the grease," I say. "They probably haven't cleaned the grill in ten years."

This is reaffirmed when I reposition my feet and the bottom of my shoes stick to the floor. Justin stops mid chew and looks toward the waitress behind the bar restocking napkin dispensers. She smirks at Justin's questioning look.

He studies his burger before shrugging. "Ignorance is bliss."

We're in the middle of eating when the kitchen doors fly open and our waitress comes running out. The diner is mostly empty, just us and another couple, as she calls out for the other waitress. Seconds later, she's at our table.

"There's a fire," she says, untying her apron.

"Fire," Justin parrots, his mouth full of food.

"Yes, a grease fire. The entire kitchen is in smoke."

It's then that we notice black smoke starting to billow from the double doors leading to the kitchen. Our waitress hops over the counter and opens the register, pulling money out and stuffing it in her bra. Justin hurries, grabbing both our cheeseburgers and fries, and I grab the drinks. We're almost out the door when Justin remembers our books. Food is obviously first priority.

taking mine

We exit the diner along with everyone else, jogging across the street to gain a better view of the building and the black smoke rising high into the air. It's kind of unbelievable we didn't have a clue what was happening, sitting and eating like everything was a-okay. All the while, an inferno had taken off. Sirens echo down the street, followed by horns bellowing. I glance at Justin and see him shoving a couple of fries into his mouth, eyes fixated on the scene before us. I had forgotten about the drinks in my hands, suddenly aware of them again.

"You really are bad luck," I say, incredulous. "I guess that's a night."

Justin looks down at me, swallowing his last bit of food. "Is your car at the diner?"

"No, I rode with Kaley to school this morning. I can walk home from here."

He draws his eyebrows together as he looks down the block. "That's a long walk."

"I walk it all the time. I'll be fine."

He leans over and drinks out of one of the cups in my hand. I'm unsure as to whose is whose at this point, but I doubt he cares.

"I'll walk you," he declares after finishing.

"That's dumb. You're going to have to walk all the way back."

My words get muffled by the sound of the fire trucks and ambulances pulling to a stop in front of us. Justin tosses the now empty basket of fries into a nearby trashcan and pulls me along after him in the direction of my house. I don't attempt to argue until it's quiet enough to be heard. We walk almost the entire length of the block before he speaks.

"I live in the apartments across from the university. I'll take a cab back."

"And then you're paying for a cab, also dumb."

He takes another bite of his burger. "I didn't have to pay for dinner. Cancels itself out." At the next cross section, we finish off what's left of our food. We're about to cross the crosswalk when a haggler approaches us, dressed in the same Batman shirt I've seen him wearing for the past two years.

"Come on, I've told you, you can't pretend to be Batman and ask for money."

He smiles. "How else do you think Bruce Wayne got his money?"

"Not panhandling, I can guarantee you." I'm already pulling open the zipper of my backpack, digging for the stray dollars I save for the vending machines at school.

Justin bends and whispers in my ear. "Do you know this guy?"

"Not really," I say. "I don't even know his name."

The man replies, "Yes, you do. It's Bruce Wayne."

"Actually," Justin says. "Bruce Wayne's fortune came from family money."

Batman narrows his eyes and throws a thumb in Justin's direction. "Who's this kid?"

I hand him a couple of one-dollar bills and pat him on the shoulder. "I'll see you next week, Bruce."

He smiles, showing his lack of teeth. "Tell your brother I could use some more socks."

"He told me to tell you he's dropping off a box at the shelter on Monday."

"Good man, there."

"It's almost curfew. You don't want to be last in for top bunk," I respond. He mumbles something under his breath, shuffling away. "He's hard on newcomers."

"New to where? This intersection?"

"The shelter is about a block that way," I say, pointing down the street. "We've been donating there for a few years now. Usually only residents come through here."

We walk a few paces before he replies. "It's strange how protective your brother is, yet he lets you wander around sketchy neighborhoods by yourself."

His words come off all knowing and judge-y, and it irritates me.

"My brother doesn't *let* me do anything. I am my own person."

Justin is surprised by my backlash. "I didn't mean for it to sound that way. It's just that I've noticed you frequent some rough areas, and you're best friends with a homeless guy who won't tell you his real name."

"I'm also walking home with someone following me without my permission," I throw back.

He laughs. "But you know I'm not going to hurt you."

Do I?

"Look," he says, stopping mid step. He turns me toward him, his hands resting on my upper arms. "At least let me show you some self-defense moves."

I roll my eyes. "Seriously? You don't think my brother's covered the basics with me already? I learned how to throw a punch when I was like twelve. You saw it for yourself."

"I saw you sloppily throw a punch. You're lucky he was drunk. He wasn't that hard of a target."

"Bullshit. It was good and you know it."

"Okay," he says, taking a step back. "Show me what you got."

"I'm not going to hit you."

"Don't worry." He smiles. "You won't."

I wrack my brain, trying to recall a hazy memory of Kip teaching me stance. But then I think, *Fuck it,* and swing. Or stumble. Justin catches me around my waist as my step hits the curb, turning me around and placing me back on my feet.

"Stop laughing," I say, embarrassed.

He wraps his forearm around my waist, his chest pressed to my back, and I feel the rumble of his laughter.

"I'm sorry," he says, trying to speak trough his hysterics.

I struggle, trying to break free.

"I quit," I say, marching in the direction of my house.

"No, no," Justin says, pulling me back by my hand. "I'm sorry. No more laughing." He crosses his chest with a finger. "Promise."

I grumble but give in. "I'm not in the right mindset," I say in defense.

"Did you have this much coordination when you were twelve?"

Maybe he can sense the amount of patience I'm working with because he straightens his features.

"No laughing," he reiterates.

When I relax, his smile reappears.

"Okay," he says, standing alongside me. "Position your feet farther apart like this." He waits for me to mirror him before continuing. "Your fist is good, but when you throw, throw across your body."

"But you're taller than me. How do I aim across if your face is an entire foot above me?"

"That's the largest misconception. People thinking hitting someone in the face draws the most damage, but really all it does is piss someone off. Aim for the throat." He taps right above his Adam's apple, effectively distracting me. "It's the most vulnerable and no one sees it coming."

I wonder if his stubble tickles when—

"Lilly," Justin says. His eyes are hooded. It's the same look he gave me at lunch, except this time he's a little less unsure of it.

"Yes?"

He swallows, positioning himself in front of me. "Get your stance right and follow through with your body."

I focus on that specific point on his throat, which surprisingly helps, considering my attraction comes with weird, violent thoughts toward him, and I swing. Not so bad this time. I manage to get close to my target without nearly killing myself, but he deflects easily.

"Pull your momentum in with your hips."

"My hips," I repeat, confused.

"Like this," he says, placing his hands on either side of me. "When you swing, turn your body with the throw."

There's a small part between his lips as he looks down. I lied. It's not his neck I want to taste, it's his mouth.

I want him to kiss me.

The feel of his hands burns through my clothes, kicking my heart rate up a few notches. His mouth falls open a little farther, his tongue barely touching the top of his bottom lip. His grip on my hips tightens,

taking mine

and I feel like he's fastening me, like I need him to be my anchor. After what feels like an eternity of waiting for him to move, I find the courage to look from his mouth. He's focused on my lips, completely zoned in on them. Instinctively, I wet mine, wondering if he's going to act on it, to show me I'm not the only one wanting this.

The action snaps him away. Closing his mouth, he drops his hands from my waist. The uncertainty that was missing from his gaze earlier is back full force this time, no mistaking the conflict in them. He backs up a few paces, putting distance between us.

"Um," he says, clearing his throat. "Want to try one last time?"

I swallow, gathering my emotions. I can't pinpoint exactly what I'm feeling, but I'd say disappointment and confusion are high up there, followed shortly by embarrassment.

"Sure."

He doesn't look at me when I swing, getting everything right, but without enough force. He blocks me but still compliments me on my form. This is the first time things have been this awkward between us. It's silent, too late in the night for traffic, and the bustle at Chuck's is too far behind us to be heard. His movements draw my attention from the corner of my eye as he pulls out a pack of cigarettes. He opens it and slips one into his mouth, the act completely habitual, something only achieved through repetition. He lights it, sucks in a deep breath of smoke, and releases.

It's like this the rest of the way. Me in my thoughts and him in his. Whatever just happened between us has effectively put a strain on our friendship, if that's even what it was, and it makes me sadder than I think it should. I hate to admit it, especially to myself, but I think I like him. Or liked. Or whatever at this point. But either way, it's obvious he doesn't feel the same or he would have acted on it.

When we reach the intersection a block from my house, I convince Justin that I'm fine walking the rest of the way by myself. A reminder of what Kip's possible reaction would be if he saw him helps my case when he wants to argue. I jog across the street when I hear my name being called.

"If you're ever in a position to, always run. Don't fight unless it's a last resort."

I smile, breaking a small chip off the large iceberg that had successfully wedged its way between us.

"I'll tuck that tidbit away just in case."

He doesn't smile, simply nods. I take a couple more steps when he calls out my name again.

"Yeah?"

"I'll forward you that practice test from Blake. You never traded emails."

"That sounds great. Thanks, Justin."

He nods again but makes no effort to move. I walk the rest of the way feeling like his eyes are burrowed into my back. I fight the urge to look until I reach my driveway and give in. He's there, standing in the same spot, new cigarette lit. I can barely make out the shape of him, only the movements of him smoking. The ember gets flicked away and I lose sight of him.

chapter 5

EVERYTHING'S PICKED UP and the shop's ready for closing. It's later than what we usually close, but we were abnormally busy for a Wednesday. Kip left about thirty minutes ago and I have to stay behind to file. At least, that's what I told him. His concern didn't help my conscience when he suggested I go home after I spilled an entire pan of grease on my shoes.

I had a meeting with my adviser earlier today and it didn't go very well. She pretty much confirmed what I already knew. Considering I was never emancipated and my brother wasn't ever assigned as my legal guardian, I have no proof of my parents' income. When I applied for financial aid before the semester began, they declined me and I had to file an appeal. The problem is, it can take up to three months to process and there's still a possibility it will be revoked. Tuition is due now, so I don't have the luxury of waiting. Loans are an option, but lenders tend to only approve students who are already accepted into law school, wanting to better their odds to see the money returned. I can change my major, but if I really want a chance at being accepted, I need to stay on course. In the end, I'm just screwed.

I poke my head into Taylor's office. "Are there any orders out yet?"

He shakes his head but motions me into his office since I'm here. "Jimmy wants to offer us a different solution to the dilemma with the Mustang."

I raise my eyebrows.

"We're still going over the logistics, but there's a catch."

"What catch? How can there be a catch? We made a deal."

"We did," he says. "But he's offering us something extra. Something beneficial on our end."

"Okay," I say, drawing it out.

Taylor clasps his hands. "But I'm fairly positive Kip isn't going to go for it."

"Can you get to the point?"

"I don't want to say too much until everything is ironed out, but I'm giving you a heads up. You know, since you are the one who got us into this mess."

"Oh, thanks," I say dryly.

"You're welcome," he repeats in the same tone.

Dan saunters in, dropping a large sum of money in front of Taylor, looking like the cat who ate the canary. Taylor looks to me and back at Dan. Getting the impression I'm intruding, I start to leave.

"Are you going scouting tonight?" Dan asks.

My eyes connect with the stack of money and then Taylor when I respond. "Yeah."

"Let Ethan know to prepare to stay late," Taylor says, directing me.

"Yes, sir," I say, feeling every bit of the place he's putting me in. Beneath him.

Taylor always walks a fine line between carefree and giving one too many shits. There is no middle ground with him. Where my brother, on the other hand, lives in the middle. After informing Ethan, I wait for Dan outside the employee entrance. He comes barreling out, an even bigger smile than before.

"What was that?" I ask.

His smile drops. "What was what?"

"Don't play stupid. The money?"

Dan lets out an exasperated breath, already tired of my questioning. "We're just doing some business on the side."

"It's not drugs, is it?"

"God, no," he shoots back, repulsed. "Lilly, I have a family. Even I have standards. Don't worry about it, okay?"

taking mine

Deciding to leave it alone for now, we part ways. It's still early. Earlier than I'd like to be looking for cars, but it's a weeknight and Kip's already suspicious. There's a motel a block away from the shelter that I used to frequent. It's mostly drug users and out-of-town laborers, but every now and then a good vehicle comes up. And there are no security cameras and they never fix the streetlights, so it's an easy fix.

It's about a twenty-minute walk, maybe a little longer without shoes. I keep my eyes peeled for anything worthy of being avoided, which is pretty much any and everything that looks questionable. Figuring since I'll be close to the shelter, the lack of shoes will help me fit in. I stop a building over from the motel, scoping out the parking lot. The building is U-shaped with the lot settled in the middle. I've been spotted here before. Someone happened to see me outside their window as I was picking the lock, but with the way the parking lot juts right up against the street, it was easy to make a run for it. And again, no cameras to identify me or to pinpoint the direction I went.

I end up waiting for over an hour, watching lights turn off one by one before I'm satisfied with the lack of traffic between rooms. I tuck my hair under a spare baseball cap I found in the break room, hiding the blonde locks that can be a giveaway. Already spotting a couple of Toyotas that look promising, I mark out a game plan. They have the best resale value for parts and there's never a short supply of buyers. The adrenaline coursing through me makes me jumpy, ready to get this over with.

It's the first vehicle in the lot that gives me pause. It's a Toyota Camry, early 2000 model, in decent condition, unlocked... with the keys sitting in the cup holder. It's not as big of a surprise as people think it is to find an unlocked vehicle, keys sitting right in the ignition, let alone the cup holder or glove box. Relatively common, actually. I've stolen a car that was left running outside of an apartment complex once.

Feeling a bit smug when no alarm goes off when I open the door, I'm paralyzed when I hear my name. Standing stock still, as casually as I can, turn my head in the direction of the person the voice belongs to.

The voice I like a little too much and almost the last person on Earth I want to see right now.

"Justin," I breathe out. "What are you doing here?"

His eyes trail from the car and back to me as he holds up a to-go bag from Chuck's. I'm momentarily impressed by how quick the diner was able to get back up and running in just five days. By the amount of smoke the kitchen was emanating, I had assumed they'd be out of commission for a while.

"Lilly," he says, his voice cautious, taking a step in my direction. "What are you doing?"

I open my mouth but nothing comes out, the red and blue lights behind him distracting me.

"LILLY." JUSTIN REPEATS MY NAME an uncounted amount of times. It takes an absorbent amount of focus to avert my eyes from the cop's direction. "Get in the car," he says.

Not giving me any more time to decide, he grips my arm and not-so-gently shoves me into the Toyota. I scramble over the center console, Justin climbing in behind me.

"What are we doing?"

He picks up the keys, adjusting his seat and starting the car.

"Justin, what are you doing?"

The cop exits his car, turning his head into his shoulder and dispatching something into his walkie. He hikes up his belt, preparing himself as he tries to get a good look inside the car. My eyes fixate on his walk toward us, his face determined.

"Justin."

"Do you want to go to jail?" His eyes are hard as he looks at me. I shake my head no.

The tires squeal as he floors the gas, bottoming out as we hit the street. I snap my seat belt on, holding on to my seat for dear life. I check the passenger rear-view mirror, watching the cop turn around and jog back to his car. We run a red light and a cascade of brakes screech to avoid us.

"Justin." His name is the only thing I can muster as we swerve in and out of traffic. He doesn't bother to acknowledge my ramblings, only accelerates through the intersections with zero disregard for oncoming traffic.

He slams on the brakes, making a ninety-degree turn onto a side street. I brace my hands on the dashboard to prevent my body from jerking forward. Justin's sole focus is on the road in front of us, his jaw clenched as we fishtail. He straightens the wheel, glancing at me for a split second; we're heading down a one-lane in the wrong direction. I alternate between wanting to see where we're going and wanting to close my eyes from terror. Risking a short glance over my shoulder, I spot the cop's flashing lights a good distance away. When I turn back around, we're approaching a four-way, all stop lights red in our direction. Justin doesn't waver.

"Hold on," Justin says a millisecond before he whips the car left. We barely managed to scrape past a van, pulling into an alley.

We park behind a dumpster and kill the engine, both of our eyes trained to the entrance, waiting for the familiar lights to pass. It takes a few minutes, each longer than the last, before the sirens approach and pass without incident. We simultaneously let out a breath.

I drop my head back against the headrest, hand clutching my chest. "What. The fuck. Was that?"

Justin eyes me from his side of the car. "You tell me."

"Me? I'm not the one who instigated a high-speed car chase."

"I'm not the one committing grand theft auto," he retorts, throwing his hands up.

For the first time in my life, I'm confronted by somebody catching me. And it's a person I know, a person who helped me not get caught. I take a breath to calm my temper, allowing some of the adrenaline to phase out.

"Why'd you help me?"

His eyes are directed out his window as he takes his time to respond, running a hand over his face. "I don't know. I saw the panic on your face and reacted."

His words leave little to discuss, and he's obviously feeling more conflicted about it than he's letting on.

"We should ditch it," I say, reaching for the door handle.

taking mine

"No. They're going to be patrolling, no doubt a dispatch is out. I say if we don't see anything in an hour or so we can go. Dawn is probably their shift change, so we'll wait until then if we need to."

Great.

Silence descends and it's stifling. There's a weird animosity between us, and I don't even know what for. We've now committed a felony together, and neither one of us wants to be first to break the standoff. It's not like I stole *his* car.

Minutes pass and all I can think about is all the food I didn't eat today. Being so stressed about meeting with my adviser and work, I skipped lunch and dinner. As if on cue, my stomach rumbles. Justin looks over at me and I start laughing.

"I can't help it."

He reaches for the floorboard and pulls out a crumpled white bag. My stomach growls louder at the sight of the bag and he laughs, halving the burger and handing it to me. He folds the bag down, shaking the fries out. I sigh in contentment as I chew my first bite.

"So." Justin swallows his before finishing. "You steal cars for what... fun?"

"No," I snap.

He raises his eyebrows.

"Sorry. I have no right to get defensive."

He nods once, accepting my apology. "Want to explain why you do it?"

Not particularly. "It's a long story."

"We have time."

I pull the baseball cap off and readjust my hair. "For now, I'm just trying to pay for school. This is the only thing I've got."

He finishes his half of the burger and wipes off his hands. "By stealing cars and doing what with them?"

My laugh is dry as I shake my head, at a loss for words.

"Lilly," he says, sensing my hesitancy. "I'm sitting in a stolen vehicle with you. I'm not going to judge you."

I can feel his eyes on me as I fidget in my seat.

"Do you sell them?" He's persistent.

"For parts," I clarify. "We break them down and sell them on the black market. They're worth more that way."

"We? Who's we? Kaley?"

I laugh. "Kaley is the least stealthy person I know. No," I say, my laughter dying off. "She doesn't know about what I do."

He looks surprised. "Then who is we?"

"This is how Kip supported us after our mom left. She left, not a word, in the middle of the night. At the time I don't think I quite understood the implications of her leaving. Kip did a good job shielding me from it. From my understanding, he went to a few local businesses, asking to work for cash. He ran across Toby's, and Taylor's dad gave him one."

"He gave a sixteen-year-old a job to steal cars?"

"Fifteen."

Justin blows out a breath, leaning back in his seat. "How come no one alerted the authorities?"

"About my mom?

He nods.

"She wasn't known to be mom of the year. It was normal for her to miss parent stuff at school, and neighbors knew she was a recluse...a drunk." I pause, surprised by the lump in my throat. "For me, life went on as normal."

He lets me finish my food in silence, even offering me the rest of the fries. It's when I prop my feet on the dash that he gives me a strange look.

"Where are your shoes?"

I laugh, forgetting I'm barefoot. "Got ruined at work."

He shakes his head, offering nothing up as to what he's thinking.

"What?" I implore.

He releases a breath and smiles at me. "Considering your history, you're surprisingly..."

"Not who'd you expect to be a criminal," I finish for him.

"Yeah," he says, smiling. "You're...."

"You can say it, sheltered."

"Protected," he reiterates.

"Kip doesn't know I've been stealing again."

"Again?"

"I quit when I started college. New beginnings and everything. I guess old habits die hard."

"You're out of practice."

I throw my head back, laughing. "You can say I'm a little rusty. Or desperate," I add at the end.

"Because you lost your scholarship," he clarifies.

"I need half of my semester's tuition paid by Monday. If it's not, then all my hard work will have been for nothing and I'll be doing this for the rest of my life. I'll be working at the shop changing brake pads and oil pans for twelve dollars an hour."

Justin breathes in deeply, like he's taking in the stress I'm letting out. I can physically see the pressure building up inside him and wonder if that's what I constantly look like. No wonder Kip's been in my space lately. I must look like shit.

I laugh.

A confused smile kicks up the side of his mouth. "What?"

"You're such a conundrum."

"I'm the conundrum," he says, pointing at his chest.

"Yes."

I don't elaborate.

His laughter gives me pause, the realness of his smile. I forgot how much I'm attracted to him. Okay, I was distracted. But he's looking at me like I'm interesting, and it sets a burn inside my chest. I have a weird urge to slap him. It hasn't escaped my awareness that whenever I can't handle my feelings toward him I become internally violent. It's like he sets all of my insides on fire, and I'm still not sure if it's a good or bad thing. Not knowing how to handle my irritation, I lean over the middle console and kiss him instead.

The second my lips meet his, his laughter dies in my mouth. There's a light hum in the back of my throat. It's a sharp, quick kiss before I pull away, stunned by my own audacity. We're both not breathing. I watch his eyes dip to my lips and he reaches to the nape of my neck, pulling my mouth back to his.

This time the kiss is edged with tension but more control. Justin's tongue meets mine, creating a deeper connection. The hand clutching the back of my neck gets tighter the closer my body draws to his. He wraps his other arm around my lower back, pulling me into his lap. It happens so quickly I don't even question it. Air hits my waist as his hand trails up my spine, drawing up my shirt along the way.

My hands frame his neck, feeling the muscles I've fantasized over more than I care to admit. There's a tug on the hair at the base of my skull, pulling my head back enough to angle my neck toward his mouth. The second I feel his open mouth place a kiss at the curve of my neck, I don't falter, instead gliding my hips over his, feeling him through the rough fabric of his jeans. Justin sucks in a shudder, his mouth open against my throat, pulling me farther down onto him.

A loud bang startles us apart. Two feral cats are fighting on top of the dumpster behind us, causing the lid to fall open and hit the metal side. After we realize we're safe, we untwine from each other. Justin's hand slips out from under my shirt, leaving a cold imprint of where it was. Tucking the loose strands of my hair behind my ear, I ungracefully scoot back over the console, straightening my top and trying to gain control of my breathing.

I force myself to look at Justin even though a huge part of me wants to ignore what just transpired. His hand is covering his mouth as if he's hiding the evidence. He runs his fingers over his lips a few times before he looks at me. My heart stalls.

"Lilly, I'm...shit." He closes his eyes and opens them again. Trying again, he says, "I'm in a bizarre place right now. If we, us, became more than friends...it would completely derail me."

I try to calmly, rationally digest his words, but I can't stop my feelings from being hurt. My ego, at the very least, is a tad bit taken back.

"We're obviously very attracted to each other," he says, stating the obvious.

It's easier to clear the air now. Get it out in the open and rid ourselves of the uncomfortable place that we've been in since the night we left Chuck's. My eyes focus on his lips for a split second before I realize what I'm doing. My brain isn't very quick to keep up.

"I get it," I say, not getting it at all. "We're both focused on school, right?"

He gives a hesitant nod. "Right."

"We'll stay friends, just like we have been, and pretend this entire night didn't happen."

Justin straightens, placing his back up against the door. "I get the feeling this isn't about our kiss."

"Kiss is a mild term for what we just did, but whatever way you want to look at it," I say.

"Are you going to continue doing this?"

"You mean stealing cars?" A logical part of me knows I should just say no, lie and go on about my business, but for some god-forsaken reason I don't want to lie to him. "Yes."

"Then I want to come with you."

I jerk my head back, confused. "What?"

He heaves a sigh. "I know that you're still going to do this even if I try to convince you otherwise. If your brother can't even stop you, I have no hope, but I want you to be safe."

"Contrary to what you saw tonight, I've done this for a long time without being caught. I got careless tonight. It won't happen again."

"It's not only that. You're in a bad part of town, by yourself, doing something incredibly stupid. As your friend, I can't let you do this by yourself."

"As my friend," I repeat.

"Yes."

Out of the corner of my eye, I see him adjust himself through his pants. The sexual tension is still there. A lot there. And he wants to be friends. Yeah, this isn't setting us up for disaster.

"We should be safe to leave, huh?"

He checks the rear-view mirror even though he can only see a tiny portion of the street from where we are. "Where to?"

"Toby's. It's the automotive shop off of Dupont."

"A certified chop-shop."

THE BACK ENTRANCE to Toby's is open for us when we arrive fifteen minutes later. Taylor is already waiting as Justin parks the Toyota in the closest bay. His gaze is perceptively cool at the sight of Justin driving.

"Who's he?" Justin asks.

I don't get a chance to respond, as Taylor's already opening my door. "Who's your friend?"

"Justin," I say as Justin exits the driver side. "This is Taylor. Taylor, this is Justin. He's a friend from school."

"Care to explain why he's showing up in a stolen car with you?"

The whole lying thing with Taylor never goes well with me. "You wouldn't believe the coincidence." Taylor's attention doesn't waver as I stall. "So, he kind of happened to be passing by when I was popping the lock."

His face tells me he doesn't believe me.

"It's not like I invited him along, okay? I'm just as thrilled as you are that I got caught."

"That still doesn't explain why he's here, with you, in a stolen car."

This is the part of the story that I'm less than thrilled about telling. If Taylor thinks I'm a risk, he'll revoke my privileges. He'll refuse to sell for me anymore.

Justin answers for me. "I didn't give her an option. I figured if I let her go, I was already an accessory, so I went along for the ride."

Taylor glares at him. "This isn't a fucking merry-go-round. You don't get to hop on and off for fun and then decide you're getting sick of going in circles. You're either in or you're out."

Justin holds Taylor's attention steady as he replies, "I'm in. Lilly knows I'm in."

I can see the metaphorical noose being strung around Justin's neck. Taylor can see it too, and his smile says it all.

chapter 7

A COUPLE OF DAYS LATER, Taylor corners me in the break room, asking if I can speak to him in his office. Ethan gives me a questioning look and I shrug. Taylor watches me approach from the other side of the glass window.

"Shut the door." Reluctantly, I take a seat, already annoyed by how often I'm finding myself in his office lately. "I need your help." The seriousness of his tone sets me on edge. "Jimmy has come through with his compromise. We have an order coming up and it's going to make us big money."

"Which is?"

"It's bigger than anything we've ever done before and it's different from anything we've ever done before. But I need your help to convince Kip to do it."

"Why? Kip doesn't deal with this stuff anymore. And it's not like you exactly need his permission. Technically, Toby's is yours."

"Kip is who Jimmy dealt with when he ordered from us years ago. He reached out to Kip about this new deal, but Kip directed him to me, said he doesn't handle this side of the business anymore. It put Jimmy on edge. He wants Kip. He trusts Kip."

"You know I can't convince Kip of anything."

Taylor twirls a pen around his fingers. "I'm hoping the money will be incentive enough to get him on board, but if not, I need you backing me. Two against one is better odds. And you'd be surprised how hard of a time Kip has telling you no."

"That's debatable, considering how many times a day he says it to me."

taking mine

He chuckles. "I'll go over the logistics with the both of you at the same time so he doesn't feel like we're ganging up on him. That way, we're all on even playing field."

"And how do you know I'll even think this order is a good idea? If you're saying it's out of the norm then it might be too big of a risk."

Taylor smiles and buzzes Kip into his office. "Because, Lilly," he says, pausing to lean back in his chair. "The kind of money Jimmy is paying is more than worth it."

Kip pauses at the door when he sees me sitting across from Taylor. "Everything okay?"

"Everything's fine," Taylor says. "I have something I want to discuss with you."

Kip looks to me for answers. "What's this about?"

I shrug.

Taylor mimics Kip's tone, sitting up tall, losing the unperturbed Taylor and replacing it with business-savvy Taylor. "I want to talk to you about Jimmy's proposition for us."

"I don't do orders," Kip says.

"And you won't have to. But Jimmy wants to know that you're okay with our arrangement before he'll give us the job."

"What job?"

Taylor pulls out a manila folder and hands it to Kip. I lean over, peeking at the eight-by-ten glossy photos of cars he's pulling from the envelope. These are not the kind of cars we deal with. My eyes bug out as one shiny new car after another runs through Kip's hands.

"What the hell is this, Taylor?"

"Jimmy wants us to transport these cars for him."

"He wants us to steal them?" Kip says, incredulous.

"Hear me out," Taylor says, gearing up to get defensive.

"He expects us to successfully pull off stealing high-dollar vehicles? We're a chop-shop, Taylor. Not fucking criminal masterminds. All of these require transponder keys."

"Jimmy has someone that will supply us the resources we need to access the cars. He has a tech guy he uses all the time."

I pull a picture of a 911 Carrera out of the folder. "How will we know if they'll be legit? A lot of the new Porsches have motion detectors inside the cab. If the key doesn't match, whoever is in the car is screwed."

"We've been guaranteed that the keys will work with the transponders. Once the car is unlocked, everything will disable."

Kip tosses the folder on the desk, making it skid to a stop in front of Taylor. "Why would a millionaire pay someone to steal cars? He can pull up to any car dealership and buy a car out right."

"It's not finding the car that's the issue. He doesn't want to have to file them with the IRS. He wants to pay cash and not be taxed for it."

"How much?" I ask.

"How much is he going to pay us for our services?"

Kip snorts. "Yeah, for our services."

"He'll pay half the base MSRP rating on each car." Kip opens his mouth to speak, but nothing comes out. Shock is a light term to describe what he's feeling. "Much more enticing now, isn't it? On top of that, he'll add an extra ten grand a piece for commandeering them." He finally releases his business tone and leans back in his chair again, believing the argument is already won.

"Oh my God." I tick off the amount of cars I saw in the folder, calculating over half a million in profit.

Once Kip finally gathers all his bearings, the sticker shock wearing off, he asks, "Where are we getting these cars from? There's not a whole lot of six-figure cars cruising around the city."

"Jimmy will find the cars, tell us where they'll be, and when they'll be there. We'll go pick them up and drive them to the shipping yard located on the west bank. He'll reserve a couple storage containers to keep them in before he ships them to one of his other properties in the UK."

"He's smuggling them," Kip states.

"He's transporting them," Taylor clarifies.

"He doesn't want papers on them because he's trying to bring them into another country illegally."

taking mine

"Even if that is his reasoning, Kip, does it matter? We steal cars to illegally sell them for parts. It's not that far off. We're not killing anyone; we're just scheming the system.

"So, to make sure I understand this," I say, garnering their attention. "Jimmy will tell us what vehicle he wants and where it is for us to retrieve it and deliver it? All we're doing is driving a car from point A to point B?"

Kip looks at me still holding the picture of the Carrera in my hand. "You're not actually considering this, are you?"

I shrug off his question. "It's kind of a hard deal to pass up. If we do this we wouldn't have to ever do it again."

"She's got a point, Kip," Taylor tries to reason.

"If it's so damn easy then why doesn't he drive the damn cars himself?"

"These are high-class cars and some of them are going to be in high-profile places. He doesn't want any connection to himself. It's our jobs to figure out how to get them. We're the leg work."

Kip runs both his hands down his face before blowing out a large breath. He takes the picture from my hand and scans it. "When's he expecting a decision by?"

"The end of the week."

Kip nods once and stands. "Okay. Let me think on it and I'll let you know."

Taylor's eyes follow Kip out of the office, returning to me once the door is shut. "Now it's up to you."

"If the money didn't convince him, Taylor, I don't know what will."

"If Kip has a weakness, it's you."

"Don't hold your breath."

I decide to wait until after work to confront Kip about the deal. It's hard not to balk at the amount of money we can make. It's enough money, even split between us, that we can put some to the side and still pay for the necessities. Like school. It can pay for school. So when I get home, I tentatively step into the kitchen. I know that whatever conversation Kip and I are about to have, it needs to be broached carefully.

Kip's breaking down and cleaning the shotgun he keeps next to his door. The kitchen table is covered in newspaper and gun residue.

This is a promising start.

"Grab the glock from the pantry," he says, not looking up from his task.

I hate the feel of guns. It's like death is sitting in the palm of my hand. But I know Kip needs reassurance that I'm capable, so I pull open the gun safe we keep stashed in the pantry and bring it to the table. I check the chamber for a bullet and drop the clip out, laying the gun and the clip side by side on the table.

"Do you remember Dad?"

Completely thrown by his question, I shake my head no.

"Not at all?"

"No."

He pushes back from the table and pulls his wallet out from his pocket and hands me a folded picture. It's an old Polaroid with a thick white crease down the middle from where it's been folded over time. Even so, it's easy to distinguish that it's a picture of our dad holding the both of us, Kip and me saddled on each hip. I couldn't have been over a year old, wearing footie pajamas, and Kip is adorned in Ninja Turtle slippers. Dad's in the middle, dressed in a mechanic's jumper with a thick mustache, but it's our smiles we're wearing that pull my attention. We're all smiling, laughing at something. It's unfiltered happiness.

"He was the best dad that we could have asked for." Kip's voice trembles. I look up to see his eyes rimmed with worry. "I know you have had to wonder what type of man could marry the type of person mom was, but she wasn't always like that. There was a time when we were all a happy family."

My fingers whiten around the picture, afraid it will somehow slip through them. "You've never talked bad about Dad. I always thought

taking mine

that maybe it was because you glorified him. Like, maybe you were too young to remember the bad."

"I remember," he says. "I'm not saying they were perfect, but they loved us."

I try to control the tremble in my voice. "Mom didn't."

Kip's breath is deep. "Sometimes I think that, too, but I think maybe she was just lost without him. He was so sure and happy all the time. He was an anchor for her. For all of us."

"I wish I could remember."

"Me too. Sometimes I wish you could remember Mom when she was sober. But maybe it's a good thing you don't. Maybe it's easier to hate her for leaving than remember her any way else."

"Because then it's just sad."

"Yeah, it's sad."

He finishes piecing the shotgun back together and reaches for the glock. Thinking the conversation is over, I stand and push my chair in. It's not exactly how I expected the conversation to go, but it wasn't awful. Kip's voice stops me in my tracks.

"I can't tell you what to do, Lilly. You're old enough to decide for yourself. But I can expect enough respect for you to be honest with me. Tell me where you are so I don't worry myself sick that something bad happened to you. Especially when I know you've been working for Taylor again."

A weight drops. "It's not what you think."

"It's not?" The level of accusation and disappointment emanating from him is what I've been trying to avoid.

"I lost my scholarship last semester. I couldn't bring up my grades in time."

"Why didn't you tell me?"

"What could you have done? Tuition is more than what both of us make combined."

"I would have figured out something. Anything other than what you're doing."

I sit back down. "And I knew you'd say that. It's not your load to carry. Like you said, I'm old enough to be responsible for myself. This is my burden, not yours."

"You're not a burden, Lilly. Don't ever think that."

"But I am. I always have been. This is bigger than today. This is my future. And I want it, not just for me, but for you. I know you hate working for Taylor, and this is the only way I can make a difference."

"It's not your job to worry about me."

"Isn't that what you've been doing all your life? Worrying about me? You hate the shop and everything it represents. From the time you started working for Taylor's dad until now. And you've done it only with concern for me."

He runs both of his hands through his hair and then folds them across the table. "It's my job to take care of you."

"No, Kip," I say, sadness radiating from my voice. "It was Mom's. Don't get me wrong, I'm so grateful to have you. Who knows where I would be today if I didn't. You've carried me this far and now I want—no, I *need* to carry myself."

"So what's your plan? How are you going to get through the next four years of school without a scholarship?"

"Well, since you brought it up, I was thinking about the offer from Jimmy."

"The one that's too good to be true?"

"Yes, that one. It's enough money for both of us to not have to worry for a long, long time."

"At what cost?"

"We don't know that there is a cost."

He looks at me with such endearment. "There's always a cost, Lil."

WHEN I MADE MY PAYMENT to the bursar's office, I thought I would feel like a weight had been lifted off my shoulders, but it doesn't. I no longer only carry school, but also Justin's involvement with Taylor. At some point in the last week, I inadvertently and effectively derailed both of our futures. Logically, I know Justin decided for himself, but it doesn't stop the guilt from settling in. How can he make a smart decision when he has no idea what he's in for? Taylor also mentioned that Justin is going to need to prove he's trustworthy.

I'm stumbling. I've been going through the motions, but I can't find steady ground where I'm secure in knowing I'm doing something right. I'll take anything at this point.

Kaley looks over my shoulder as we're walking toward the courtyard, looking at the grade scrawled across the paper. "Lance told me he informed you about what was going to be on the test."

I yank the sheet from her view, crumbling it into a ball. "Yes, Kaley. Thanks for the reminder."

She's quiet from the backlash and I immediately feel bad, but not enough to apologize.

"Why don't you go out with us tonight? Forget about all the worrying and really let go. Maybe even have a drink or two."

I give her a look. She knows I don't drink. If I do, it's very rare.

"At this point it can't hurt you more than help you."

Stopping in the middle of the courtyard, letting Kaley walk ahead of me, I try to recall the last time I felt like I could breathe. The last time it didn't feel like I was doing everything on default. A quick image of me straddling Justin's lap runs through my mind, and I have to force myself to divert my train of thought.

Kaley finally notices that I'm not walking next to her and turns around. She raises her hand to shield the sun from her eyes, squinting at me. "You coming?"

She's my ride home, but I just need...air.

"No," I say, pulling my phone from my back pocket. "Go ahead. I'll text you later."

"You sure?" she asks, concerned.

I roll my eyes, giving her enough reassurance to continue without me.

And then I text Justin.

The apartment building Justin lives in is located right off campus. It's a hot spot for students who want to be close to the university but don't want to live on campus and deal with campus regulations. It's cheap housing with free cable. Makes it kind of hard to pass up.

As I'm ascending the stairs that lead to his apartment, I tamp down the doubt floating around in my head. We're friends. He said so himself. There's no need to overanalyze why he's the person I want to be around right now. None whatsoever. He answers the door with a lopsided smile, and it eases some of the uncertainty I had mere seconds ago. Stepping to the side, he lets me in.

"I'm sorry I'm kind of dropping in on you last minute," I say once he shuts the door behind me.

"Is everything okay?" He watches me so intently. It's a part of who he is, I think. Observing people, emotions.

"Yeah," I say, breathing in the smell of his apartment. "Can we..." I trail off, dropping onto his couch, past the point of wanting to stand. "Can we just hang out?"

He raises his eyebrows, running a thumb across his bottom lip. "Yeah, sure. We can do that. What would you like to do?"

"Anything, nothing. I don't care as long as I don't have to think for a little while."

This brings a small smile to his face. "The last time I tried to distract you, a restaurant caught fire and you said I was bad luck."

"First of all," I say, holding up a finger. "You said you were bad luck first. Second, Chuck's is already back in business, so no harm done. And third, saving me from the cops is enough retribution in my book."

"But you still think I'm bad luck?" His smile is teasing as he stands. It's now that I notice he's wearing flannel pajama pants and a black t-shirt, his scruff a tad bit longer than he normally allows it to get.

"Were you sleeping?" I ask, suddenly uncomfortable in my jeans and v-neck.

He looks down at his clothes as he scrubs his cheek, trying to hide the color in them. "Uh, no. I'm ashamed to admit I haven't put on real clothes all day. I kind of played hooky."

"I wish."

"Anytime you need a breather, you're more than welcome to come hang out." He digs around in the fridge. "Want something to drink? I've got water or beer."

"Water is fine."

"I was about to order dinner. Does pizza sound good to you?"

"As long as I get to pick the toppings." He gives me a hesitant look. "Extra cheese and pineapple."

"No," he says, horrified. "Absolutely not. We'll do half and half."

He tosses me the remote while he orders the pizza. I take a sip of my water and look around his apartment. It's a small one-bedroom layout, just enough space for one person. The kitchen takes up the entire back wall with a low breakfast bar separating it from the living area. His furniture consists of a navy blue couch and matching recliner, a small coffee table, and a mounted flat screen. There's nothing else of significance.

"What," he says after he hangs up the phone.

"How long have you lived here?"

He thinks for a moment. "About a year and a half. Why?"

I make a point to look around the room. "There are no decorations."

He glances at the empty space around him and shrugs. "I'm a guy."

It's not just that though. It's the lack of knick-knacks. There's no loose change or receipts or loose items of clothing littering the floor or hanging up. There's nothing to distinguish that someone actively lives here.

He runs his thumb over his lip again, and it dawns on me that it's a nervous tick. He catches me staring and drops his hand.

"This is weird, isn't it?" I say, facing the issue head-on.

We stare at each other in silence.

"This is not going to be weird because we're not going to let it," he says, an air of authority in his voice. "I'm going to go outside and smoke, and when I come back things are going to be normal."

I nod in agreement.

I wait until the door shuts behind him before sagging back into the couch. This is proving to be more awkward than I thought it would be. Why am I doing this to myself? An annoying voice in the back of my mind whispers, *It's because he makes you* feel, and it sounds like the creepy creature from The Lord of the Rings.

Shaking off a chill, I straighten myself, determined to not over think anything. Literally, my goal for the night is to think about as little as possible and still be considered a living entity.

Justin comes barging back inside, this time a pizza box in hand. "One pizza pie, half amazing goodness and half nasty Hawaiian shit." He drops the box on the coffee table and points at me with new energy radiating through him. "I'm going to change. Be ready to leave when I come out."

"Wait, what?" I say to his back as he's already walking away.

"Five minutes," he says in warning.

"What about the pizza?" I yell loud enough for him to hear me through his bedroom door.

"Bringing it with us. The food at the bowling alley is stupid expensive," he calls back.

"Why are we going bowling?"

This time I don't get a response.

"BOWLING IS THE BEST American sport there is. Other than baseball, of course."

"No it's not," I say, lacing up my shoes. "Bowling predates America. They found artifacts dating back to before Christ."

He stops tying his shoes, turning to look at me. "You've just had that stored in your head?"

I shrug. "I took Sports History my freshman year. It was one of the things that stuck for some reason. Ask me what I had for breakfast—couldn't tell you."

"A blueberry muffin and coffee with cream."

My heart stops.

He rolls his eyes. "You have the same thing every morning at the cafe. I think you're the only one who doesn't realize it."

Justin makes the smoothest transition from unmanageable awkwardness to easygoing effortlessly, and it occurs to me that he can make my mood reflect his. It's hard not to smile when he smiles, hard not to laugh when he laughs. He's contagious.

I've caught the type-A strand of the Justin-flu.

"I hate to tell you this," I say as I watch him put our names up on the board. "But I'm about to school you with my bowling skills."

"Oh, yeah," he says, smiling. "Sports History must be really hands-on."

"Come to think of it, the teacher was kind of touchy-feely."

He takes a seat on one of the plastic chairs, waving me first. "Show me what you got." I sift through the bowling balls, trying to determine the one that feels best. "Today," he says, sarcasm dripping from his voice, urging me to hurry up.

I sneer at him, choosing a random ball near me. "You can't rush perfection."

He snorts.

Holding the ball close to my chest, I let out a breath as I move forward, releasing it at just the right angle. It's a strike. My smile is cocky as I turn to face Justin. "Did I mention I'm going to kick your ass?"

"I thought you were joking."

Justin looks slightly less intimidated as he stands for his turn. He takes longer than I do to pick a bowling ball, his face serious as he decides.

"Today," I tease, laughing when he shoots me a look.

His first bowl only knocks down half the pins, and I bite my lip, fighting back a smile.

"Just getting warmed up," he says, rubbing his hands together.

This time, he knocks down the rest of the pins, garnering a spare. He beams a triumphant smile as he turns around, dancing to the pop music playing overhead. I laugh, impressed by his smooth moves. His dancing is reminiscent of an eighties version of Michael Jackson, just a little less coordinated.

"It's on," he says, dropping onto the seat next to me.

"I'm still ahead of you."

"Not for long."

We spend the rest of the first game volleying back and forth. Anytime either one of us pulls ahead, the loser definitely knows it. The teenage girls next to us certainly enjoy when Justin is ahead and they're graced with his awesome dance moves. I enjoy them too, but not enough to go easy on him.

We're on the last frame and we're almost tied. Whoever scores the most on this bowl wins. I'm gearing up to throw a second strike when I trip over something invisible, causing me to drop the ball. It spins in the wrong direction and rolls into the gutter. I look down, trying to find what made me stumble, and see my shoelaces are untied.

Justin starts laughing.

"This isn't fair," I say, not stopping the whine coming through. "Why didn't you tell me my shoe was untied?"

"Then I would have missed the wonderful sight of you failing," he says, a very pleased smile gracing his lips. "Now, step back so I can show you how it's done."

I'm angry. Losing over something so incredibly dumb leaves a bitter taste in my mouth. Refusing to be outdone, I sneak behind him as he positions to throw and I grab the ball. It causes him to lose his grip, and the ball slips from his hand, rolling straight into the gutter, leaving the score in my favor by four points.

"Hey," he barks, incredulous. "Now that's not fair. I get a redo."

"Nope," I say, covering the reset button on the console when he reaches for it. "I won fair and square."

"You cheated!"

Playing coy, I shrug. "Prove it."

He can't believe my audacity, his tongue shoved into the side of his cheek. "I'll prove it," he says, right before he throws me over his shoulder.

"Justin, put me down," I shout, trying to sound authoritative upside down.

"Admit you cheated."

"Never."

"Have it your way, then." He repositions me on his shoulder and begins walking as he yells, "I've got a cheater over here!"

"Justin!"

"She's really awful and mean and downright—"

"Okay, okay," I yell, trying to cut off the rest of his words with mine. "Okay, I cheated. Put me down."

As he bends over and sets me upright, all of the blood rushes from my head to my feet and I'm dizzy for a moment. But it doesn't take me long to notice the people staring. Not to mention the group of girls next to us giggling like hyenas.

I glare at him. "Asshole."

His mouth drops open, huffing out a laugh. "I'm not the asshole, cheater," he says, poking me in the shoulder.

I slap his hand away. "You're just a sore loser."

He gives me a look, and I already know I'm going back over his shoulder. I don't fight it this time, enjoying the shape of his butt through his jeans. His hand smacks my backside and I yelp from the sting.

"And now you've got a sore ass."

SOMEHOW I MANAGED TO CONVINCE Justin that the soft serve ice cream at the food counter is worth the five-dollar price tag, and we're camped out on the roof of his Jeep, musing over the last three games we played.

"I don't think we're going to be allowed back in." The shift manager spent the entire time giving us the stink eye after the cheating debacle.

Justin smiles. "He's just pissed he's going to still be here in twenty years, trying to figure out how come he never did anything worthwhile with his life."

My smile slips. That's my biggest fear.

"That's not going to be you," Justin says, dipping his eyes to meet mine. "You've just got to believe in yourself. Stop worrying about what your future is supposed to be, and start listening to what you want today to be." Judging my mood, he switches tactics. "Let's play a game. If you could steal one car in this parking lot, which would it be?"

"For myself or to sell?"

"Either."

That's easy; I don't even have to think about it. "The new Cobra parked under the awning would be nice to have. It's fast and has a really good safety rating, so if I ever crashed I wouldn't die. To sell," I say, pointing with my spoon. "The beat-up Firebird parked two rows over would probably be a good payout, especially if it has anything original. And by the looks of it, the owner couldn't have changed much."

Justin squints, trying to pinpoint where the Firebird is located, partially hidden behind a Dodge Ram. "You didn't even have to look. When did you spot it?"

"I don't know," I say, shrugging. "I just saw it."

He leans forward, draping his arms over his knees. "Let's do it."

"Do what? Steal it?" He nods and I shake my head, pointing above us. "There are two security cameras on the building, one on each light post, and one taking video of our faces when we entered the building."

He takes a moment to pinpoint the cameras. "It's second nature to you. To assess the surroundings and determine how viable it is to get away with stealing something."

I digest his words. "I guess it is."

"You never noticed?"

I shake my head. "I suppose it has a lot to do with all of Taylor's constant reminders to know my surroundings."

"He's the one who showed you what to do?"

I nod. "I knew Kip would never agree to it, so I asked Taylor."

"How old were you?"

"Seventeen."

His voice is low when he asks, "Why? What made you decide you wanted to do this?"

"At the time, I was bored. Kip was even more protective then, always on my case about what I was doing, especially once I started hanging out with Kaley. I think I wanted to do something just to go against him, to piss him off."

"Typical teenager," he says with a smile.

"Yeah, but then I think I got addicted to the thrill of it. Every day I looked forward to getting out of school and going to work, knowing I was going to go do it again that night."

"So it wasn't about the money?"

"Not then, no."

As a matter of fact, it wasn't until right when Dan and Melanie found out they were expecting. They were close to the age I am now, both working minimum wage jobs. I had caught Melanie meeting Dan in the employee parking lot. She was crying because her parents had kicked her out, and Dan was freaking out because he shared a one-bedroom apartment with Ethan. I was looking for an excuse to steal, looking for an excuse not feel bad about myself, and I had found one.

It's powerful in its own weird way. I have the power to take something. I suppose I could psychoanalyze how it can relate to having lack of control in my everyday life, but that's all mumbo jumbo. It's a rush. It's doing something and having zero repercussions for my actions. The act of being devious is greater than the actual worth of the item. It's doing something just because I can. Or, it was. Now, it's much greater than that.

I think back to late middle school when I began to steal petty things and how much simpler it was for me then. I began with small stuff—pencils or concession money—and then it slowly progressed to cell phones and wallets in high school, eventually landing me at the feet of

Taylor. It got to a point where even stealing an unlocked vehicle wasn't worth the challenge. I'd want the car that I knew I would struggle with. It only pushed the desire to do it higher.

I nudge his shoulder with mine, breaking him from his thoughts. "Are you going to tell me about your criminal past, Sherlock?"

"Who says I have one?" he says, nudging me back.

"I don't care what you say; no one has the balls to run from a cop unless they've done it before. And you're incredibly nonchalant about working for a chop-shop. So, spill."

His smile is tight lipped. "I went to prison when I was seventeen for aiding and abetting an armed robbery." He laughs at my reaction. "It's not something I broadcast, okay?"

Crossing my legs, I face him. "Elaborate."

He smiles at my eagerness. "My parents were going through a tough time, always fighting. My dad was an alcoholic and he'd take it out on my mom. She was working three jobs trying to support us."

I sit as still as I can, not wanting to disrupt him, almost trying to disappear so he's comfortable. "So, my mom was always gone. My dad stayed in the house most of time, leaving me and Jacob alone to entertain ourselves a lot."

"Jacob?"

"My little brother. He's a little younger than me, about your age. We ended up doing a lot of bad stuff just to kill time. And mostly because we could. We were out one night with a group of guys we hung out with, and we were on our way to a tiny bar on the outskirts of town that served alcohol to underage kids. My friend Tommy said he wanted to stop and swipe some beer. We stopped at this small tin store right by the county line, leaving Jake in the car.

He takes a break to dig through his pocket and produce a pack of cigarettes. He lights one and inhales before he continues, his voice a little bit lower in timbre. "I'm in the back, shoving these ice cold bottles down my pants, when I hear yelling. I look around the aisle and see Tommy holding a gun up at the clerk, telling him to give him all the cash in the register. Not knowing what to do, I ran to the car."

"So you weren't the one to actually rob the store?"

"Other than the beer, no. Tommy came out of the store right as the cops showed up. Several squad cars poured in and I panicked. I took off. I was driving this beat-up Isuzu, barely topped out at eighty, and I knew we were going to get caught. I jutted into a cane field and dropped Jacob off."

"He was what, fourteen?"

"Fifteen. It was his birthday. I admit I wasn't the big brother I should have been, not like Kip is. I always figured since he went with me everywhere I could keep him safe. I was wrong, but that's the way I looked at it."

I nod, wanting him to know I hold no judgments.

"Once I got back on the main highway. I surrendered."

"How long were you in jail for?"

"I was sentenced to four years but got out early for good behavior. A little over a year and a half in all."

His eyes are cast off, looking at nothing in particular, and I'm reminded of how much older he looks. It's daunting. Wanting to break the mood, I quip, "Now I know where you got your mad driving skills from."

He throws his head back and laughs, smiling from ear to ear. When he looks at me, his eyes are lighter, making me smile with him. "I doubt my one outrun from the law makes me an experienced driver."

His laughter dies down and it's replaced with silence. This time it's comforting. And it's now I realize that every breath I've taken since leaving Justin's apartment hasn't felt like it's been trying to kill me. I breathe deep, relishing the feel of...contentment.

It's close to midnight when he drops me off a block from my house. I'm about to open the door when I have a question I need answered. "Why did you agree to work for Taylor?"

"I ask myself that," he says. "Sometimes I think fate is giving me a lousy hand."

"Is it the money?"

He shrugs, his arm draped over the steering wheel. "Life has a way of putting me in places with you when it knows I can't have you." He looks up from my feet, his gaze gently sliding up my legs and over my body, stopping once he reaches my eyes.

I clear my throat, forcing myself to speak. "A goodbye would have been fine."

He smiles.

chapter 8

PROFESSOR WHITTICKER DISMISSES the class with a final warning that fraternizing with student teachers is forbidden and can lead to being dropped from the class with a failing grade or expulsion.

"There goes my chance at passing." I shove my notebook into my backpack and wait for Kaley to finish reapplying her lip gloss.

"Mm, I highly doubt Lance is good at obeying." She smacks her lips together and shuts her compact.

"Ashley might be. This is her career on the line."

"For some reason I can't believe that any girl who falls for Lance's charm is a studious rule follower. And if on the off chance she is, I have faith Lance will find a way around it. He's sleazy like that."

The chilly air blasts us when we step outside, whipping our hair into disarray. It's the first day of fall when the temperature is cold enough to wear a jacket. I pull my hood up as we trek across campus. Everyone agreed we were spending too much money at the café, so the study group decided to convene in the courtyard. And Lance kind of got us kicked out when he hacked the café's Wi-Fi and changed their music station. None of the employees could actually prove it was him, but when he started dancing to a song about anacondas, they had a good idea.

The low temperature is pushing people to actually use the campus grounds again. The courtyard is chock-full of people lying out, eating, studying, and a small group is throwing a football around. Lance comes barreling toward us, looking over his shoulder as he catches a perfect spiral inches from our faces.

Kaley holds a hand up to shield her face. "Watch it."

He's undeterred. "Mornin', ladies. Care to join us in some tag football?"

"It's too cold to move," I say.

"That's why you need it," he says, squeezing my upper arms together. "Get those juices flowing."

"I'm good, thanks."

He looks to Kaley and she rolls her eyes. "Fine." She says it like she's doing him a favor.

Lance tosses the ball to Kaley and winks. "Do you even know how to play?"

I hear Kaley growl as she throws the ball at Lance's face and he ducks right as it zooms over his head. His eyes are huge when he looks up at her cocky glower. I laugh.

I find Blake sitting against one of the oak trees and make a spot next to him, clearing out some of the leaves and debris.

"Didn't want to play," he asks, greeting me as I sit.

"Nah. You?"

"Heck no. They've argued for the past twenty minutes on whether or not the ball was inside the end zone."

I look up and see Justin explaining the parameters of the makeshift field when Lance chimes in, shaking his head and pointing out new grounds. Justin pulls the football from Kaley's hands and places it down on the field, done with Lance's insistence and wanting to start the game. The two teams consist of six players each; Kaley and Courtney are the only girls participating.

"I'm guessing we're not studying today?"

"Doesn't look like it."

Leaning against the tree, I put in my headphones and huddle under my jacket. Kip's been staying up late with me, helping me with practice questions and making flashcards. This morning he gave me an impromptu quiz and rewarded every question I got right with bacon. Between him and the study sessions, I feel better about my academic standing.

taking mine

I can do this. I'm moving forward and there's a real possibility I can bring up my GPA enough to apply for law school in the fall of next year.

But for now, I'm focused on graduating, and I'm breathing, and that feels perfect.

I don't know how long I'm out for, but when I open my eyes, Justin's naked torso is the first thing I see. He crouches down in front of me, pulling the earphones from my ears. The sun is out and the clouds from earlier have dissipated, leaving a mild warmth in the air. Suddenly stuffy, I pull down my hood and my hands from my pockets, a thin layer of perspiration coating my skin.

But mine has nothing on Justin's.

His chest and shoulders are covered in dribbles of sweat, beads of them falling onto the ground at his feet. There's a small bit of hair that's scattered around his navel and disappears under the hem of his blue jeans.

"You missed your second class."

My eyes jump to his eyes. "What time is it?"

"A little after noon. You looked comfortable, so I told Blake to let you sleep. He left a while ago."

Rubbing the sleep from my eyes, I sit up, trying to deflect the sun's glare. The football game is much larger. The population of players has doubled since I fell asleep, with most of the male players shirtless. "Everyone's still playing football?"

He looks over his shoulder for a second. "No one wanted to go to class when the weather's so nice." *Very nice*, I think as my eyes trail up the arms he has braced over his knees. He grins. "Everyone's going to go grab lunch. Want to come?"

"I've got class in ten minutes."

He shrugs, and it's like all the muscles in his body shift with the movement. "Skip. Take a sick day."

"Yeah," Lance says, jogging to a stop above us. "Everyone's meeting in the cafeteria."

"Everyone's skipping school to spend the day at school? Does anyone else think this is stupid?"

Justin rolls his eyes, tugging me up with one hand and impressing me with his strength. "Come on. Stop being a Debbie Downer."

"Gee, thanks, when you put it that way."

He smiles, throwing his arm over my shoulder and putting his sweaty body next to mine. "You're grouchy when you wake up."

Lance follows behind us, tossing the ball into the air as we walk across the courtyard. "It's probably because the first thing she saw was your face."

Justin releases me from his side, and I instantly resist the urge to rub myself into him like a cat seeking attention. "Don't you have Kaley to piss off or something?" he says, pulling his tee back over his head. I stand between them getting dressed, and I keep my eyes diverted, trying hard not to stare.

"She loves it."

Justin raises his eyebrows. "Yeah, like when she slapped you across the face when you *manhandled* her right before the end zone."

Lance rubs his cheek, a smile of adoration in place. "It was a tackle. That's the game. She was just mad because I got sweat on her."

"It's touch football, Lance. There is no tackling."

He waves the football around dismissively, and I'm struck by how alike he and Kaley are. "Semantics."

Everyone files into the lunchroom from outside, and it sounds like a cacophony of voices, everyone in good spirits with the beautiful day. A couple of guys fall in line behind us and give Justin and Lance praises for such a good game, and I'm kind of sad I missed it, especially because I didn't know they were going to be playing shirtless.

Kaley comes barreling through the crowd and screeches to a stop. "Knee-Slapper Tommy," she says, right before she launches her lips onto Lance's without a second more to explain. Justin takes a step back, his eyebrows hitting his hairline as he looks from them to me.

Their lips are moving so urgently that I feel like I'm watching a freak show. I catch sight of Tom, in his blue-jean-shorts glory, watching them. Disappointment flashes across his face before he shrugs and walks away.

"Okay, he's gone."

They separate as fast as they joined. "One of these days I'm not going to save you," Lance says, wiping excess saliva from his face.

"You wish," she says, winking at me before marching off.

"How many times has she pulled that maneuver?" Justin asks.

"Lost count."

We retrieve our lunches and manage to squeeze into a table toward the back.

"Oh," I say to Lance. "I forgot to mention that Whitticker's on to one of his student teachers releasing information to the student body. He threatened expulsion if he finds out who it is."

"Oh, yeah," he says, unimpressed. "Whitticker's just jealous he can't tap it. Ashley told me he's made passes at her when they've been alone. Pervert."

"Why doesn't she go to the dean?"

"Because he's a good reference on a résumé. And she feels like she's getting retribution by releasing information." He shrugs. "Either way, I'm not worried."

A fry flies through the air and nails Lance in the face. Justin and I both start laughing when we pinpoint where it came from.

"And that's for the uncalled-for tackle," Kaley yells from down the table.

"What the fuck, Kale. You got it in my eye." Lance rubs his eye, blinking repeatedly.

"We would have won that last game if you hadn't cheated."

"Remind you of anyone?" Justin says, leaning into me.

"Yeah," I say. "It reminds me of ninny babies who hate it when they're beaten fair and square by a better player."

He digs his tongue inside his cheek, just like he did right before he threw me over his shoulder at the bowling alley, and I already know I have something coming for me. I just didn't expect for it to come from behind. The second Lance's pizza hits the side of my face, the entire table falls into silence as Lance scoots down a seat, putting distance between us.

Justin runs a finger across my cheek and sucks the marinara from his fingertip. "You were saying…"

I wipe the grease off of my cheek. "Nothing."

Half the table is disappointed by my response, including Justin. "That's it?" he says, skeptical.

"No retaliation?" Lance laments.

I shrug. "It's a losing battle."

After a half hour of being paranoid, Justin begins to loosen up, laughing with a guy across the table as they discuss Tony Romo's quarterback skills, and Lance is knee-deep in conversation about strippers with the girl next to him.

Someone slides into the seat Lance vacated, placing a large salad onto the table. "Can I sit here?" He's stocky, his body most likely perfected to be the muscle mass it is, and at complete odds with his cheery smile.

"No, but since you're already sitting, be my guest."

He smiles at my sarcasm. "I didn't know if you'd need extra room to sleep." I'm confused until he says, "I saw you sleeping outside. You snore."

"I do not," I protest.

"Don't believe me, ask your friend." He nods in Justin's direction.

Now I'm questioning myself. I've never snored before. At least, no one's told me I have. Kaley's the only person who's actually slept next to me, but she would have told me…right?

"You're so full of shit," I say, calling his bluff.

He laughs, mixing the greens in his paper bowl. "I had you for a second."

"No, you didn't." He gives me a look and I relent. "Maybe."

He reaches his arm across his chest, holding his hand out for me to shake. "Matt," he says in greeting.

"Lilly."

"Like the flower?"

"No."

"No?

taking mine

"Nope," I reiterate.

"Alright. Well, in case you were wondering," he says. "I'm Matt like Matthew except without the hew."

I smile, because I've got to give him credit for trying. "No way."

"Unbelievable, I know."

We smile at each other, not saying anything. It's kind of awkward, kind of comfortable, and it takes Lance's laugh cutting through our silence to break it.

"So, you're new here?" I ask, reaching for a conversation starter.

"Yeah, how did you know?"

I pretend to smell the sleeve of his shirt. "You've got that newbie smell."

He sniffs his shirt, a touch of self-consciousness creeping in. "Like grass and sweat?"

I laugh.

Matt manages to keep an entire conversation going about daffodils and somehow still keeps me interested. Apparently his mom is an avid gardener. Our table stays occupied long after the lunch rush blows through, leaving the janitors sweeping around our feet.

"You're leaving," Justin asks, looking up from his seat as I stand.

"Yeah, I'm going to try and get some studying in before work tomorrow."

"I'll walk you," Matt says, standing up. He doesn't ask or wait for my reply as he piles his napkins and trash into his long-empty salad bowl.

"You don't have to," I say.

"I'm done and headed that way, anyway. Might as well walk together."

It's as if Justin just realizes that I had someone the size of a linebacker sitting next to me this whole time as he gives Matt a look-over, perplexed by who he is and why he's so nonchalantly offering to walk me to my car.

"I'm sorry," Justin says, turning to face us. "Who are you?"

"Matt," he says, holding his hand out in the same manner he did to me.

Justin looks at Matt, ignoring his outstretched hand. "I'm sure you're a nice guy, Matt, but I'll walk her."

Matt pulls his hand back, caught off guard by Justin's hostility. At this point, Justin's slacked off all pretenses of being nice and is outright glaring at Matt, all the while sitting. Matt looks to me, but I'm too busy shooting daggers at the back of Justin's head. "Matt," I say, picking up my books. "Can you wait for me outside?"

He nods. "Yeah, no problem." He gives Justin one last glance before making his way to deposit his trash and walk out the door.

Everyone's eyes are on us as I pull Justin up by the sleeve of his shirt and out of hearing range. "What is up with you?"

"Nothing," he says with a purposefully blasé shrug, serving its purpose to piss me off.

I raise my eyebrows. "Oh, okay. For a second there I thought you were acting like a dick."

His eyebrows meet. "The dude is for real creeping on you."

I'm taken back by his response. "Let's say he was hitting on me—"

"He was."

"*If*," I correct. "It's up to me whether or not I want to test that theory, okay?"

He crosses his arms and runs his thumb over his bottom lip, looking over my head when he replies. "Fine, but don't say I didn't warn you."

"Fine," I concede.

I don't wait for him to say anything else as I head to meet Matt outside. I'm half expecting him not to be there, knowing there's a good chance that Justin really did scare him off, but he's posted against the wall, thumbing through his phone when he sees me exit the lunchroom doors.

"Everything alright?"

"Yeah." I don't elaborate as we begin walking toward the student parking lot.

"He's not...your boyfriend or anything...or if he is, 'cause that's okay, I just..."

"No, he's definitely not my boyfriend. Just a friend. A weird, overprotective one."

He blows out a breath of air. "Good, 'cause I'm not into stepping on anyone's toes."

I freeze.

He stops and gives me a weary look. "That is, if I'm taking a step at all."

"Is that a very veiled way of asking me out?"

"I think so?"

We pick back up our pace and I mull it over in my head. I glance over at him and he looks up from our feet in the same fashion. He's followed me to my car by the time I come to a conclusion.

"Yes," I say. "I'll go out with you."

His eyes light up, but he masks it well with a smile. "You had me worried."

"For a second?"

He shrugs. "Maybe."

We trade numbers and plan on setting plans for later. It's not until I'm in my car and pulling away that it occurs to me that I've never been on an actual date before. I text Kaley.

KIP IS WATCHING TV in the living room when I'm about to leave. He must have just got home from work, judging by the red bandana still tied around his forehead.

"Going out?"

"Yeah," I say, slipping on my cotton jacket.

"With Justin?"

The tone in his voice throws me off. "A group of us is studying at his place. Why?"

"Dan told me Justin showed up at the shop with you in tow. Said Taylor had a talk with the both of you."

Sighing, I drop down on the couch beside him. "Justin lifted a car with me."

"Since when?"

"Only once."

"And he was just like, 'Committing felonies is rad'?"

"No one says rad anymore, Kip."

"Lilly." He says my name in warning, having no patience with my deflecting.

"He doesn't want me to do it by myself. He thinks it's dangerous."

"And you trust him?"

Trust. The word in itself carries the implication that I know what I'm doing when I say, "Yes, I trust him," when really, I have no idea.

Kip finishes his beer and stands, walking into the kitchen. I hear the glass bottle hit another in the trashcan, and he reemerges with the glock by his side. "I want you to keep this with you."

"Kip."

"Put it in your car for now until I can sign you up for a concealed weapons class."

"Justin's not going to hurt me," I say in defense.

"It's not for Justin. Taylor's getting desperate for this money and I don't like it. Please, just do what I say and give me a little more peace of mind." I take the gun from his hand. "Remember what I taught you?"

"Only point if I have intention to shoot."

chapter 9

"CAN WE TAKE A BREAK?" Kaley slides from Justin's couch like a slinky.

Lance throws his pen down. "I second that."

Kaley managed to corner Justin into allowing a study session in his apartment. Justin couldn't blame them when he and I had been skipping sessions to study alone in his apartment or at Chuck's. It was more of my doing than Justin's because of my desire to avoid putting him and Kaley in the same room.

Ever since she picked up the change in our dynamic, she's been grilling me. And if she's not bugging me with incessant questions, she's throwing out sexual innuendos whenever Justin and I are within ten feet of one another. Things went back to normal after bowling night, except now there's more apprehension. Everything we do, we do with caution. If he's sitting on the couch, I take the recliner. If I'm in the kitchen, he'll wait until I'm done before entering. There's too much tension now. I feel like we're a bomb. And I'm scared Kaley has the remote to trigger it.

"My brain hates me. I've read the same page twice and I can't recall a single sentence." Courtney massages her temples.

Blake hops up. "Anyone want something to drink?"

"I'll take one," I say, raising my hand.

He looks around the room, one by one, double-checking. He gets to Justin, who still has his head down. I say his name and his head snaps up.

"Want anything to drink?"

He shakes his head no. He's been moody, barely putting in any effort to socialize. He's probably said all of three sentences combined since everyone arrived. Everyone's just kind of avoided interacting with him. I've caught him staring off into space more than he's actually studied.

"Let's go out," Kaley says, looking to Lance. She knows he's her best bet at rallying the troops.

Justin is already rubbing his eyes from exhaustion. Next week is midterms, and we're all cramming. College is basically a massive test to see who can retain the most information without actually understanding it.

"A hangover isn't conducive," Courtney says.

Lance wraps an arm around her shoulder, teasing her with a little shake. "Courtney, ever the voice of reason, we can go to the bar a few blocks over and have a chill night. No dance clubs with strobe lights or EDM music."

"Only middle-aged men looking to score. I'll pass, thanks. But I do think I'm going to call it a night."

Lance drops his arm in defeat. Turning to Blake, he pushes on his bicep. "What about you, buddy? Up for some pool?"

"No, man. Not tonight."

Kaley gives me a poignant stare, nodding her head in Justin's direction. I shake my head no. She silently stomps her foot. I shake my head no again. She holds up her hands, pleading with me in prayer.

I throw my hands in the air. "Justin, do you want to go?"

He doesn't look at me but shakes his head no.

"It's okay," Lance says, patting him on the shoulder as he walks toward the door, Kaley following right behind. "We'll have fun without you."

"Come on, Lilly."

I give her a look. "I never said I was going."

"You've been MIA since the semester started. You kind of owe me, especially because you've been ditching me to spend lunch with Matt."

taking mine

Her deviousness is astounding in the most horrific way. On Monday, I canceled lunch with her to finish a paper that was due, and I happened to run into Matt in the library. When Kaley brought me a smoothie out of the kindness of her heart and saw me sitting with him, she was kind of pissed. She didn't say she was, but it doesn't take a rocket scientist to figure out when Kaley's being pissy. Like right now.

"Fine," I say. "I'll meet you there."

I wait for everyone to leave so that I can try to talk to Justin alone and figure out what's going on with him. I pack up slowly, not wanting to jump him with questions the second we're alone. He's tapping his pen against the arm of the couch, staring at the wall on the other side of the room, not making a move.

I clear my throat. "Justin." My voice is low, but it still sounds like a wrecking ball came in and demolished half the apartment.

"Lilly."

"Is everything okay?"

He looks at me, his face purposefully blank. "Are you seeing that Matt guy?"

I'm so caught off guard that it takes a second for me to register what he said. It's almost as if he's...jealous.

"We haven't made any official plans or anything."

He nods once and stands, dropping his books on the coffee table. "Have fun tonight."

And that's all he says as he walks into his bedroom and shuts the door behind him, leaving me to excuse myself.

THE STING OF JUSTIN'S DISMISSAL lingers as I walk into the bar. It's empty, considering it's the official start of finals week. Lance is already talking up a girl by the dartboards, and Kaley's in the midst of some jocks. Of course they're not worried about midterms when half the professors pass them regardless. But overall, nothing special or interesting is happening, and the last place I want to be is here.

I'm already taking a step backward when Kaley spots me. "Oh no you don't," she says, linking an arm through mine. "You've been MIA since the beginning of the semester. Tonight, you're obligated to have fun."

Grudgingly, I let her lead me to the bar. I think about planting my feet and finding out how far she's going to take this. I smile at the image of her dragging me across the floor as I try to claw my way out.

"Margarita on the rocks?" the bartender says, already familiar with Kaley's drink of choice.

"No," I say for her. "I'm not carrying you home tonight."

She holds up her hands in surrender. "A beer, please."

The bartender looks to me and I order a cherry soda.

"What's the obligatory amount of time I need to be here?"

She muses, touching the tip of her chin. "Until I'm satisfied that you've made a valiant effort."

Figuring I'm going to be here for a while, I go ahead and take a seat on one of the barstools. The bartender slides each of our drinks over and begins wiping the already clean countertop, busying himself for the slow night.

"Are you going to tell me what's going on between you and Justin?"

"Nope."

"It's socially unjust to withhold this kind of information from your best friend."

"There's no information because there's nothing going on."

"Sure, and that's why you're always staring at each other when you think no one is looking."

That's not true.

"It's true," she says, reading my thoughts.

One of the jocks calls her name, needing another person for a game of billiards. She's indecisive, torn between the fun on the other side of the bar and really getting the inside scoop on my nonexistent love life.

"Go," I say, shooing her away.

"Are you going to leave?"

I roll my eyes. "No. Now go."

She sighs, and for a moment I wonder if there's another reason she wanted me to tag along, but she leaves before I get the chance to explore further. I'm left with me, my drink, and staring at my reflection in the mirror behind the bar for company.

"Your friend ditched you?" the bartender asks, picking up my drink and wiping away the condensation underneath it.

"It's okay. It's kind of her MO."

"Sounds like a great friend."

"She's not so bad. We've both been kind of flakey lately."

He stops cleaning and leans on his elbows. "That explains why I've never seen you around. Your friend comes in a few times a week."

That's more than I was aware of. I look over my shoulder and see her laughing at a guy demonstrating a trick shot behind his back. The number of males currently vying for her attention is ridiculous.

"She comes alone?"

He nods in Lance's direction. "They always come in together, but they don't always leave together."

I don't need him to elaborate. "You're just full of all kinds of nifty information, aren't you?"

"My life consists of this bar five nights a week. Watching people drink is the only hobby I have time for." He smiles, a little bit of shyness creeping in.

He's charming. He knows how to put just the right amount of effort into a smile to be likable. And it's so much different from Justin's, where he only smiles when he feels like it, and it's always genuine. He has no charm, at least in the sense that being himself leaves more to the imagination than the boy standing on the other side of this bar.

"You forgot to mention flirting with customers."

Almost as if my thoughts had conjured him, Justin takes the seat to the left of me, shooting daggers at the bartender before landing on me. The dark circles under his eyes throw me off. In the hour we've been apart, they appear to have gotten darker than when we were at his apartment. I knew he was tired, but I didn't know he was *that* tired. I can't recall his eyes being so deep.

"You know him?" The bartender leans back and points at Justin.

Justin doesn't give me a second to speak, ordering a whiskey on the rocks. It's more of a demand, but the bartender drops his towel, reaching for a bottle under the counter.

"Single malt?"

"Bourbon," Justin says, his tone sedated, holding no weight.

"I didn't know you drank hard liquor," I say, watching the auburn liquid being poured.

The glass is placed in front of Justin and the bartender walks away, picking up his rag to continue his ritual. "Yeah, well," he says, taking a gulp of the liquid downing half the volume in one swallow. "There's a lot you don't know about me."

A slew of words fly through my mind that I'd like to say to him, but I tamp them down, figuring he's got to be like this for a reason. I quit trying to figure out Justin weeks ago. Sometimes he's happy-go-lucky, other times serious, but rarely has he been this down.

I signal the bartender, smiling at his reluctance as he walks toward me, and order myself the same drink. Well, though. 'Cause let's face it: I'm cheap.

Justin watches me sniff the dark liquid and take a sip. He cracks a smile when I choke.

"Why can't you pick something fun to drink? Like a mimosa."

He downs the rest of his glass and signals for a refill. "I need a reminder of why I hate alcohol."

"Because you don't want to be like your dad?"

His head snaps in my direction, eyes hard. It's the first time I've been on the receiving end of his anger, and it's more potent than I thought. He doesn't say anything as he finishes off his second drink. "I'm going to call it a night. I'll see you later."

I reach for his shoulder, catching his t-shirt in my hand. "You just got here."

"And now I'm leaving."

"Not until you talk to me." His entire body tenses, readying for a fight.

taking mine

"Talking isn't going to fix anything, Lilly. If that was the case, I would fucking talk you out of my system."

I release the grip on his shirt. "You're right."

All the fight I had in me a second ago diminishes as quickly as it came. I pick up the remainder of my scotch and throw it back. A groan rumbles from Justin, annoyance being its epicenter. He wraps his arm around my waist, lifting me off the barstool and placing my feet on the ground.

"What the hell."

He grabs my hand, pulling me toward the exit. I stumble over my feet, trying to keep up. Kaley shoots daggers at him as we pass the pool tables, and I shake my head at her to stay.

"Justin," I say, trying to keep my voice calm even though I'm shaking. Not from anger but adrenaline.

"I'm not going to leave knowing you're just going to get shit-faced drunk and there's no one to look after you."

"I'm old enough to take care of myself."

"It's not you I'm worried about."

"Haven't heard that before. If I wanted another overprotective brother, I'd just clone Kip."

He stops mid stride, making me run face first into his chest. His laugh is almost manic. "I guarantee you I'm the furthest thing from your brother."

Without another word, he turns back around and heads back to his apartment. We're already at the halfway mark. I know Justin won't actually force me anywhere. If I choose, I can turn back around, go back to the bar or to my car, and call it a night. On second thought, the whiskey seems to have settled in my stomach, leaving a wake in my head. Driving probably isn't in my best interest. Deciding the latter, I trudge on behind him.

By the time we reach his apartment, neither of us has spoken a word in the entire block over. His posture is wrung tight, like a rubber band stretched to its capacity. It's like we ran the entire way here instead of walking, considering our breaths are harsh, anger still very much alive. I don't even flinch when he slams the door behind me.

I walk straight to his fridge and pull out a beer. I open it by the time he reaches me, and he pulls it from my lips. "Stop."

"You stop," I say, pulling the beer back.

I'm poking the bear, I know this, but I really, really want to. Call it the weeks of pent up frustration, or the countless times I've replayed our kiss in my head, or it very well could be the teasing words he said the night he dropped me off from bowling. Hell, it might be his freaking pen chewing. Call it retribution. But at this point, I'm the one about to snap.

He rips the bottle from my hand and throws it in the sink, making glass and froth splatter up against the backsplash. "You're acting like a child."

"Stop treating me like one."

"Since when does making sure you get home safe make me the bad guy?"

"Since you refuse to tell me what the hell is going on with you."

He pinches the bridge of his nose, taking a step away from me. He lets his arm drop, insolent. "What are you talking about, Lilly?"

"I don't know," I say, throwing up my hands. "How about why you've been walking around like someone killed your dog? Or why you're so adamant to defend me when you don't even want anything to do with me? You don't get the right to chase off someone who's flirting with me when you've made it perfectly clear there's nothing between us."

"There it is," he says, pointing at me. "This has nothing to do with me trying to make sure you're safe. Why can't you listen to me when I say I can't do a relationship right now?"

"Who said I ever wanted a relationship!"

The silence that descends after my outburst is deafening. His face is red, partially due to the amount of alcohol running through him, and partially due to the amount of yelling that just occurred. A vein throbs on the edge of his temple. Acting on impulse, I place my thumb against it, trying to slow the pounding there.

"I'm sorry," I whisper. "I'm sorry for whatever you're going through right now. I'm sorry you feel like you have to go through it alone. And I'm sorry I'm making it worse. That originally wasn't my intention."

His mouth is opened slightly and our breaths converge between us. He pushes me up against the counter, and less than a second later his lips are on mine. Our mouths clash, uncoordinated, and our teeth hit from the force. His tongue immediately pushes into mine, and it elicits a moan. His hips press hard against mine, pinning me back as I tug on his shirt, pulling it up. He pulls back long enough to help me, but he doesn't waste any time before his lips are back. Forcefully, he lifts my shirt up over my chest, exposing my bra.

Lifting me, he places me on the breakfast bar, making my chest level with his. His lips trail over my neck and skip over the shirt bunched there, pulling my bra down to expose my breasts. Maybe it's the alcohol, but all I can think is how incredibly hot this is. His mouth lands on one breast and he wraps his arms around my back, arching my body into his.

He nips me, and I grab his hair, yanking his head back. My teeth clamp down on his lip in return. He takes my punishment with a guttural sound, only making me want more. I lace my fingers through his belt and undo it, pulling it through its loops. He finishes off my work, undoing the button and pulling down the zipper as I undo mine. He grabs the back of my knees, pulling me forward, causing me to lie back against the cool tiles. I lift my hips as he drags my jeans over them until they're on the floor with his shirt.

I'm waiting on a comment about my lack of underwear, but when I look down, I see nothing but fire in his eyes. There's something dark. Need or something he's chasing. But I'm pretty sure I'm chasing it, too.

"Shit," he says, running his hand down his face. And it's the first sign of hesitation. Stopping it mid thought, I sit up and pull his mouth to mine.

His kisses are slower, more controlled, so I nip at his neck, trying to get the fire back. He tightens his grip on my hips. "Lilly..." Deciding on another tactic, I slide my hand down his pants. His hips jerk against the feel of my palm on him. I stroke him leisurely a few times before I give him a strong pull. "Fuck," he hisses through his teeth.

He retrieves a condom from his wallet, pinning me back to the table. "I'm sorry," is the last thing he says before he pushes into me. I have no time to decipher the meaning before my back arches off the table. Justin's forearm is banded around my lower back, pulling me down onto him. He doesn't bother to muffle his response, and it's like throwing fire onto my already scorched body. I've never experienced being with someone in this way. It's raw, uncoordinated, and fucking fantastic.

We're gripping each other so hard I'm positive there's going to be bruising, neither one of us letting up. I trail my hands over his shoulders, feeling the muscles of his back as he pushes into me. And every push is a means to an end. There's no other thought but getting what we both desire in one another.

I don't have one coherent thought. Nothing else exists for these blissful moments. I was wrong when I said I felt like I was going to snap. No, it's now, most definitely now. My entire body locks around his, chasing this spark until the edge when he meets me at the same point. His teeth clamp down on my shoulder, and I dig my nails into his sides, wanting this feeling to last forever.

We lay unmoving, him on top of me, our arms still around each other as we catch our breaths. He makes the first move, placing an open-mouth kiss on my shoulder, in the same spot he bit. He pulls away and helps me sit up, never taking his eyes off of mine. I keep my emotions in check, hoping I don't show the amount of unease that seeped in with his departure. He disposes of the condom and pulls his pants up from around his thighs as I fix my shirt and bra.

"Shower?" he asks, unsure.

I pull some of the damp hair off my neck and nod. "Please."

Laughing, he helps me to my feet, and I wince. "Are you okay?"

taking mine

It's my turn to laugh. "I think my entire body is going to be sore."

His cheeks are tinged red, a flush covering his chest and neck. "The bathroom is in my bedroom to the right. Give me a second to clean up our mess."

Walking with as much dignity as I can muster, I march my bare ass to his bedroom and I don't stop to look at the queen-sized bed or dresser. Being alone is my only goal, and I shut the door behind me. It's tiny, with a pedestal sink and the same tile on the walls as the kitchen. Sterile is the best word to describe Justin's bathroom. Everything is plain, white, and extremely clean.

I cut the water on, adjusting the temperature as I get the remainder of my clothes off. A bottle of all-in-one body wash sits on the shelf next to the showerhead. I take a sniff, expecting it to smell like Justin, but it doesn't. Justin smells clean but earthy. This smells pungent and closely resembles the horror of anything Axe.

"What are you thinking about?" Justin asks, pulling the shower curtain back and getting in. His arrival soothes some of the hurt from the kitchen. I stand with my back to the spray, slowly running the remaining soap from my hair. Instead of answering, I shake my head, half in confusion and lack of words to process it.

His eyes take me in and I do the same. We didn't have a chance to take a moment to appreciate each other. I've never been particularly insecure. Only in times when I've had to stand in a room full of women did I ever feel judged for my body. But in front of Justin, I want to be perfect.

To fight my desire to cover my flaws, I reach out for him instead, placing my hands flat on his chest. His muscles jump underneath my touch. I don't look up at him as I trail my hands up and over his shoulders, and down his arms, stopping when I see the marks. Nail marks cover his sides from his ribs to his shoulders.

Without the hurry from before, Justin leans his face into the crook of my neck. His chest rises deeply against mine as he breathes in. "I don't want to say anything to ruin this," he says into my shoulder. "But I need to tell you that I didn't mean for this to happen."

My breathing stills against his.

He lifts his head from my neck to look at me. "I tried to keep my distance from you, to not let it come this far, but I literally can't stay away from you."

Little droplets of water gather on the tips of his eyelashes, each blink releasing more. The dark circles under his eyes are still there but less visible than before, and I smile because I know that I eased whatever was troubling him, even if it wasn't in the smartest way.

"I never asked you to stay away."

"I know." His fingers trail the bite mark above my breast. He outlines the two crescent moons that face each other. Turmoil lurks behind his eyes as he starts in on the second bite on my clavicle.

Pulling his hand away, I run his fingers over my lips. "Quit thinking."

"That's funny coming from you."

His face is stoic, his eyes jumping over me. He kisses me. It's chaste, a small kiss, but he's close enough for me to feel him. "Let's get cleaned up and watch a movie."

"A movie?" I laugh.

"Got a thing against movies?"

"It's just, I figured, you know, that I'd go home…now."

"We've both been drinking. I don't think driving is a good idea, and it's too far to walk."

"But isn't this crossing a line? Staying after sex?"

"Lilly," he says, a resigned smile on his face. "We're watching a movie, just like when we've watched Family Feud and pigged out on potato chips." Turning me around, he pins my body up against his and I can feel every inch of him. "Besides, we blew the line up when I fucked you in my kitchen."

THE ROOM IS ENCOMPASSED in darkness when I awake alone in Justin's bed. I'm completely cocooned within the blanket, hiding any bit of skin from the whirl of the ceiling fan. I went to bed with the fan definitely off, but apparently it was turned on in the middle of the night. Justin sleeps with every appendage stretched to its max capacity, and he ended up kicking the mountain of covers to my side. I don't understand why he even has them if he refuses to use them.

Justin's voice trails in from the crack in the doorway. Unsure of what time it is, I decide to get up and find my phone. I use the bathroom and redo my hair, thinking of saving Justin from my morning bed head and scarring him for life. Peeking out the door, I see him pacing the living room on the phone. Identifying that it's safe to come out, I wrap the comforter around myself. His back is to me as I wade across the living room to get to my phone off the coffee table.

"I'm not sure," he says into the phone. He rubs his eyes like he does when he's particularly tired. "I haven't figured that out yet." His words clip off when he catches sight of me. "Look, Mom. I've got to go, but I'll call you later, okay?" He doesn't wait for a response before he hangs up.

"You don't have to get off the phone because of me."

"I needed an excuse to get off, anyway. I don't know how long I could hold off the Spanish Inquisition."

"She worries a lot about you?"

"You have no idea," he says, shaking his head.

I scroll through my texts, getting more anxious with every missed call from Kip. "My brother's going to kill me."

"Seems like we're both dealing with overprotective parents this morning."

He's leaning his back against the bar, the same one we…yeah, he's drinking a cup of coffee. Nothing strange about this at all. And I feel like a complete pervert that I can't seem to find the will to think about anything other than touching him. I consider actually doing it, seeing where it goes, but he's completely dressed and ready for the day. I'm the one still nude. I text Kip and glance around the room and into the kitchen. "What did you do with my clothes?"

"I folded them. They're sitting on top of the dresser."

"Oh, I didn't see them." I walk past him to get to his bedroom, and we hold eye contact the entire way. Granted, it's like six steps, but it's long enough for me to see the heat in them. He turns away and walks into the kitchen.

When I do finally get dressed and gain the nerve to step out of the bedroom, I find him microwaving Pop-Tarts.

"You don't have a toaster?" He jumps at the sound of my voice and I laugh. "You're kind of jumpy this morning."

He takes a bite of his Pop-Tart. "I like my Pop-Tarts warm, not crunchy."

"Noted."

"Want one?" he asks, holding out its pair.

"No thanks. I've got class in an hour and I still need to go home and change. I can't think of anything worse than taking the walk of shame to class." I expect a laugh, or at least a half-assed chuckle, but all he does is nod. "So...."

His phone rings, interrupting the awkward silence. He pivots around and grabs it off the counter. "Fuck," he says, reaching for his keys and packet of cigarettes on the breakfast bar. "I've got to take this. We'll talk later, okay?" He's at the door when he says, "Lock up on your way out."

Disappointment. It's a resounding feeling that echoes in my chest, in the same cavity that holds my breath and my heart. I'm aware of it even though I'm not a hundred percent sure I understand it. Technically, nothing was promised and false hope wasn't given. It's not one of those predicaments. Which kind of makes me feel worse about it. Justin's too good of guy to do those things, and I'm too impetuous to stop it. It's as much my fault, if not more so, that I'm feeling let down by him.

When I walk the two blocks back to the bar to get my car, it's nowhere to be seen. I check the back parking lot even though I'm positive I didn't park back there. I walk around the entire building before I notice the sign on the side of the building. After business hours, vehicles are towed upon discretion.

Fucking fantastic.

chapter 10

"HOW MUCH MONEY?"

"Five hundred." Taylor counts out five one hundred dollar bills from his wallet and hands them to me. Confronting Taylor for money isn't something I wanted to do, but having my car impounded took the last few I had.

"Have you talked to Kip about the offer from Jimmy?"

"I'm going to tonight."

He's not overly enthusiastic with my answer, but it pacifies him for now. "Kaley's been waiting for you. She's in the lobby."

"Why?"

"Hell if I know. Just don't forget about talking to Kip."

I roll my eyes.

I find Kaley and Kip arguing, and I'm immediately positive it's concerning my whereabouts from last night. They both look up at me when I walk in. Kip's expression is livid whereas Kaley's is a mix between fear and anger.

"Where the hell were you last night?" Kip's voice reverberates through my chest. It's louder than when he found out I started working for Taylor in high school. And I'd thought it couldn't get louder than that. "I went out with Kaley to a bar by the University."

"Don't treat me like a fucking idiot, Lilly. Tell me the truth."

"Justin's."

"Justin's," he repeats. He eyes me for a moment before diverting his attention. Kaley and I wait in stony silence for him to say something else. "I want you to come straight home after work." His tone is abrupt and to the point.

"What, are you punishing me?" I say, half laughing at the assertion.

"You can't punish her," Kaley yells in my defense.

"We agreed you'd be honest with me." That's all he says before he leaves, throwing the guilt on thick.

"She's twenty-two, for God's sake," Kaley yells at Kip's retreating back.

Dan opens the shop door, peeking his head in. "Everything alright?"

"We're fine," she snaps, and he throws his hands up, letting the door fall back in its place. "It's ridiculous how he tries to control you."

"It's fine, Kale. He'll go home and calm down and we'll talk it out. We always do."

"So," she drawls, turning the conversation around. "Justin's?" I walk away, not giving in to her curiosity. The last thing I want right now is to relive the atrocity that was this morning. "Oh, come on," she calls at my retreating back. "Was it good?" I open the shop door. "Give me a thumbs up if it was good," she yells in a last ditch effort, so I flip her off.

TWO DAYS LATER, Kip confirmed with Jimmy that we were in. I wasn't there for the actual conversation, but I was there when Taylor received the news. The entire shop was stunned by Taylor's generosity to buy everyone lunch from the pizza shop down the street. Kip made the comment about counting chickens before they hatch, but nothing could have stopped Taylor from celebrating. Or Dan. His smile was large enough to blind someone. And so help me, I couldn't shake off their enthusiasm either.

That's why I thought about skipping tonight, but Taylor insisted I should still cover all of my bases. Given the lenience from Kip, Taylor asked Dan if he'd seen any good finds while out scouting. Dan said he spotted this Chevy Impala and the owner is a well-known dealer on the East bank. He frequents a residence there every Monday. The only reason they haven't made a move is because he's in and out quick.

taking mine

I'm at a park about a football field's length away. I have about a five-minute window. The neighborhood is upscale, on the more residential side of town. Suspicious activity is more likely to be reported. I check my phone. Dan said the dealer gets here between ten and ten thirty. It's 10:05 and he still hasn't arrived. It's hard to tell whether or not he'll show. I'm nervous this time. Off kilter. The close call with Justin has me on edge.

"I was hoping I wouldn't find you here."

Justin's voice pulls my attention away from the time ticking on my phone. We haven't spoken since I left his apartment, so I don't why he's here. Not because we're avoiding each other, but because we've been genuinely busy. Finals week just ended, and we're now in the start of fall break.

And it clicks. I don't bother to ask how he knew, already suspecting Taylor and Dan. How convenient that they had a car already lined up for me. This isn't for me; it's for Justin. It's a final run-through to see if Justin has the balls to go through with it twice. And this time, the stakes are a little higher. Taylor needs another hand with Jimmy's offer coming in.

"Because you don't want to see me or because you don't want me to do what I'm about to?"

He sighs, taking a seat on the swing adjacent to mine. "I always want to see you. That's the problem." He pulls his cigarettes from his pocket and lights one.

"Sounds utterly conflicting and annoying at the same time."

He laughs through his nose. "It is. You have no idea."

"You're right, I don't."

His smile fades. "Can you trust me?" A nearby streetlight casts an orange glow on the both of us. "Trust me when I say you don't want anything to do with me."

I don't react to his words, internally or externally. "That is kind of funny." I pause to gather my thoughts. "I do trust you, you know. I mean, technically we barely know each other. A couple of months. And yet I feel like if I gave you my life," I say, pulling his hand toward me, palm up. "And placed it right here..." I close his hand into a fist. "It'd be safe. You'd never let anything bad happen to it."

I lift my eyes and he's staring at my hand wrapped around his. I can see the swallow of his throat. "Lilly." He says my name like he's in pain.

"Its fine, Justin. I'm not asking anything from you."

I release his hand from my grasp and we sit in silence. He smokes slowly, and I inhale the smell of it as it billows my way. He doesn't ask questions as to what we're waiting for, and I don't say. It's a little past ten thirty when the dealer makes his appearance.

He stands when I do. "It's the Impala?"

"Yeah. We only have about a five-minute window."

"Okay," he says, stubbing his cigarette out.

I pop the lock and climb to the passenger side. Justin follows suit without any direction. I hand him the wire strippers and I keep a watch out as he opens the ignition panel and cuts the wires. The car comes to life and we pull away from the curb in record time. It's incredibly efficient with an extra person helping.

"Are you sure you don't do this often?"

"More often than I'm proud to admit." He side-eyes me. "Not recently."

"You're doing it right now."

"Besides now."

"Because of me?"

He adjusts his seating and places one arm along the window. "Because of you," he says. His eyes shift from the road, to me, and back again.

When we get to the shop, Dan and Ethan are waiting for us, ready to break the car down. Ethan is more of the silent and get-down-to-business type. I think he's only ever spoken to me when I've addressed him first. It comes as no surprise when he ignores Justin with no questions asked. Dan, not so much.

"Taylor wants to speak with you before you go," Dan says, motioning over our shoulders to Taylor's office.

"Yeah, I'd like to have a talk with him as well."

taking mine

"Want me to wait here?" Justin says.

"No," Taylor's voice cuts in from behind us. "This concerns you, too."

We crowd into the small office space, and Taylor remains standing as Justin and I take our seats. Taylor jumps right to the point, saying nothing as he turns his computer monitor toward us. Three of Justin's mug shots stare back from the screen. His age shows in all the pictures, indicating they were taken a long time ago. Justin sits a little straighter.

"You have no right," I accuse Taylor.

"It's a matter of public record, Lilly. Anyone can access this information for a small fee. I'm going to look into the person who's been spending so much time with someone I'm close to, especially someone who makes a habit of engaging in criminal activity."

I roll my eyes so hard I give myself a headache. "Get real, Taylor. Cut the intimidation tactic. What do you want?"

Taylor finally sits. "There is no tactic. I'm offering him a job."

All the breath leaves me.

"What job?" Justin asks, leaning forward.

"No," I cut in before Taylor can respond.

He continues, acting like he didn't hear me. "I assume Lilly's told you what we do."

"You're basically blackmailing him."

Taylor cuts his attention to me. "I'm not blackmailing anyone. I'm showing him that he has nothing to hide from me."

"No, you're implying that his past dictates his future."

"I'm giving him a choice, Lilly. The same choice I've given you."

"This isn't about me. This is about him."

"You're right. You can leave my office."

"Lilly." Justin's voice cuts through the sound of blood thumping in my ears. He's telling me to trust him. I see it. It's ironic considering the conversation we just had. I told him that I did trust him, and now I have to prove it.

Shoving up from my seat, I point a finger in Taylor's direction. "Don't forget that you wouldn't have this job if it weren't for me."

Taylor gives a nod of acknowledgment. "And for that I'll give you the full profit from the Impala after I pay Dan and Ethan their share. I'm only holding Justin to the same standard I hold you, Lilly."

And that's the problem. I hold him higher than me.

I help Dan and Ethan box up the parts as they dismember the car. I struggle through listening to Dan goad Ethan into talking about a girl he brought home the night before, only for Ethan to repeatedly tell him to shut up. My eyes wander to the window to Taylor's office, as if I can see through the blinds and get a feel on the conversation. It's a full twenty minutes later when the door opens. Taylor shakes Justin's hand, and he gives me a smirk as he shuts the door and Justin walks away.

I place the last box of parts into Dan's van for him to deliver, and Justin reaches over and pulls the door shut for me. "So," I implore.

He shoves his hands into his pockets, making his cotton t-shirt give a little and pull tight over his shoulders. "Think you can give me a ride home?"

I want to immediately jump into questions.

"Can I smoke in here?" he asks as we get in my car.

"Yeah."

He holds his hand out the window, trying to prevent smoke from getting in. Smoking really is his stress relief. I figure I can withhold the interrogation until he's done, no matter how much I'm itching on the inside.

His face is deceiving. To the world he looks like an easygoing guy, but underneath that, I've seen a mirage of hardship and a sense of desperation. I feel like he's hiding something. I don't push. I really wouldn't know where to start if I did. The only thing I know is that I trust him. And maybe his heart, even if it's so conflicted.

"Is your brother going to have a problem if I work for Taylor?"

"Kip doesn't have much to do with this side of the business anymore."

"Why's that?"

taking mine

"I think he wants out. He's never actually said it, but I can tell. The minute he made enough to support us managing Toby's, he quit dealing with the orders."

"And Taylor's okay with that?"

I shrug. "I don't know. I think he prefers it this way. He's never been as interested in running Toby's as he is selling parts. Toby's was only supposed to be a front, a well-do business to hide the internal affairs, but Kip has pushed to make it as authentic as he can."

I pull into a parking spot across from Justin's apartment, but he makes no move to get out as he finishes smoking.

"Why'd you say he wouldn't have the job without you?"

"Because I convinced Kip to do it. Jimmy wouldn't give us the agreement without Kip on board, and I pushed Kip to say yes."

"You want out from under Taylor. This can make enough for you to quit."

"Yes," I say. "For the both of us. Kip wants this too."

For the first time since coming out of Taylor's office, he looks at me. It's the same look he gave me when we were in the shower. Sad. Possessive. Proud? There's a tiny part of me that recognizes we're connected in a strange way. The insinuation that I can read his emotions as well as he can mine is staggering.

"It's hard to turn down so much money. And it's hard to feel bad when we're going to be stealing from rich assholes," he says.

"Yeah."

A crowd of students stumble past my car, rocking the vehicle back and forth. Laughter filters in from the outside. "Want to come inside?"

It's only been a few days since Justin and I were alone in his apartment together, yet it feels like a lifetime. But in that lifetime, the disappointment lingers. For whatever reason holding him back, I can't fix it or force it. It's something he has to figure out on his own.

I read in a case study once where the defense won based on the concept of mamihlapinatapai. It's when two people look at each other and both of them are wishing the other would initiate something they both desire. Right now, he wants me to say yes, to give in. He's torturing himself and, in turn, torturing me.

"No, I think I'm going to head home."

I can see the small amount of anticipation he had diminish, and I instantly want to retract. I've relived our time together, and I want it. Bad. It's really all I can think about. And that's the scariest part. So, I hold on to my resolve and bite my tongue.

"Okay. I'll see you at the next study group?" It's a question, so I nod. "Okay," he repeats as he gets out of my car.

He's halfway across the parking lot when I remember there's a very important question I still have yet to ask. I roll down my window and yell, "Justin." He turns to me. "What did you say to Taylor?"

"Yes, on one condition… I go with you."

I smile. I can't help it. He winks at me before he ascends the stairs, skipping every other step.

THE FIRE IS STARTING TO SCORCH my skin, so I take a step back, letting the cold settle back in. I'm on my first date with Matt, if you can call it that. We're at a party off campus. Some rich kid down the street from Kaley's house decided to throw one last minute. When Matt texted and asked me to hang out, this isn't quite what I had in mind, but it's everything I ever expected a kegger to be.

Girls are dressed in their skimpiest outfits, sitting in the living room and watching a group of jocks play beer pong. Girls in short shorts, girls in bikinis, girls in no bikinis, and considering it's freaking cold, it's fucking ridiculous. The backyard is big enough for an in-ground swimming pool and a fire pit and that's it.

"Lilly."

I blink as I focus on Matt next to me, the flicker of the flames casting shadows against his face.

"I'm going to go grab another beer. Want one?"

I shake my head.

He gives me a tight-lipped smile before departing toward the house.

We've been here for over an hour and I've stood in the same spot the entire time. Figuring we're not leaving anytime soon, I might as well take a seat. Before I know it, Matt's returned with his beer and a canned drink, which he hands to me. He's nice. He insisted on staying outside with me when I opted out of staying inside. The music's too loud and it's crowded to the point I feel like I'm breathing in everyone else's breath.

"You're not having fun, are you?"

"I'm relaxing. People-watching."

He looks around the small fenced-in yard. "Sometimes I forget what these parties look like to someone who hasn't experienced them before."

I shrug. "It's not that special."

He doesn't reply and instead takes a sip of his drink. My phone buzzes in my pocket.

It's from Taylor. He wants me to meet him at Toby's ASAP.

"Let me guess, you gotta go," Matt says, smiling at me.

"It's not like that," I say, defending myself.

"It's okay. Go." I don't move and he pokes me in the side. "Go."

I stand. "Thanks for understanding."

He shrugs. "I'm about to kill a game of beer pong."

I smile, he smiles, and it's safe to say we won't go out again, but it's been an insight to the strange world of college dating. A girl in a bikini runs by and a person in a gorilla suit follows shortly behind. Matt laughs along with everyone else, and I'm lost in the humor. Maybe it's a rich people thing.

ALL THE LIGHTS ARE ON at Toby's when I park next to Kip's truck, and I note the absence of Dan's van. Even when we're closed, he's usually here doing stuff. I hear Taylor talking when I enter the shop. His office door is open, letting his voice echo along the walls.

"I agreed to the job on one condition, and that was that Lilly wouldn't have a part of it." Kip yells over Taylor's voice.

"She's not going to agree to that."

"It's not her decision; it's mine."

I knock on the open door, letting them know I arrived. "What's going on?"

Kip's face is so red I know he is beyond the stage of irritated and crossed into pissed off territory. "You're not running the cars for him." Kip points at me, drilling in his point.

I look at Taylor for more clarification. "Kip, we need her. There's no one else we trust enough to do it."

"Do what?"

Kip's face is pained as Taylor describes it to me. "Our first order is due in 24 hours. That's by midnight tomorrow. The car is scheduled to be in valet parking from about nine to midnight at a charity event at the LeRouge."

"It doesn't have to be her," Kip seethes through his teeth.

Taylor continues, "We originally planned that Dan and Ethan would go on the first run. This being unknown territory, we didn't want to put you on the front line. However," Taylor draws out. "It's a black tie event. Ethan isn't old enough to attend, and Dan doesn't look the part."

"I'll go." Kip says it like he's already repeated it multiple times.

"It's too risky for one man. And no offense, but you don't scream upstanding citizen, either."

Taylor is right. The harsh lines that outline Kip's features can only be a side effect of carrying a stressful life. It doesn't say money. "Then we don't do it," Kip says in finality.

Taylor scoffs. "It's an Italia. That's 100k, Kip. Even you're not stupid enough to pass this up."

"A Ferrari?" The office goes quiet at the entrance of Justin.

"You called him in?" Kip looks at me accusingly.

"I did," Taylor interjects, daring Kip to challenge his authority. "I would never send Lilly in by herself."

"I would like to think you wouldn't send her in at all."

"This is the info we've received on it." Taylor hands Justin an envelope.

Justin leans against the wall next to me and pulls out the contents. Images of a bright yellow Ferrari Italia covers the first page. He shuffles through more, giving an outline of the building and parking garage. The last page lists some employees and valets who are staff that night. He dumps the envelope over and lets a clicker fall into his palm.

"This is detailed," Justin says, stuffing the papers and key back into the envelope. "How does he get this information?"

"Don't know, but that's not our job to worry about."

Kip looks at me in aspiration. He really can't believe Taylor's comprehension of the entire deal. Justin looks to me. "It's your decision. I'll do whatever you want."

I blow out a mouth full of air. "It's going to be hard to pull off." Justin nods in agreement. "How is the money split?"

"Right off the bat fifty goes to you and Justin. That's twenty-five grand a piece. The remainder will be split between the rest of us. Ethan, Dan, Kip, and myself. The same will go on the next run."

"Lilly—"

"It's my decision, Kip."

He sighs, taking the package from Justin and handing it to me. "Study this. Detail it. Know every camera angle, every shift change, everything. Do you hear me?"

"I didn't agree—"

"I know you. You can't turn it down and I don't blame you. But this is your only run. After this, no more." Kip hands me the envelope and looks to Justin. "I'm trusting you to protect her."

I've never seen Justin look more serious than when he nods at Kip in understanding. Kip leaves without another word.

"He'll come around," Taylor says, trying to convince himself. "Once the money starts coming in, he'll be thanking me."

"We're going to need dress attire," Justin says.

I nod. "I'm sure Kaley has something I can wear."

Taylor pulls a couple of hundreds from his wallet and hands them to Justin. "Go rent a tux. Something designer."

Justin nods and walks out, leaving me alone with Taylor, when a thought occurs. "What about traffic cameras? Driving a bright yellow sports car through downtown is going to be obvious."

"Not once you're over the river," he says. "There aren't a lot of taxpayers on this side, and once you're out of the city, there's not a business for miles."

The hypothetical aspect of simply driving a car from one destination to another seems simple enough, but there are so many factors at play that make it high risk. And essentially, when it comes down to it, if we're caught, whoever is driving the vehicle is going down for it.

Not Taylor.

So I'm not sure whether I believe him. I'm starting to see Kip's reluctance. Taylor's pushing more than normal.

I DON'T KNOCK AS I WALK into Justin's apartment, past the point of niceties. He looks up from his stance at the breakfast bar, a beer settled in front of him, evidently waiting on me to show. He downs half the bottle in the time it takes me to walk toward him. Passing him, I open the refrigerator and retrieve a water. He shuffles around the envelope's contents, spreading out the paperwork one by one.

"I think we need to start with the layout of the parking garage," I say, leaning against the counter. "Ins and outs, cameras."

He braces his palms on the counter. "Where were you?"

Confused, I screw the lid back on my nearly full water bottle. "What?"

He shifts a picture over, pretending to inspect it. "Before Taylor texted you."

I shake my head and look back at the papers in front of us. "Justin, we really need to study—"

taking mine

He turns to face me. "At least tell me why you look so nice." He picks up a strand of my hair and lets it fall between his fingers.

I wore it down for the party instead of in my usual ponytail. The amount of effort I put into it is laughable in comparison to the other girls there. It only adds to the reminder of who I am not.

"Were you on a date?"

I slam my hand down. "Good God, Justin. Can we focus on the job at hand? This isn't child's play."

"I feel like it is," he says, leaning into me. "When I had you right here..." He points to the counter. "Right here two weeks ago."

My face is hot from anger. I know he's trying to rile me up. He's picking a fight and I'm not going to give it to him. Instead, I point to the exit ramp on the garage blueprints. "The entrance requires a keycard, but the exit ramp is pressure activated. No keycard or security access needed to get out, just in."

His eyes are like flint when he takes a step back, finishing off his beer and slamming the bottle down on the counter. He disappears into his room and shuts the door. A minute later I hear the water cut on in his bathroom and I sigh, relieved to have a reprieve. I take a few breaths and steady my racing heart. It's so hard to not fight back. It's easy to give in to the hope that comes with fighting him. It's harder to be indifferent.

I pull my hair back and settle myself onto one of the barstools, determined to focus. I study the entire garage and bottom floor of the hotel. The shift changes and breaks are scheduled upon request or when slow. There are always at least two valets manning the front entrance, three when busy. The only way into the parking garage is through the front with a keycard, and it's a huge cause of worry. One camera points at the front entrance and one at the rear. The lone camera in the garage is pointed in the general direction of the cars but far enough away to get away without being pictured. I check the employee staff rooms and see that those are void of any surveillance.

The water shuts off from the other side of the wall, and I brace myself for his reemergence. There's shuffling, drawers opening and closing, and then his door opens. He runs his hands through his hair a few times before settling onto the stool in front of me.

"I'm sorry," he says.

I nod. "Okay."

He pulls my notes toward him. "This is all based on circumstance."

"I know, but it's the best I can come up with."

"There are too many variables."

"Fine," I say. "You come up with something better."

His eyes stray and linger on me, noting how I put my hair up, before he squeezes them shut. "Jesus Christ..."

I give him a sad smile. "You can't leave it alone, can you?"

He rubs his fingers over his eyes. "At least tell me if you were with him."

"No."

"No you weren't or no you won't tell me?"

I'm silent and he throws his hands up. He stands, once again retrieving a beer. On his way back, he grabs me by the waist, spinning me around until I'm facing him in his arms. My arms are pinned between us as he leans us back against the counter. My heart thumps furiously in my chest. I want him to lean me back like last time. I want it so bad I can feel my knees shaking.

His lips are so close to mine that I don't dare move because I can almost taste him. "When he touches you, think about how you feel right now. Does he make you want him like I do? Does he make it hard to breathe because you're scared you'll give in? Do you want to give in?"

He presses his lips to mine for a split second, enough for me to think he's really going to kiss me, and then he pulls back just out of reach. I place my hands on his chest, feeling his heartbeat as his breathing increases under his shirt.

"Bastard." I push him back.

He pulls my face to his. "I know," he says. He pushes his lips into mine. It's the same desperate need as last time but stronger. This time we've had a foretaste of what we're like together, and it only adds more fuel to the fire.

I gather more willpower than I knew I had, and I push him away, covering my mouth from his onslaught. "No, you don't get to do this. It's not fair to me."

"You have no idea what's not fair."

"What do you want from me?" I yell. It makes my throat raw and I'm immediately ashamed of my emotional outburst. I turn away from him, trying to gain control of myself.

"Hey." Justin follows me through the living room. "Lilly."

"I'll meet you here tomorrow," I say, picking my keys up off the coffee table. "If you come up with something better, let me know."

"Lilly, wait. Please, let me explain." His hand appears from behind me, shutting the door when I try to open it. "I'm sorry. I know this isn't any easier for you than it is for me."

"But why? Why is this even difficult in the first place?"

"It's hard for me to explain."

"Try."

He drops his forehead against the door. "You don't understand."

"You know, I don't get why you're so hell-bent on staying away from me." I don't know what makes me say the words, but I hate them immediately. I suck at keeping my emotions in check. Going so long without having to deal with them, and now they're like wild chickens and I'm scrambling to catch them before they fly the coop.

He's completely still next to me.

I shrug out from under him. "After we do this run, we should take some time apart."

"Lilly." His voice is desperate as he lets me open the door.

"And you should cut ties with Taylor," I say. "He's only going to bring you down."

chapter 11

KALEY FINISHES THE WAVES of my hair and places her hands on my shoulders, looking at my reflection in the vanity mirror. The antique furniture is polished to shine. Anytime I've ever looked in it I've felt like a farce, like only people of class and notoriety got the privilege of laying eyes on it. That's how I've felt since the first time I walked through Kaley's front doors. I've heard that people eventually get used to it, being surrounded by opulent things, but I'm still waiting for that day to come.

"You look beautiful." Kaley's smile borders on motherly and I avert my eyes, not used to her affection. If Kaley isn't insulting you, she doesn't like you.

I can see myself from the chest up, the neckline of my gem-colored dress scooping across the bottom of the mirror. My hair is pulled to one side of my neck, tendrils sweeping around my face. After much bargaining, my make-up is perfect, nothing overdone or dramatic. And for the first time ever, I feel honored to sit down at the two-hundred-year-old oak table, onto the carefully preserved cushioned stool, and stare at the person in the mirror. The stranger before me resembles someone of monetary value. If I were kidnapped, my kidnapper would send out a ransom note, believing I was worth something.

Kaley's face starts to wane, losing the touch of pride in it. "Do you like it?"

I take in a breath and force a smile. "It's amazing, Kaley. I can barely recognize myself. You did great."

Her smile returns. "All we need now is the shoes." She disappears into her closet and emerges with a pair of nude heels, aka my worst

taking mine

nightmare. She hands them to me and I slip them on, stretching my toes as much as I can to gain room. "Stand so I can get the full effect." A little wobbly, I stand, turning so she can see me from all angles. "You're all grown," she says, her hands clasped in front of her mouth and her eyes a little watery.

"Get it together," I say, snapping my fingers.

She shakes her head, clearing her vision. "Excuse me for being excited about the first time I get to squeeze you into a dress."

"Forcibly."

"Stop. You're going to have so much fun."

I told Kaley that I needed a formal dress for a date with Justin tonight. The last thing I wanted to do was stir the pot, but it's better than telling her the alternative: the truth. I had to listen to thirty minutes of her explaining how she *knew* Matt was going to be the catalyst for Justin to finally make his move.

"Don't be nervous."

I snort. "Now that you say that, all my anxiety has suddenly disappeared."

She rolls her eyes. I head out of her bedroom and slip off my shoes, knowing there's no way I'm going to make it down the marble staircase in four-inch heels.

Kaley pads behind me. "You need to practice," she admonishes me.

"You're right, but falling twenty feet to my death seems counterproductive."

"She's got a point, Kaley."

Mr. Monroe is waiting at the bottom of the stairs, bags by the door, as he shrugs out of his overcoat. He shakes my hand, reaching out for a hug from Kaley.

"I didn't know you were coming home," she says, mildly baffled by his appearance. "Where's Mom?"

"She flew to see a friend in the Alps. I decided I'd been gone long enough, so I came home. Someone has to keep an eye on you."

He winks at Kaley and she basks under his attention, and I'm reminded how charismatic he is. I've only met Mr. Monroe a handful of times, but every time I'm caught off guard by his magnetism. He's incredibly smart, and you only have to look at him to know it.

"You look beautiful, Lilly. Where are you headed off to?"

"She's got a date," Kaley answers for me.

He smiles. "That's not surprising in the least."

Where Kaley basks, I'm intimidated. I duck my head, trying to hide my blush. "You should go," Kaley says, rescuing me. If anyone understands what it's like under her dad's scrutiny, it's her. "You don't want to be late."

"Yes, well," Mr. Monroe says, standing a little taller. "Most men know the best women are worth waiting for." I feel my cheeks reddening by the moment. "Have a good night, Lilly." He dismisses Kaley and me, leaving us to ourselves. Kaley's eyes follow him out the grand foyer, a frown across her lips.

"It's a good thing he's home, right?"

She sighs. "Not if Mom isn't here." She opens the door, distancing herself from further discussion. "Call me tomorrow and give me all the details," she says, returning to her normal self.

I roll my eyes. "I'm sure you'll call me."

"And I'm going to want my dress back." She gives me look insinuating I better not ruin it.

Gathering up the material, I slide into my Honda, feeling like a modern day Cinderella. It's a cliché rendering, but it's fitting. Except I'm not going to steal a prince...

I'm going to steal an Italia, which is way cooler.

JUSTIN IS WAITING FOR ME at the foot of the stairs, leaning against his jeep when I arrive at his apartment. The tux he's wearing is tailored to him. Every line curves to his body from his shoulders to the taper at his waist. He stands with a hand in his pocket, the other with a cigarette pinched between his fingers, blowing smoke into the night air. The normal scruff that accompanies his features everyday is shaved smooth, giving him a more boyish charm than he normally has. James Bond would be jealous.

He squints when he sees me walking up, almost like he doesn't recognize me. He assesses my hair and make-up, finishing his perusal down the frame of my body, stopping at the tips of my shoes. "You look…" he says, trailing off.

"Beautiful. Flawless. Every man's dream," I finish for him.

My attempt at humor falls flat when he brushes a strand of my hair back. I clear my throat and open the passenger door of his Jeep. Spurred into action, he helps me up, holding the length of my dress for me.

"Thanks," I say as I take the material from him.

He walks slowly to his side of the car, head down, contemplative. I take deep breaths, trying to prepare myself for the night. Life is about to get complicated as hell, and I don't need to be focused on my emotions.

Justin gets in and situates himself by unbuttoning his tux. His hand hovers over the key in the ignition. Letting out a breath, he turns his head to look at me. "Ready?"

Not in the least, but I nod in acquiescence.

The charity event is being held at a historic building downtown that was later converted into a modern day hotel. Classic Greek architecture with large columns and fountains take up the front entrance. It's in complete contrast to the modern buildings surrounding it. We wait in the precession for the valet.

"Aren't they going to run everyone's license plates once they realize a car is missing?" I ask.

"Most likely. That's why Taylor mocked up a fake temporary one."

Women in expensive dresses step out of vehicles valued close to six digits, adorned in costume jewelry, except the jewels aren't fake. I run my fingers over my throat, subconsciously checking for an imaginary necklace that's sitting there without my knowledge.

"Don't worry, you look amazing," Justin says, and I drop my hand. "Are you nervous?"

"A little. This isn't like anything I've ever done before."

"If we stick to the plan, we'll be fine."

I raise an eyebrow. "I thought my plan was too circumstantial for your liking."

He weighs his head from side to side. "I may have just been trying to goad you."

"No," I say in mock astonishment.

He gives me a look. "Stay by my side once we're in."

We slowly roll toward the entrance, moments away from making our appearance. Security guards stand out front wearing tuxes, earpieces in, overlooking the small walkway where press is taking pictures. This isn't a small event, not in the least. No doubt some important people are going to be in attendance, and it only inflates the rising panic in my throat.

"So we can scope out the employee rooms?"

"That," he says in confirmation. "And because every man in the place is going to be looking at you." At some point my hand must have returned to my neck because he pulls it away, giving me an admonishing look. "You don't need diamonds."

I'm partially grateful and annoyed that he can read me so well. "How long do you think we'll need to stay?"

"An hour, maybe less. Just until the entrance dies down a little. Not so much activity at the front."

It's our turn to exit and a young valet opens my door. I immediately memorize his name. Dalton. Nineteen. Shift ends at midnight.

He gives me a flirtatious smile and holds out a hand for me. Putting my game face on, I return his smile full force. "Welcome to the LeRouge."

I show a little more skin than need be as I exit the car and give Dalton my full attention. "Happy to be here." I smile brightly at him.

He tears his eyes away from my legs as I let my train fall onto the small carpeted runway. "Let me know if I can be of any service."

Justin pushes his way through the both of us and holds his arm out for me to take. Dalton winks at me as I'm whisked away. We stop at a podium, an older lady and a security guard standing behind it, checking off names on the invitation list. This is the first real test that determines whether or not Jimmy is actually dependable when he says he's going to take care of everything. He set up the invite, getting alias names on the list.

Justin pronounces our names and the woman smiles sweetly at us, handing Justin two admittance tickets. I notice the camera mounted at the entrance of the hotel lobby at the same time Justin does, and we both duck our heads as we walk through the metal detector. There's a small portion of the entrance reserved for press, and we walk around it, opting out of getting our pictures taken. I struggle to keep up with Justin's pace in my heels.

"Can you slow down?"

He stops right as we enter the grand ballroom. "I don't want to risk being pictured."

The ballroom is the largest room I've ever been in. The ceiling is so tall I get vertigo as I look up. Everything is accented in gold, the color of wealth. Tables line the back wall with a dance floor in place in front. On either side of the room, two different cars are blocked off with velvet ropes

"Is that what they're holding for auction?"

Justin leads us in the direction of the small crowd gathered around one of the vehicles. A lotus, the softest shade of pink only discernible under the glare of the chandelier light, sits nestled inside velvet ropes.

"What's the charity again?" Justin asks.

"Breast cancer research."

"It looks like a life-sized Hot Wheels car," I say, unimpressed.

Justin smirks at me. "I don't think pink is your color."

We read the specs and take a look at the silent auction list. The first bid already began with six figures. "There are a lot of deep pockets in this room."

"Mm," Justin hums. "Pretentious people showing off. I doubt anyone in this room actually cares to have a pink Lotus. It's all for show."

Justin keeps his hand firmly placed on my lower back, staying with me wherever I go. We round the entire ballroom, checking out our surroundings. Justin picks off a couple champagne glasses from a passing waiter and holds one out for me.

"You need to drink something or your nerves are going to get the best of you." I'm once again floored by his ability to recognize my emotions before I can even register that I'm feeling them.

"I don't think alcohol is going to help me take my mind off of it."

"I beg to differ," he says, hiding a deliberate look behind his champagne flute.

I take the glass from him and take a sip, ignoring his smirk. "I'm just ready to do this. The waiting is killing me."

"Patience," he says. He finishes his drink, disposing of the glass on a nearby table. He does the same to mine, taking it from my hand and setting it next to his before pulling me toward the dance floor. "If a drink won't help, maybe some dancing will."

"No," I say, trying to plant my feet, which proves to be ineffective in high heels. "I'm not dancing."

"Yes you are," he says, not bothering to look at me.

By now, a small crowd of people are slow dancing to the twinkle of the orchestra music playing overhead. Justin pulls us right in the middle, making no excuses along his way. He pulls me closer to him, cradling my hand in his, and I'm dancing before I even know that I am.

"You are so stubborn," he says at my refusal to smile.

"You're so overbearing."

He maintains his expression as he sways me out from his body and back in. "Influential," he counters.

And it's true. He has the ability to influence the people around him. I've seen Lance subdue his antics whenever Justin is being serious. I've seen Courtney and Blake pay close attention whenever he talks, like whatever he says is worth listening to. Hell, I've seen Kaley stop and acknowledge Justin like I've never seen her do with anyone besides her dad.

But it's so much more than just the people he surrounds himself with; it's how the maître d' beamed under his smile. Or how Kip saw the honesty in him when he and Lance brought Kaley and me home. He has a way of gaining reverence and it's polarizing.

He pulls us closer, fitting me into him. "If you could have any superpower, what would it be?" he says.

I breathe deep, relishing his scent masked by a hint of cologne and cigarettes. "To have the ability to make people happy," I say, maybe swayed a little by Justin's abilities.

His arm seems to tow me even closer, closer than I thought we could get. It's comforting here. The grandiose ballroom is marginally less daunting in his pretend shelter.

"To make other people happy or to make you happy?" he says, looking at me with such endearment it hurts.

I swallow and focus back on the pulse point on his neck, the one right below his ear. "What about you?"

"Mine is much less noble than yours." He spins me. "You know how when you're watching a cooking show and the food looks so good, even if you're not hungry or you don't particularly like what they're cooking, you want it anyway? How awesome would it be if I could reach through the TV and pull out whatever food I want?"

He's so proud of the thought that I can't help but laugh. "That is a pretty good superpower. You could feed the world."

"Yeah," he says, much more subdued. "And I could have steak whenever I wanted. I would record all my favorite dishes."

We continue to dance in a small circle, watching people come and go during the constant stream of music. We don't speak but keep a small motion back and forth enough to be considered dancing.

"It shouldn't be much longer now. People are already sitting. Once they call for dinner, we'll make our move."

"Okay. Let me use the bathroom."

"We can check out the storage room on the way back."

The stalls are occupied, so I wait at the sinks. I adjust my hair and try to tame frizz and gain traction from my time spent in Justin's arms.

I'm disarmed but slightly less unstable than when the night started. I've traded one predicament for another. I use the bathroom and reemerge, finding Justin waiting outside the door.

He gives me a questioning look. "Are you okay?" I nod, not wanting to give voice to my fears. "We don't have to do this," he says.

I don't tell him that stealing the car is only half my problem. "I'm fine. Have they started dinner yet?"

His eyes jump back and forth, trying to gauge my honesty before he gives in. "Yeah," he says. "They're on the first course."

We turn right, following the directions from the copy of the layout we studied. At the end of the hallway, there's a maid and storage room. We wait until the hall is empty and disappear inside. Justin locks the door behind us. The room is filled with laundry. Most of it is guest towels and robes, but one small hamper is filled with employee uniforms, or most important, valet uniforms.

"Dan said he left a bag behind the washer."

Justin retrieves it and produces the key fob and keycard to access the garage ramp. I didn't want to risk bringing them through security, so Dan made a run today to hide them here. Justin takes off his tux and slides on one of the valet jackets from the hamper. He digs around for the gloves to match but comes up empty handed.

"I shouldn't need them," he says, and I'm not quite sure if he's reassuring me or himself.

"Give me fifteen minutes. Hopefully I'll come up with something by then."

He hands me the valet ticket, draping his tux over my shoulders. "Breathe."

"Breathing."

He smiles and releases my hand.

Opening the door, I step out of the employee room, trying to quiet my shoes on the marble floor. As carefully as I can, I pull the door shut behind me. A soft click resounds through the hallway.

"Can I help you?"

My heart drops as I look up to find a young waiter watching me. I'm not sure what my best smile is, but I put it on. "I was looking for the bathroom."

The waiter points to the door to his right.

It's obvious I should have seen it in passing by, and it makes me look like a dumbass. I giggle. "Must be the champagne. I don't know how I missed it."

He nods, evidently used to dealing with drunken girls wondering about. He watches me enter the bathroom and I shut the door, hoping like hell he doesn't go into the storage room to discover Justin. I give it a few seconds before I peek into the hallway and discover it empty.

I make my way to the entrance, making sure to keep close to the building and out of sight of the cameras. I peek around a column and see Dalton and another young valet standing behind the hostess stand. They're joking about something, their laughter wafting through the air as one of them holds up a cell phone. The maître d' is gone, but the security guard still holds his place next to the podium, looking incredibly bored.

I take a breath and come into view from the shadows. The sound of my heels gets their attention as I approach. Dalton's smile grows as I get nearer. Feeling brave, I toss my hair over my shoulder.

"Hi." Dalton smiles. "Do you need us to fetch your car?"

"I do." I hand him my ticket.

Dalton nods to his coworker. "Hey, Jess. 233." Jess opens the lock box and produces the key to the Jeep, disappearing into the outlet of the parking garage. "Didn't stay very long," Dalton says, taking notice of my early departure.

I catch a glimpse of Justin rounding the corner behind the guard and know I need to come up with something quick. "Um," I say distractedly. "Yeah, kind of boring."

Dalton gives me a grin that's all cheese, and I cringe. "What happened to your date?"

"My date? Oh, no. That's my brother."

He pulls a lock of my blonde hair out from under the tux. "You don't look anything alike."

"Adopted." It's the first thing out of my mouth, and I instantly regret it. It's an obvious lie.

Dalton's smile only grows. "Want a private tour of the spa?"

This kid is a sleaze, probably used to getting attention from rich socialites. "I don't know," I say, trying to draw out my time. "Won't you get in trouble?"

"Jesse will cover for me. We're slow right now."

He slides an arm around my waist, and I internally fight the urge to punch him. We're about to enter the lobby and I'm in full panic mode, trying to figure out some way to distract the guard, and quickly. The heel of my shoes catches on the edge of the red carpet, and I fall forward. Dalton tries to catch me but fails against the flailing of my arms, and I land on the palms of my hands.

"Are you okay?" the guard asks, helping Dalton lift me to my feet.

"Yeah," I say, straightening out my gown.

"Are you sure?"

I look up at the guard and catch a glimpse of Justin disappearing around the side of the building, just in time for Jesse to pull up in the Jeep, and for the first time in my life I am appreciative for having no idea how to walk in high heels.

"Yup," I say, my face about to break from my smile.

"Ready?" Dalton is pleased I'm not hurt, ready to continue on with his "private tour."

"Actually," I say, pulling away from him. "I should probably just go. I'm feeling a little tired." His face falls and I smile apologetically.

"Sure," he says, stuffing his white-gloved hands into his pockets.

My heart is jack-hammering; the thrill of possibly getting away with this is making me giddy. I walk to the Jeep, or skip, basically, and get in, trying to suppress my smile. It's the first relief I've felt in two days, and I breathe it in. I pull away from the curb and dial Justin.

He answers.

"Everything's okay?"

taking mine

"So far. I'm headed to the shipping yard. Are you on your way?"

"Yeah. I'll be there right behind you."

The good thing about leaving cars at the docks is that it's only ten minutes away from Toby's. The river flows directly between the city, and it puts us driving on the outskirts, away from traffic cameras and businesses.

The shipping yard is on the smaller scale, a stopping point along the river, mainly used for storage. It's privately owned, and the owner has never had much incentive for high security measures. It's unmanned at night with a minimal chain link fence as its best line of defense. It's about a two-mile drive from the main road, and the drive turns from pavement to gravel along the way. The gates are open, but I park across the street, deciding it's best to wait on the outside just in case.

Ten minutes pass and I'm starting to worry. I text Justin, asking him what's taking so long. I keep my eyes peeled for any movement nearby, but nothing is visible except for the one small light pole near the entrance. I decide I can't wait any longer and get out. I remember the container number and keep to the far side of the light pole, wanting to keep my face obscure. Not that the gold dress I'm wearing wouldn't give me away or anything.

Using the flashlight on my phone, I search down the first row of containers, holding the train of my dress in my other hand. It's dead silent, not a single sound, and the ringing in my ears only accentuates my anxiety. I'm just about to give up and head back when I turn down a row and see a crack in one of the containers, light pouring into the darkness. I check the number, confirming it's the right one, and step inside.

Justin's back is to me and he's pulling at the trunk of the Italia.

"What are you doing? What's taking so long?"

He turns at the sound of my voice. "Lilly, you shouldn't be here. The plan was that you'd wait outside. There's no point in risking both of us being seen."

"I didn't know if you were okay. You never responded to my text."

He pulls his phone out of his pocket and looks at it. "No reception."

"Is it nice?" I ask, rounding the side of the car, checking out the interior.

"Oh yeah," he says, his voice full of awe. "But look, there's already another car here." Another Corvette, a Grand Sport, is parked in front of the Italia.

"Do you think Jimmy has someone else pulling cars for him?"

"I don't know." He cups his hands and tries to peek inside the passenger side window. "Or maybe whoever was working for him doesn't anymore."

"Why would someone quit?"

"I don't think it would be voluntary." The meaning of his words sinks in and a new onset of nervous energy runs through me. "Come on, we shouldn't hang around too long."

He shuts the door to the Italia and flicks off a switch, cutting the lights, and waits for me to exit before locking the doors behind us.

"Were you trying to open the trunk?"

"Yes," he says. "The key we were given is a valet key. It only opens the driver side door and starts the ignition. I couldn't access the glove box either."

"You think that means something?"

"Maybe. Maybe not. Jimmy might know someone at a dealership that ordered the key for him and that's how he gets access to transponder keys."

"Or," I say, knowing there's another theory.

"Or he's hiding something and he doesn't want us in the storage compartments."

IT'S NOT UNTIL WE'RE BACK in Justin's apartment that we speak again. We were told that Jimmy would contact us when he confirmed our job was complete and that a package of cash would be dropped off to Taylor immediately following. Kip insisted I wait it out here. He doesn't want me to move around too much just in case.

Justin smokes one cigarette after another in the open doorway of his apartment. His dress shirt is unbuttoned with the sleeves pushed up to his elbows, his bowtie hanging undone around his collar. He's paced the living room since we arrived over an hour ago.

"Can you sit? You're making me nervous."

Justin stubs his cigarette out and shuts the door behind him. "It was too easy. It doesn't make sense."

I stop myself from admitting that I've had the same thought. "Smoking yourself to death isn't helping anything."

He wipes his hand across his mouth and takes a seat next to me on the couch. I flip through the channels on TV, trying to find something worthwhile. "Right there," Justin says, prompting me to stop on a fishing show.

"Fishing?"

"Yeah." He shrugs. "I like to fish."

"Since when?"

"My dad used to take me and my brother when we were little." He senses my confusion and says, "Before he started drinking."

"What's your dad like now?"

Justin kicks off his dress shoes and props his feet up on the coffee table. I gather the material of my dress and fold mine under me. "He's better. Been sober for five years now."

"You don't talk about him much."

"Eh." Justin seems uncomfortable. "We don't have much of a relationship. Even before he started drinking, he was never home because of his job." I remain silent, prompting him to keep going. "He was a cop."

I scoff, smiling. "Isn't that kind of ironic?"

He smiles back. "You have no idea."

I toy with my cell phone, flipping it over and back in my hands, unsure of how much I want to divulge. I've never cared to tell anyone about my past. It might be because I've never had someone to tell, but for some reason I want to tell Justin. He's always held no condemnation against me or my brother for the lives we've lived, and that's comforting. He's the first person I've felt free with.

"My dad was killed by a cop."

My words snag his attention away from the TV screen, where the fisherman is struggling to reel in a freshwater fish of some sort. "What?" he says, stunned by my admission.

"My dad was walking home from work one night when a cop approached him. They went through the whole spiel, why he was out this late on the wrong side of town, why didn't he take the bus, etc. Wasted fifteen minutes of questioning before he asked for my dad's identification. My dad's jumper didn't have pockets, so he always kept his wallet on the inside of his zipper. When my dad reached for it, the cop drew his gun. Claimed he thought my dad was reaching for a weapon."

"Lilly, I'm so sorry," he says, something akin to pity.

I shrug. "It took me a long time to remind myself that all cops aren't him, that one deputy who turned my family inside out, so I get it. I know it's not the same, but I get it."

There's so much intensity in Justin that I have to stand to get away from it. Both of our phones ding in succession, but Justin doesn't move to look at his.

"Taylor says the money is waiting for us at the shop," I say, reading the text. "I think it's safe for me to leave." I look up to find Justin standing from the couch and making his way to me. The look in his eyes stops me. I'm frozen as he advances, only stopping once he's standing inches before me. "Justin," I say in warning.

"Lilly," he challenges me back.

"Don't." I hold my voice firm, but even I can hear the wariness behind it.

I'm weak.

"Don't what?"

"Don't do whatever you're about to do."

He cups my face in his hands. A small smile plays at his lips like he's holding a secret he knows I'm dying to know. "This has already

taking mine

gone too far. I've been trying to stop my feelings for you, but I think we both know it's too late for that. And I think it's too late for you to stop them either."

I'm torn between preventing him from going further, not wanting to be disappointed again, and wanting to hear the rest.

"One day you'll realize what a prick I am, but today I want to prove to you that you mean something to me. That I can't stand the thought of you with someone else, and I won't let you walk out of here without knowing you're with me."

My phone dings a few times in my hand, and Justin pries it from my fingers, tossing it on the couch. I'm spaghetti as he pulls my arms around him. We're both dressed in our finest, barefoot in the middle of his living room. I'm looking up at him, not sure what to say, and he doesn't expect me to say anything. He dips his head down slowly, giving me ample time to stop him, glancing from my lips to my eyes under his lashes.

He places his lips on mine, unmoving, and we breathe each other in. I know he's waiting for me to make the next move, to push us further. The thing is...I feel too much with him. It's like I'm thrown from one extreme to another. Without him, I'm fine, indifferent mostly. With him, I'm in a whirlwind of emotions.

I'm happy. I'm angry. I'm content. I'm disappointed.

He's the furthest thing from indifferent, and it's amazingly awful.

His eyes stay locked on mine as I run through my emotions. He knows I'm sorting through my feelings. He can see through me.

I'm transparent.

Pushing all the apprehension away, I squeeze my eyes shut and push my lips into his. I can feel his smile ease against my lips and he reaches down, never releasing me from our kiss as he picks me up from under my thighs.

"Stop me if I'm being presumptuous," he says against my lips as he carries me to his bedroom.

"You are, but I'm not going to stop you."

His smile grows as he lets me down in his bedroom. The only source of illumination comes through his open door. He shrugs out of his button-up and reaches across his back to pull off his undershirt. His movements aren't slow, but they're far from the hurried pace we were in last time. A wave of excitement filters through my body at the thought of what's about to happen. I've worked so hard the past few weeks trying to block the images of that night out of my head. It left me confused. It left me wanting it more and more every day and hating myself for it. I wanted to remember every aspect but wanted to forget it ever happened at the same time.

Justin leans down and places a kiss on my exposed shoulder. "Let me undress you," he says into my skin. I turn to the side, giving him access to the zipper. As he pulls the zipper down, he runs his hands over my hips and down to the train. He lifts the fabric, trailing his fingers up my legs. He smirks when he reaches my underwear.

I smile when he slides a hand over the satin fabric. "It was laundry day."

He removes the rest of the dress, and neither one of us moves. "I've wasted more study time than I'd like to admit wondering if you were wearing anything or not."

"That's funny," I say. "I fantasized about stabbing you in the eye with your pen."

His touch halts. "Wait, what?"

I laugh. "You don't want to know."

He looks at me with a confused smile but doesn't push. His smile slowly slips and his mood shifts to a more serious nature. He turns me with my back facing him, and I feel his hands travel over my hips, moving up toward the clasp on my bra. He undoes it, and I let it fall from my shoulders. It's as if he knows this time I'm a little shy, giving me time to adjust. He kisses my other shoulder this time, and up my neck. My inexperience weighs heavy as I adjust to his assured movements.

Once he reaches the farthest kissable point along my throat, he follows the path to my lips, turning me around with the motion. I force myself to relax, enjoying the taste of him, something I've desperately tried to forget. My breasts are pressed up against his bare chest, and his arms are completely surrounding me, like he wants every inch of me to be imprinted on him, and it's a euphoric sensation. He walks me backward to the bed and picks me up, situating me against the pillows.

Kneeling above me, he unbuckles his belt, giving him more room. I can't take my eyes off of his hands. The way the tendons stretch along his hands and forearms at the movement is tantalizing. His hands freeze and I look up. There's a confident smile in place as he slides his pants off. Not wanting to just lie there staring, I sit up and touch him. I hear more than see his intake of breath. His hips push into my hand as I stroke back and forth.

"Lilly."

The way he says my name gives me just enough confidence to place my lips around him. I don't get a chance to taste him before I'm pushed back onto the bed and he's over me.

"Next time. I want to do this right this time, and that won't help me." He kisses me one good moment before moving down my body. I already know where he's going, and I instinctively close my thighs. He looks up at me from his position. "What's wrong?" His question is ironic given he wouldn't just let me go down on him.

I shake my head.

"Lilly," he says, leaning up on one arm. "Are you nervous?" I don't need to say that I am. I know he sees it, and a small amount of fear seeps into his features.

"I'm not a virgin or anything, or wasn't before, you know..."

Justin licks his lips and kisses the inside of my thigh one time before replying. "How much experience are we talking about here?"

"A few," I answer vaguely. His teeth nip a little bit of skin in the same spot in warning. "One boy in high school. We only actually had sex a handful of times."

He kisses the inside of the opposite thigh, a tad bit closer to his destination. "Was he your first love?"

"No."

He smiles at my irritated reply before sucking again, but closer this time.

"Then why'd you give him your virginity?"

My thoughts are scattered as I feel his teeth once more. If there's anyone anywhere who can hold a conversation with Justin between their legs, they should be honored. Seriously.

"It's not like I gave it away. I wasn't holding on to some idea of what my virginity meant to me." And if I'm completely honest, Kaley had me convinced that sex was the best thing she'd ever experienced. It's something I chased all three times. An idea that I was missing out on something that couldn't be put into words. And all three times I left feeling bored. That's when I came to the conclusion sex couldn't compete with the thrill that stealing gave me.

"Was the first time you came during sex with me?"

Justin's voice pulls me from my thoughts. "Yes."

His face loses all playfulness as he leans back and pulls the small bit of material down my legs. His eyes stay on me. Even when I feel the flat of his tongue hit me in just the right place, he doesn't break contact. Then he moves a fraction and sucks—hard.

And I break.

chapter 12

"I'M NOT ASKING YOU to leave the apartment; I'm asking you to come eat breakfast." Justin gives me a look. "Or dinner, whatever time it is."

"I don't need food, just you." I pull him by his arm and he catches himself from landing directly on top of me.

We spent the entirety of the night doing nothing but feeling each other. One more time turned into two more times before the sun came up. Then we spent the entire day sleeping, only getting out of bed to use the bathroom.

"You need food." I attempt to pull up his t-shirt and we struggle, battling each other. I get the shirt halfway up when he pins my hands back. "Don't fight me. You'll lose."

I lean forward and bite his forearm.

He grunts and repositions our hands wider, out of reach of my teeth. "You don't even have to get dressed." He gives me a swift kiss before leaping from the bed, escaping my grasp.

I huff out a breath as I roll over and swing my feet onto the floor. I find my underwear and pull them on. "I want you to know I'm doing this against my will."

"Duly noted."

He opens his dresser and produces a plain white t-shirt, holding it out for me. I try to take it and he hides it behind his back. Smirking, he kisses me. I try to press further, but he steps back, breaking the kiss, tossing the shirt at me.

"Now hurry before the food gets cold."

I'm halfway to the kitchen when I feel the sting of his palm against my ass. I squeal in shock.

"That's for biting me." He kisses the side of my neck before sitting at the breakfast bar. He places a pile of pancakes in front of me while I rub the sting out of my right ass cheek. "I should let you starve."

"Where in the hell did you find the ingredients to make pancakes?"

"They're beer pancakes. Main ingredient: beer. Instead of syrup, we've got some peanut butter that expires in a week, so you better eat all of it." He folds a pancake and dips it into the peanut butter, holding it up for me to take a bite.

"This is actually really good, and I hate beer." I tear off a piece of his pancake and eat it. I leave Justin to his breakfast and locate my phone shoved between the couch cushions.

Three messages from Kip asking if I'm staying at Justin's, threatening me if I don't reply, and then insisting on coming to get me. I text him back, reassuring him that I'm alive.

"I need to go. Kip's freaking out because I haven't messaged him all night."

"Hold on," Justin says, shoving the rest of the food into his mouth. "I'll go with you."

Showing up at home with Justin after spending the night at his place may be pushing Kip a little further than what he's comfortable with. "No, it's okay. He's still not really on board the Justin train yet."

"I'm a train? Is that why you like riding me?" My mouth drops open and he laughs, picking me up and throwing me over his shoulder.

"Justin, you're not coming."

"Fine," he says, entering his bedroom and tossing me back onto the bed. "But I'm going to come one way or another."

"Oh. My. God. Who are you?"

He places an open-mouth kiss on my stomach. "You like it."

And help me, because I do. The weariness he's been carrying around with him the past couple of weeks has disappeared almost completely. The fun-loving person who stripped during lecture is back. The guy who played Family Feud with me between classes. The one who taught me to play pool and schooled me in bowling. I hadn't realized he'd disappeared until now. Looking up at Justin, I notice his dark circles are almost nonexistent, and it's like I'm seeing him for the first time again. Except better. He's still has a sense of brooding hanging over him, but right now, he seems happy.

THE YELLOW ENVELOPE is packed to the brim in cash. Twenties are stacked in thousands by rubber bands. The weight of twenty-five grand is roughly two pounds, give or take a few ounces. I shake it around a little. "I feel like I'm missing something."

Justin glances at me from the driver side of his Jeep. "I don't think it's sunk in yet. It's a lot of cash."

I place it against my window, using it as a pillow. "I'm not even sure what I'll do with it."

"I thought you were going to pay for school with it."

"Duh, I just don't know what to do with it in the meantime. Do I place it under my mattress? I don't have a cookie jar big enough."

"You could keep it at my place. Really, I'd feel more comfortable if you kept it at my place."

I give Justin an accusing look. "Of course you'd want me to let you keep it."

He laughs. "You know I wouldn't touch it."

"Do I? I heard you've robbed a gas station before."

He gives me a look, brushing off my small dig. "I don't like the idea of you harboring so much money in your house. What if someone breaks in?"

"No one knows I have twenty-five grand sitting under my bed."

"Who hired you in the first place?"

"Why would the person who hired me take the money they paid me with? That makes no sense."

"Jimmy obviously has someone who was working for him before. What happened to them, huh?"

"I don't know. Maybe they quit."

"And walk away from this type of easy money? No way."

"Maybe they got caught."

"People squeal when faced with prison and would sell their own mother's soul to get a lighter sentence. There's no doubt that Jimmy would do any and everything possible to make sure that wouldn't happen."

He's got a point.

"Look, I'm not saying that anything is going to happen, but I'd feel better if you let me keep it.

I pick up his package of money, and with mine, I sandwich my head between them. "I can't wrap my head around it."

He laughs.

"Fine," I relent. "Only because it'll make you feel better."

"And because you trust me."

"And because I trust you," I repeat.

He brings my hand to his lips. "Thank you."

It's weird, being so openly affectionate. It's not something I'm used to. I've never really had a boyfriend, and it's not like I had affectionate parents due to not having any at all. And my brother is my brother. Affectionate in the only way he knew how to be. By supplying for me. So the repeated feel of Justin's lips, his touch, is different, and I have to stop myself from pulling away. I understand that this says something about my psyche. Like, some hypothetical therapist somewhere is making notes on a notepad.

"Are you going to tell Kip?" Justin asks.

"That there might have been someone working for Jimmy before?"

He nods.

"No. I don't want to worry him. He stresses too much as it is."

We come to a stop sign and Justin pulls me into a kiss, holding my face between his hands. "You have such a good heart."

My heart skips. It's tender in a way that I surprisingly need. To be told I'm good inside. That through it all, I'm an okay person. I give him a tight-lipped smile in return. It's scary that I suddenly feel lost. It's not normal that a compliment makes me doubt myself.

"You do." Justin's words pull me back to the feel of his hands on my cheeks and his breath on my lips. "You may not see it," he says, touching the small space above my heart. "But I do."

I've never ever questioned myself before, but confronted by the reality someone thinks highly of me, I'm very sure I'm not sure at all. I've never made excuses or blamed people who are better off. I've just been reacting to my environment. Right? But maybe I've been wrong. It's the thought that I have never bothered to study myself in the first place, to look inside and figure out who I am.

Maybe I don't have a good heart.

TODAY IS ALMOST LIKE THE FIRST day back from fantasy land. Other than going home to check in with Kip and picking up our packages from Taylor, we've spent every waking second of the weekend together. And when I say together, I mean *together*.

I spent the majority of class daydreaming, a permanent blush permeating my cheeks. I'd be more put out by it if I weren't in a constant stage of bliss. It should scare me that he's so good with my body, a woman's body, but then again I could care less how he gained such skills as long as he continues to use them on me.

Justin beams when I meet him in the courtyard, and I'm positive my expression matches.

"I was thinking we could skip class today and go somewhere," he says. "Got anything you need to stay for?"

"Where are we going?"

"The shipyard. I want to get a better look at the cars."

"Isn't that kind of risky? How are we going to get in without being noticed?"

"The entire place is crawling with people. No one is going to second-guess what we're doing."

"What about Jimmy? I'm sure he doesn't want us snooping around."

"Exactly."

I understand Justin's skepticism. Everything inside of me is saying something isn't right about this entire deal, and for that exact reason, I don't want to dig any deeper. If we dig and find something, then all the money could disappear right before my eyes. How long do I want to stay ignorant?

Apparently not long enough to leave Justin to do this alone.

The shipyard is teeming with people. Half the workers are wearing yellow hard hats. I'm not sure what determines who wears one or not, but it kind of makes me question my safety as large cranes pass containers high above our heads. Justin's right when he said no one will give us a second glance as we beeline it to our destination.

Justin hands me a duffel bag filled with tools he thought we might need as he spins the combination into the lock. He pulls it and it doesn't give. He tries again only to get the same result.

"The combination isn't working. This is a different lock. They changed it sometime since we left."

He bends down to get a closer look at the lock and starts to slowly spin the dial, eyes closed as he concentrates. He spins it one way until he feels what he's searching for and then starts in the opposite direction. It takes a few fails before he gets it right and the lock pops open.

"Where did you learn to do that?" I ask, equally impressed and skeptical.

"My mom kept a lock on the medicine cabinet," he says, pulling open the door. "Dad never showed a particular interest in pharmaceuticals, but she didn't want to risk it if he ran out of liquor before she got home." He walks over to the Italia and reaches under the tire wheel. "They took the key."

He pulls the duffel from my shoulder and digs through it. "I brought an air wedge, but I don't know if the alarm will sound..."

Just out of curiosity, I pull the door handle and it clicks open.

He raises an eyebrow. "Or that works, too."

I slide in the passenger seat. "So, what are we looking for?" I routinely check under and behind the seats, coming up empty.

Justin kneels outside the door next to my feet and begins unscrewing the door panel starting with the lock mechanism. It pops off, and he slowly, carefully pulls back the plastic and leather panel. He squeezes his hand inside the metal interior of the door.

"I feel something, but I can't reach it."

He pulls his hand out and I reach mine in. "A bag? Feels like canvas or something."

"Can you get it?"

I tug, and the pack falls farther into my hand. I wrap my fingers around it the best I can and yank. I get enough of the fabric pooled through the hole that I can see a zipper.

"It's a gun."

Justin looks up at me. "Can you get it?"

As carefully as I can, I pull the gun out of the bag. Cautiously, I open the chamber and check for ammo. I drop the clip and hand the gun to him.

It takes me a moment to realize he's looking at me. The gun is stilled in his hands and he's smirking. It's like he finds me cute. "What?" I ask self-consciously.

He shakes his head, returning his attention to the gun. "Looks like it's police issued. The serial number has been scratched off."

The black metal catches the light as he turns it over. It's the same type of gun that was used to kill my dad. The last thing he saw was the black barrel in the hands of someone who was supposed to protect him.

"Lilly." My name reverberates inside my head. "Are you okay? You look like you've seen a ghost."

I force a smile. "I just really hate guns." I stick my hand back in the bag and feel another object. "I think there's more. The bag takes up the entire door."

"Can you get another one?" After a few minutes of maneuvering, I manage to free another gun exactly like the first. Justin repeats his examination of the gun and hands them both back to me. "Put these back. I'm going to see if I can find anything in the trunk."

"What if the alarm is on?"

He reaches under the steering column. "I'm hoping that if I use the emergency lever it won't sound."

"Well, that sounds super smart. Let's pull the alarm and just hope it doesn't go off. Stolen guns aren't stored inside of it or anything."

Her ignores me but winces as he pulls.

Nothing happens. The sound of the trunk releases, and we let out a collective breath.

Justin walks around to the front of the car. "Holy fucking shit." The words out of his mouth and the alarm behind them send ice through my veins.

Please don't be a body, please don't be a body, I repeat as I look over the hood. Justin has both of his hands laced on top of his head, staring at whatever is in the cargo space. His eyes meet mine and I know whatever it is, it's bad.

It's staggering. Plastic-wrapped blocks of cocaine are stacked in every inch of the space.

"They're transporting cocaine," he says.

"How can Taylor have let us do this?" I say, unbelieving.

"You think Taylor knew?"

Taylor's insistence to take Jimmy's offer, the repeated reference to the money, all the times he brushed off significant details.

"He had to," I answer.

Justin inhales a large breath. "We're middle men. Someone working with Jimmy drops a car somewhere and we transport it here. We're not actually stealing anything." He paces with his hands on his hips before stopping next to the Corvette.

"What do you think happened to whoever put that car here?"

He tugs on the door handle, but it's locked. "I don't know, but we should probably keep this between us."

"No way. Dan and Ethan are making a run this weekend. I can't not tell them."

"And how do you think Taylor's going to take that? Hm? I don't think whoever he's doing business with is going to suddenly take no for an answer."

An ache forms between my brows, and I press the heels of my hands to my forehead to suppress the headache building. "I can't let them go in blind. Dan's got a family. I'm sure a judge would totally overlook arms and drug trafficking."

"Hey, hey, hey." Justin places his hands on my shoulders to stop my panicking. "Breathe. Let's get our stuff together before we jump the gun. Do you have any inclination if Kip knows?"

I scour my brain. The only thing that sends a red flag is his insistent need for me to carry a gun. "I'm not sure. He couldn't. There's not a chance in hell he'd let me be a part of this if he knew. Or anyone for that matter."

"Not even for the money?" His face gives away his doubt.

"There's no way."

Justin releases his hold on me and stalks away before coming back. "Taylor was pushing the idea of you going first."

"What does that have to do with anything?"

"I don't know. I think we should talk with Kip before we decide anything."

"Okay, yeah," I say, nodding. "That sounds good."

"Trust me, okay? We'll figure this out."

WHEN I WALK INTO THE KITCHEN, Kip takes one look at me and knows something is very, very wrong. When Justin follows in right behind me with an equally serious expression, it only makes it worse. Kip automatically takes a seat. He already knows he needs to be sitting for whatever we are about to tell him.

"Did you know?" I wasn't planning on my words coming out as harsh as they do, but my mouth has plans of its own.

"Lilly." Justin says my name in a warning tone.

"Did I know what?" Kip releases the bandana tied around his neck.

Justin looks to me, asking if I'd rather him speak first.

I nod.

Justin pulls out a chair for the both of us. Once we're settled and he feels like I've calmed down, Justin speaks. "We have strong reason to believe that the cars we're transporting for Jimmy are a cover-up."

This gets Kip's attention, prompting him to sit a little straighter. "What do you mean?"

"We're transporting weapons and drugs." Justin pauses, taking in Kip's reaction, trying to gauge whether or not Kip had any inkling of the sort. The level of shock and anger that resonates in Kip tells us it's safe to assume no, he had no clue. "Specifically," Justin continues, "cocaine."

Kip's eyes explore mine, looking for confirmation. "How do you know this?"

"We went back to the shipyard and took apart the Italia. We found police-issued guns packed in fleece bags in both doors and the cocaine in the trunk."

Kip sits back in his chair, looking from me to Justin before standing. He paces much like Justin and I both did when we discovered the drugs. It seems to be a common reaction.

"Taylor knew," Kip states after a moment.

"That's what Lilly assumed. We wanted to talk to you before we did anything."

"Nothing," Kip says, sitting back down.

"But Dan and Ethan—"

"I know. I'll figure something out before then. For now, stay away from the shop and Taylor. Don't tell anyone."

"There's something else you should know," Justin says. "Jimmy had someone working for him before. There was already a car in storage when we dropped off the Italia. We couldn't get in it, but I think it's safe to assume we'd find the same."

There's a long pause before Kip replies. "And it's safe to say whoever was working for him before isn't working for Jimmy anymore."

"Not likely."

"Okay." Kip looks to me. "Pack up some stuff and stay at Kaley's until I say otherwise."

I'm already rolling my eyes, ready to argue, when Justin says, "She can stay with me."

Justin's words stop not only me, but Kip, who gives Justin a look of disbelief.

"Kaley lives uptown, and I'm right across from the school. I can keep an eye. It'd make me feel better about the situation."

"Make you feel better?" Kip says, his voice tight with indignation. "This isn't about you. This is about keeping my sister safe, and the last person who should be protecting her is the punk who goes for joyrides in stolen cars."

Justin's temper flares. "With all due respect, I'm not the one who got her involved in this fucking shit in the first place."

I leap from my seat to stop Kip's advancement on Justin, placing a hand on his chest. "Stop." He ignores me and tries to navigate around my small frame. "I said stop." My voice makes him pause, but he doesn't pull his attention away from Justin.

Justin runs his thumb over his lip, giving away his nervousness. "I'm sorry. I'm out of line. I know you've done everything you can to supply for Lilly, and that's admirable. My biggest concern is that Lilly is safe. I'd never want to lie or deceive you in any way, and I don't think it needs to be said that she stayed with me the past weekend." Justin rushes on, not wanting to dwell on his last sentence. "Regardless, it's not my decision; it's Lilly's."

It's not a statement to Kip, but a question for me. Would I rather stay with him? We've literally been together for three days, barely a minute more, and he's asking me if I want to move in with him. It would be temporary, but it doesn't lessen the amount of pressure it puts on me...on us. He's looking at me as if he's torn between understanding my hesitancy and his desire for me to say yes. *Impossible.* I shake my head as I look away. He can't care for me that deeply. *Three days,* I repeat to myself.

"What do you want, Lil?"

Justin's voice is unsure, possibly with a hint of fear, either of what my answer will be or the level of vulnerability he just allowed me to see. The question in itself represents something much larger than him asking me where I'm planning on staying.

"I'll stay with Justin," I say to Kip, watching the tension fade from Justin's features. "But only until we know everything is okay."

Kip gives me a quick smile, his blessing of sorts. "Okay. I'll let you know when I do."

He gives Justin a nod of acknowledgment that Justin returns, and leaves the room. Silence descends on us and I busy myself, pushing in the chairs to the table, avoiding eye contact at all costs.

"Lilly," he says.

I hum an acknowledgment. I'm stalling and he knows it. He stops my fiddling with a hand around my waist. His chest presses against my back as he places his lips on the curve of my neck.

"It's okay, you're scared," he says against my skin.

"Everything will be fine. Kip's always taken care of everything."

"Not that," he says, spinning me toward him.

I know he's referencing his feelings.

Or maybe it's my feelings.

Whatever. It's all the fucking feelings in this damn kitchen.

I let my forehead fall on his chest so I don't have to look at him. "I don't want to talk about it." I focus on his breathing and the steadiness of his heart underneath my touch. He's so calm, like talking about this doesn't affect him.

"You don't have to say anything."

I huff in amusement. "Of course I don't. You're going to say whatever the hell you want to anyway."

His chuckle vibrates through my cheek, and I find the courage to look up through his laughter. "Lilly, I..." He stops for a moment, and I can hear him swallow before he continues. "I've asked you to trust me multiple times."

"You have."

"I need you to trust me when I say my feelings for you are genuine. I know the only person you've ever really trusted with all your heart is Kip—"

"That's not true. What about Kaley? Or, hell, Taylor? If I hadn't trusted him, we wouldn't be in this mess."

"But only to an extent. You've never told Kaley about what you do, and you've always been skeptical of Taylor's choices." He tugs on a lock of my hair. "You barely trust yourself. You've always trusted Kip to decide for you, and I understand it. I do."

He just pointed out a major character flaw in me that I've never even noticed before. It's a small revelation, but it's also not. I don't trust anyone. Not really. It wasn't an active choice or a conscious decision; it was a survival mechanism. I keep people at arm's length because the truth of the matter is, I don't know how to make decisions for myself. I haven't had to.

Since as long as I can remember, Kip has prepped me for everything in life. He taught me how to read, ride a bike, and get my first job. He's the one who enrolled me in college. He asked me what I thought I'd be interested in, and the next day I had a packet full of college applications sitting on my bed, ready for me to pick from. I filled them out, handed them back to him, and he sent them off. When acceptance letters started rolling in, he picked the best university that offered me a scholarship and was close by.

It's not like I'm incompetent. I've always fared well in school and worked hard to make good grades. I'm the only girl my age who knows how to change her own oil and rotate her tires. But I've never had to make any major life decisions outside of what Kip has done for me. And I trusted him enough to do that. That's more than I can say for myself.

"That's why when you told me you would put your life in my hands, it made it that much harder to stay away from you. I don't deserve you,

Lilly. I know that." I attempt to cut him off, but he silences me. "Just trust me when I say that I don't. But also trust me when I say that I will give anything to make sure you're happy."

Kip's footsteps bellow through the house. No doubt a warning on his behalf to let us know he's approaching.

"Lock up when you leave, yeah?"

"Sure."

We watch him pull out of the driveway before we confront each other. I open my mouth, but nothing comes out.

He smiles, amused by my speechlessness. "I'll wait in the Jeep until you're ready." He places a quick kiss on my forehead and walks out, leaving me with the mess of feelings he doused me in.

I walk to my room and pull out a spare backpack and begin folding clothes. I'm a few minutes in when I find myself opening and closing dresser drawers repeatedly and doing the same to my closet door when I realize that my wardrobe only consists of blue jeans and cotton t-shirts. In the bathroom, I do the same, looking through the medicine cabinet for anything I may need. Toothbrush, hair ties...tampons.

Should I bring tampons?

I count the days in my head and decide no. I shouldn't be there that long, and nothing screams overly attached like stocking his bathroom with feminine hygiene products. I pack a few more items I think I'll need and walk down the hall to the kitchen. I leave my keys hanging on the wall by the refrigerator, just in case Kip needs them for anything, and a thought occurs to me.

Opening the fridge, I smile.

When I finally climb into the Jeep, Justin gives me a strange look. "You okay? What took so long?"

Pulling the leftover pizza slice out from behind my back, I shove it into his face, laughing as it sticks.

He peels the pizza away, and a hefty amount of marinara and cheese remains with a pepperoni slice dangling from his chin. He holds the pizza in both of his hands, staring down at it with one eye open, dumbfounded.

taking mine

"Gotcha," I say, pointing a finger gun at him.

He licks his lips, a smile finally appearing. "Okay, I'll give you that one," he says, wiping the sauce from his one eye smeared shut. "I didn't see it coming."

I shrink back, suddenly scared of retaliation.

"No, don't worry, you're safe for now. When I do get you back, you'll least expect it." He takes a bite of the pizza, mostly just dough, and puts the jeep in gear. "You'll have to sleep at some point."

chapter 13

THE MICROWAVE DINGS and I retrieve the carton of noodles. It's a little after midnight. I'm pulling an all-nighter for Whitticker's test tomorrow and I need fuel. Watered-down processed noodles is my obvious go-to. It was that or leftover pizza and, for the love of food, I am tired of pizza. I never thought I'd see the day that pizza would make me nauseous, but that day was a week ago.

Staying at Justin's comes with its advantages and disadvantages. The lack of home-cooked food is definitely a disadvantage. I can make fajitas and sandwiches and that's about it. Kip does most of the cooking at home because he hates fast food. Unsurprisingly, I find I'm spoiled in that department. Actually having to find food when hungry is a chore all in itself. Having to concoct something that takes longer than three minutes to cook is enough for me to decide I'd rather not eat.

Feeling like a study break is in order, I resume my position on the couch and flip to a rerun of Family Feud, turning down the volume so it doesn't wake Justin up. I've learned he's a light sleeper and an awfully cheerful morning person. Those two traits combined are hard to get used to when I've only ever shared a space with Kip, who's super quiet. Every footstep Justin takes sounds like he's Godzilla, stomping everywhere he goes. If I don't wake up to him trying to get in between my legs, which is almost every morning, then he's trying to tickle me awake. Imagine the worst possible way to wake up: that's it. I read somewhere that tickling serves no purpose other than to help build a bonding experience between two individuals, which I think is hilarious because it makes me want to commit murder at seven in the morning.

taking mine

I finish off the episode of Family Feud, allowing Steve Harvey to draw out a closing as a family celebrates their win in the background. Procrastination is a vile character trait, and I fight it as I pick up my notes, forcing my brain to kick into gear. The rest of the night goes by slower and much less successfully than the beginning did, and I catch myself fighting more and more sighs as the morning approaches.

There's a rustling of covers from the bedroom, and I know Justin's awake. His footsteps, loud as usual, announce his arrival as he makes his way to me. His eyes squint against the light and he runs both his hands over his face.

"Lilly, it's four in the morning."

"No point in going to sleep now," I say.

"You need to at least get a nap in before class or you're going to fall asleep while you're taking the exam."

I try really hard to stop the yawn before it escapes but fail miserably.

His sleepy face takes on the domineering mode he goes into when he's determined to get his way. "That's it, you're done," he says, closing and stacking up my notebooks, easily dodging my attempt to stop him.

"Justin, let me go through it one more time, please."

"If you don't know it by now, Lilly, you're not going to. You need sleep." He pulls me up by one arm, catching me as I start to lose balance, and shoulders me to him.

"You're ridiculous," I say as he deposits me on the edge of the bed.

"Yeah, well, I can say the same about you." He lifts my shirt over my head and pushes me onto my back.

I huff. "I can undress myself." But I make no attempt to move as he pulls my yoga pants down. The next thing I know I'm flipped on my side, covered head to toe in blankets, just how I like it. Quicker than I thought I could be, I'm halfway asleep in moments. I'm about to give up the fight, letting the comfort lull me to sleep, when I remember something. "Alarm," I say, words barely pushing past my lips.

"Don't worry, I got it covered," he says, placing a kiss on top of my head. "Sleep."

And with that last demand, I relent, falling into darkness.

MY LIDS ARE HEAVY as I force them open, something startling me awake. Sunlight filters through the small window on the opposite wall and it takes a second before I realize that sunlight means I'm late. Really late.

"Fuck," I cuss as I struggle from Justin's grasp.

He sits up, alarmed by my panic. "What's wrong?"

"I'm late," I yell as I fly off the bed, picking up the clothes from yesterday and shoving myself into them. "I thought you said you set an alarm?"

He checks his phone on the end table. "It's dead." Confused, he follows the power cord. "It must have come unplugged."

"Just great. Just fucking great. How come the one day in the history of ever you don't wake up at the break of dawn is the one day that I need you to?"

"You still have time if you hurry."

I skip brushing my teeth, fixing my hair as I exit the apartment, not bothering to bring my backpack.

"I'll drive you," he says, keys in hand, following me down the stairs in nothing but his pajama pants.

The cold burns my skin, the yoga pants and t-shirt doing very little to protect from the wind. "It'll be quicker if I run."

"It's too cold, Lilly. Let—"

"I don't have time to argue with you. I'll see you after class, alright? You're going to be late to your own exam if you don't hurry."

He stops at the bottom of the stairs and watches me jog across the parking lot. "You're so hardheaded," he says, his voice muffled by the wind in my ears.

"Yeah, and you're an asshole who doesn't double-check his alarms."

"Love you, too," he yells.

And my heart stops beating for all of two seconds, long enough for me to pause and wonder if it'll ever pick back up again or if I'll drop dead in the middle of the crosswalk. It's meant as a joke, a ribbing, but it sets off a whole new level of emotions inside me that I don't have time to analyze.

I stop in the middle of the intersection and look at him. He's still standing on the bottom step, leaning his forearms against the railing, smiling like a jackass. I flip him off and he tilts his head back, laughing. I can hear it even though we're almost a football field away from each other. A car horn honks, and I flip him off, too, done with people at this point of this craptastic morning.

Whitticker gives me an irritated look as I enter the auditorium but hands me the exam, holding up five fingers to let me know I've lost precious time already. Kaley raises her eyebrows at me as I take the seat next to her with only a pencil in hand. Taking a deep breath, I write my name, calming the racing of my heart as I begin. A hundred questions and a short answer determine my fate. I smile as I read the first question.

I think I've got this.

AS I'M EXITING THE BUILDING, I catch Justin leaning against one of the pillars outside. His back is to me as I walk up.

"You have no right to throw that at me." I can vaguely make out a woman's voice on the other side of the phone. Not wanting to intrude, I take a step back...until I hear my name. "Lilly has nothing to do with it." Another pause before he says, even more irritated, "Yes, but you're putting me in a bad spot."

He waits a few more beats before throwing his hands in the air. His body is poised to turn around when I take my final steps toward him. His eyes widen slightly as he takes me in.

"Look, I've got to go. I'll call you later." He ends the phone call and pockets his cell phone.

"I'm sorry. I didn't mean to overhear."

His motion is stiff as he shrugs, and I can tell he doesn't want to discuss it. "Did it go well?"

The test was brutal, but overall, I feel relief. Sweet, unparalleled relief to know I'm done with Whitticker. At least for now. "I really just want a shower and a nap."

"Your wish is my command," he says.

We walk across campus in silence. Since we've been together, I've noticed more than a few stares aimed at us. Or him, I'm not sure. I've never been particularly observant, but now it's hard not to. I find myself paying close attention to the way the wind dances across the front of Justin's shirt or the check pattern on the blanket a couple is sitting on. Or my nails. Yes, my nails. They're frayed and ragged around the edges. Somehow, I've missed how absent-minded I am. I don't know if it's a psychological thing or what, but I feel like I see things so much more clearly with him by my side. Including myself.

Justin gives me a cursory glance, confused by the stupid grin on my face, and throws his arm over my shoulder.

"You're beautiful," he says.

And next to him, I feel beautiful

The first thing I do when we're back in Justin's apartment is brush my teeth and shower. Turning on the faucet so the water can warm up, I start to peel off my clothes and shove a toothbrush in my mouth. Living in an apartment building apparently means always waiting five minutes for the water to get hot. Justin stands in the doorway and strips his shirt off.

"My mom wants me to go home for Thanksgiving," he says.

Other than the little bit Justin's told me about his dad's drinking and his arrest, I know very little about his home life, but I've gathered that he hasn't been back in a while. I'm not quite sure what he wants me to say, so I spit the toothpaste from my mouth. "That's good, right?"

"Depends," he says, holding the shower curtain back for me, getting in behind me. "Would you come with me? My mom wants you to come with me to visit her."

"Is that who you were arguing with on the phone?"

taking mine

"Sort of," he says, cupping my neck between his hands. "Stop avoiding the question."

"I heard my name. Was it about me?"

He runs his hands up into my hair and I tilt my head back into the spray of the water. "I tried to explain to her that you have a lot going on right now and I wanted to be here with you."

I open my eyes. "You told her about me?"

His smile is genuine. "Of course."

I pour shampoo into my hands and begin massaging it into my scalp, but he forces my hands away, taking over.

"So, would you be interested?"

"You make it sound like a job application."

"Technically, in my mother's eyes, you're kind of applying for future daughter-in-law material," he says, half grimacing and half smiling.

"That's not at all daunting. Sure, I'd love to be scrutinized by your mother." In a mock motherly tone, I continue, "So, Lilly, what do your parents do for a living?" I switch voices and say, "Oh, I don't have any, but my brother is known to dabble in trade smuggling. It's actually a family affair. You know, just paying the bills."

He huffs out a laugh and runs his hands through my hair, expelling the remaining soap. "When did you become such a drama queen?"

I bite his arm, and he hisses through his teeth against the pain.

"What was that for?"

"I'm not a drama queen."

"Right, 'cause inflicting physical pain isn't dramatic at all." I make a move to do it again, but he blocks me, spinning me around and pinning my back to his front. "I'll let my mother know that my girlfriend has come down with some sort of rabid disease and she won't be able to make it."

"Make sure it sounds fatal."

His laughter tickles the hairs on my neck, and I try to squirm away. "I texted Kip. He thinks it'll be a good idea to get you away for a few days. One weekend, that's all I'm asking."

I lower my guard, defeated. "If this doesn't sound like a setup, I don't know what does."

He bites my neck and I yelp. "I'll set you up."

"Oh my God. Never say that again."

He evil-villain laughs as he picks me up and pins me against the shower wall.

"STOP POUTING."

I glare at Justin as he puts my bag in the back of his Jeep. "I'm not pouting. I'm worried."

"Kip's explained everything to them. They know what they're doing. Kip just needs a little more time to talk to Jimmy."

I already know all of this, but it still doesn't ease the weight in my stomach. Kip talked with Dan and Ethan separately, explaining what we found and our suspicions. They both agreed to keep it between us before making any rash decisions. That means doing a lift while Kip attempts to set up a meeting with Jimmy. That's an entirely different worry all in itself. Neither Kip nor Taylor has ever met him in real life, and now that we know he's most probably a drug lord or something, it's that more daunting.

"Plus," he adds as he shuts the back of his Jeep. "We made a run and it was fluff."

"And they're grown men, Lil," Kip adds for extra emphasis.

"And I'm a grown woman. Yet you had a conniption fit when I went."

He thumps me on the forehead. "Which I had every right to, considering we had no idea what we were getting into. Still don't."

I roll my eyes and hug him bye. His point is valid, and I know there's no argument to be won.

"We should get there around four. I'll text you when we arrive," Justin says.

Kip releases me and slaps Justin's shoulder. "Drive safe, wear your seat belts."

Justin does the same to Kip and says, "Will do."

It's weird and comforting all at the same time to see them getting along so well. In the time since we revealed our findings to Kip, they've been in almost constant contact. Whether in regards to my well-being or Kip's progress on figuring out a solution to all our problems, they've texted back in forth all week. I just haven't figured out which feeling is more dominant.

It's about a two-and-a-half-hour ride to Justin's parents' house. His home, depending on how you look at it. I spend the better half of the ride going over different scenarios in my head. His mom can dislike me on sight. She'll take one good look at me and know that I'm a bad influence on her son. She'll be psychic and detect that I've gotten her son mixed up with the mafia. Or whatever shit Jimmy is.

Justin reaches over the seat and slowly runs his hand up my thigh. "You're legs look amazing."

His fingers are a few shades darker than my pale legs, and a thought occurs to me. "Your mom isn't super conservative or something, is she? Should I put on pants?"

He throws his head back, laughing. "I'm feeling you up and all you can think about is what my mom thinks?"

"Well, should I?"

"I don't think it's my mom that I'm worried about," he says, reaching a little higher."It's my brother."

I stop his hand. "Don't patronize me."

He leans over the middle and kisses me. "You're perfect."

"Thanks, you've been very helpful."

"You're thinking too much." I give him a look and he's not at all affected by it, smiling at my nervousness. "If I can win over your brother, there's no doubt you can handle my mom."

He has a point, but still, not very helpful.

The driveway to Justin's house is long and winding, filled with woods on both sides. Tall pine trees loom high above us, creating a tunnel effect and blocking the sunlight. The gravel road dips and turns periodically with no end in sight.

"You're not bringing me somewhere to kill me, are you?" The automatic locks click down around me. "Funny," I say, giving him a dry look.

"I thought it was."

"How much farther?"

"This long," he says as we emerge from the pine trees.

An entire expanse of land lies before us. It's an orchard of some sort. Trees line row after row behind a small bungalow-style house, old but kept up nicely. Justin parks next to another, older-model Jeep in front of the porch. Potted plants sit along the railing, and wooden chairs occupy the space between.

"I thought you said you didn't have a lot of money growing up."

"We didn't," he says, taking in the view with me. "Not until my dad sobered up." He opens his door and I am immediately bombarded with the smell of lemon and pine.

They're lemon trees.

Justin already has our bags unloaded when the front door of the house swings wide, banging off the siding.

"Three years is too long."

A statuesque woman walks down the stairs, her dark brown hair pulled back into a long ponytail, and I quickly take note that her shorts are comparable to mine. She pulls Justin into a tight embrace, with watery eyes and a shaky smile.

"You look like a grown man," she says, wiping away tears.

Justin's smile is a tad steadier as he pulls away. He lets her hold him at arm's length, looking him over. I stand off to the side, holding my backpack in front of me awkwardly. When she finally releases him, he takes a step toward me, wrapping an arm around my waist.

"Mom, this is Lilly. Lilly, this is my mom, Teresa." I feel like an object he's presenting to the class for show-and-tell.

"Lilly, call me Tess."

taking mine

There is no hug or handshake in greeting, and I'm silently grateful. Although, at the same time, I'm alarmed considering her more than welcome greeting she had for Justin. It is her son, but still. I focus on Justin's presence next to me and the calming circles he's drawing on my side.

"It's nice to meet you," I say with a smile.

A younger male's voice pulls our attention back to the house. "Not as nice as it is to meet me."

"Jake," Justin says with one of his rare, wide-eyed smiles. He releases me and meets his brother halfway up the porch steps in a bulldozer type of hug. They slap each other on the back a few times before letting go.

"Mom's right. I think I see some gray hairs, old man."

Justin slaps Jacob's hand away and pulls him into a headlock under his arm. "What did you say?" Justin says, tightening the hold.

"I said," Jacob wheezes. "You look good, man."

"That's what I thought," Justin says, releasing him.

"Boys," Tess says, trying but failing to reprimand them through a smile. "Bring the bags inside."

Jacob skips down the porch steps, stopping before me. "Jake, at your service," he says, swooping into a bow and taking my backpack.

"Where's Dad?" Justin asks, a hesitant look on his face.

"He's checking the irrigation system at the end of the plot. He'll be back by dinner."

She leads the way, evidently expecting me to follow. I look over my shoulder and catch Jacob playfully shoving Justin as he picks up my duffel bag, throwing him off balance.

"Put Lilly's bags in the den," she tosses over her shoulder.

"Mom," Justin says daringly. "We don't need to stay in separate rooms."

I cringe. He basically just told his mother that we have sex all the time.

"I don't care. In my house you'll respect my rules." Tess's words leave no room for negotiation.

"I've been living by myself for—"

"Justin," she cuts him off.

He gives me a repentant look and I smile, silently give him props for trying.

"Someone's not getting any tonight." Jacob's smile flees from his face the moment Tess pins him with a look. "What?" he says, shrugging one shoulder with a playful smile. "He's not."

She shakes her head despairingly and spins back around, but not before a ghost of a smile appears on her face.

"I'll stay in the den, Mom. Lilly can have my room."

We enter the foyer and she gives him a proud smile. "You're such a gentleman. Show her to your room and then meet me in the kitchen. Dinner is already on the stove."

The inside of the house looks exactly like what I'd expect: eclectic in the sense that everything serves a purpose.

The walls are bare, leaving the furniture as the only decorations, and it reminds me of home. Justin leads the way up the flight of stairs. He waits at the top of the landing, letting me pass. "To the right." Justin motions to a door with a crook of his head, both hands weighed down by bags.

I hear Jacob whisper something and a smacking sound makes me turn around.

"Quit checking out my girlfriend." Justin is glaring at him.

"She's closer to my age than yours, old man." Jacob is unapologetic as he shoots me a wink, quickly ducking into the next bedroom.

"Little shit," Justin says, dropping my bag on the twin-sized bed.

Justin's room matches his apartment, completely void of all personality. The walls are pale blue, probably the same blue they were painted when he was a baby.

He sits on the quilted bedspread and I say, "Your mom is…"

"Intimidating," he fills in for me.

"That's a good adjective."

He smirks and pulls me between his legs. "She'll loosen up. She's putting on a good show."

"How long has it been since you've been home?"

"Technically, three years, but even before then I wasn't really here. After I got out I rented a small apartment from the neighbors."

"Why?"

He breathes in and out a few times and then pushes his face into the softness of my belly. "My dad went to rehab right after I was sentenced. Apparently he blames himself for me getting in trouble. When I got out, he claimed he was sober and wanted to pick up a relationship with me out of thin air. My mom expected me to greet him with open arms, like he wasn't the broken man I saw all my life. And I couldn't do it."

I run my fingers through his hair, trying to grasp what it would be like. I think about my mom and how I'd feel if she wanted to pretend she'd never left, that even before that she never drank herself to sleep every day, and I already know it wouldn't be possible.

He teases a kiss under my shirt. "We should get downstairs before your mom gets suspicious."

"My mom can take a chill pill." He kisses a little higher up, my shirt inching along with his lips.

"She hasn't seen you in years. Be a good son and spend time with her."

A voice comes from the doorway. "Listen to her." A tall, wiry man leans against the door, wringing a towel between his hands. I quickly tug my shirt down and move away from my close proximity to Justin.

"Dad," Justin greets him, monotone.

"It's good to see you, son. Been too long."

Neither one of them makes a move toward the other. It's the polar opposite of the reception he got from his mother.

"Hi, I'm Lilly."

"Bruce," he says with a genuine smile.

There's a moment of silence and I clap my hands together to try and break the awkwardness, "Well, I don't want to keep your mom waiting."

Justin doesn't bother for niceties, standing as he ushers me past his father and down the stairs. We're greeted with the smell of dinner and my stomach rumbles, having long missed the smell of home-cooked food.

"Chicken spaghetti?" Justin asks, a small amount of excitement filtering into his voice.

Tess and Justin share the same megawatt smile as he dips his finger in the sauce and tastes it.

"Figured I had to bribe you to come home more often," Tess says, watching her son.

"You'd figure my handsome face would be incentive enough," Jacob says, bounding into the kitchen. "But now I see why you didn't want to come home…scared I'll steal your girl."

"Can I help with anything?" I ask, feeling out of place.

"You can help Jacob set the table," she says, pointing at the cupboard.

Jacob divvies out plates, bouncing his eyebrows up and down as I take them.

"If you don't keep your eyes to yourself, I'm going to shave your eyebrows off again," Justin warns.

This spikes my interest. "Again?"

"Oh yeah. I spent my freshman year of high school a virgin because my brother was an asinine dick."

"The bastard wouldn't stay out of my room," Justin says in defense.

Jacob leans into me and whispers, "He had the best porn mags."

"Which you stole," Justin accuses.

"What else was I supposed to do when I looked like a naked mole rat?"

"Boys," Tess says in warning.

Justin hugs his mom around the shoulders. "Lighten up. I'm sure Jake doesn't have them anymore."

Jacob agrees. "It's been a long time since I've needed—"

"That's enough," Tess says, fed up with their antics. "You owe Lilly an apology for being so crude."

Jacob rolls his head dramatically, throwing his arm over my shoulders in the same fashion. "Sorry, Lilly." Justin walks over and pops him in the same spot as he did earlier. "Ow, quit doing that or I'm going to have permanent brain damage."

"I warned you."

"You said I couldn't look at her. You didn't say anything about touching her."

Their dad strolls between them, preventing Justin from advancing on Jacob, and greets his wife with a kiss on the cheek. "Tess, it smells wonderful."

Justin distracts himself by kissing my neck, tickling me with his chin hairs, earning a look of admonishment from Tess.

"She's my girlfriend, Mother," he says with a hint of derision.

"And you're under my roof."

Justin's dad speaks up. "Tess, he's not a little boy anymore." This placates her, but only marginally. Her lips are thin as she turns away and continues stirring dinner.

I have to fend Justin off multiple times, and I can see the playfulness that Jacob has in him. The only difference between Jacob's and his is Justin's is weighted down. It's more subdued, a litter rougher around the edges, where Jacob's is untainted and boyish. I look to his dad, smiling at Tess's failing attempts to discipline her children, and Jacob's mission to annoy Justin at all costs. I can't see the man who Justin hates. And I have a hard time picturing Tess staying with a man who was less than stellar to her kids. The image before me is muddled by what I know Justin has told me.

We spend the rest of the evening laughing at Justin and Jacob banter back and forth. They spit insults and retell childhood memories, almost every one of them ending in pain or humiliation. I learn about how Justin got the scar on his lip and a crooked nose—a story including a jealous girlfriend, a bicycle, and scratch-n-sniff stickers. Tess has given up on attempting to get them to behave, simply enjoying their happiness.

Justin's dad doesn't say much of anything, but his laughter joins the rest of ours. He and Tess share thoughtful looks and smiles, and I find Justin looking at me in the same way. He's happy that I enjoy being with his family, even if he's not at peace with the man sitting at the end of the table.

I hold steady to Justin's side when he turns down his dad's offer to have tea on the back porch. There's hurt in his mom's eyes, disappointment in his dad's, but it's his choice. Jacob avoids the entire situation with his head down, charging up the stairs ahead of us.

"You okay?" I ask once we're back in his bedroom. He gives nothing away as he shuts the door and pulls me down with him across the bed. "We're going to get in trouble."

"What's she going to do? Kick me out?"

"She might kick *me* out, and I want to make a good impression. And you didn't help with pushing her buttons."

"The only impression you need to make is on me. A strip tease should work."

I roll my eyes and swat at his chest as I sit up. "Justin, seriously."

He breathes in the way he does when he's annoyed by something. It's usually directed at Lance during study group. "I'm not going the entire weekend without touching you."

"You went weeks without touching me. You'll be fine."

I rest my head in the palm of my hand and lie down next to him. We're silent, and I study his profile as he stares at the ceiling, thinking about so much. I run my fingers across the knuckles folded across his chest.

"Your dad doesn't seem so bad."

"No, I guess he doesn't."

I don't press the issue as I continue to put gentle pressure against his hands, trying to give him solace. He continues to stare at the ceiling as I wait for him to voice his thoughts.

"He was an angry drunk." I hold my breath at his words. "He was verbally abusive to my mom, sometimes physically, too." He can see the question behind my eyes, the fear in them. "He didn't touch me or my brother. Only once when I was older we got in a fistfight. I couldn't hold my tongue anymore, and I knew just what to say to set him off."

"You wanted a fight."

He nods. "I was angry. I wanted to hurt him as much as he'd hurt me, as much as he'd hurt my mom, and for everything my brother and I had to see. I'd been waiting on the day I could stand up to him."

"Years worth of anger."

"It was the same night of the robbery."

The glimpses he's shared with me are falling into place like puzzle pieces. "That's what triggered him to get sober?"

"Supposedly."

I lay my head down on his chest, letting the rhythmic rise and fall soothe the both of us. He runs his fingers up and down my side, easing me.

"Do you believe love has conditions?"

My question stirs him out of his thoughts. "What do you mean?"

"Do you think you can only love someone if they're good to you? Can you love someone despite their wrongdoings?"

He takes a moment to think about it. "I think love is love. Even if you try to convince yourself it's not, it's still there."

"But what if that person never loved you in the first place?"

He shifts to where he can see my face, pulling my chin upward. "Where's this coming from?"

I shrug. "I understand how hard it is to forgive your dad. My mom was an alcoholic. After my dad died, she quit being a mom. She wasn't mean, necessarily, just neglectful. Kip says she wasn't always that way, but I don't remember her being a mom, you know? How do I even know if she loved me?"

"Lilly," he says, hurt lacing his voice. Hurt for my hurt.

"But I still feel like I love her. I don't know if I forgive her for leaving us. I just kind of feel like she wasn't emotionally there to process everything."

He runs his fingers through the hair tucked behind my ear. "I can't speak for your mom, but I can't imagine anyone incapable of loving you."

"But she still left."

He doesn't respond, most likely unsure of what to say. It's hard to justify a mother leaving her children regardless of the situation. He wraps his arms around me, pulling me as close to him as we can possibly fit.

Momentarily, I'm guilty for directing the attention to my problems when we're currently living in his, but I think it's what he needs. He needs to focus on something to lessen his afflictions. A sense of belonging fills my chest, and I never want to be without it.

The feel of his lips against my forehead is the last thing I feel before I fall asleep.

A LOUD BANG SHAKES US from our sleep, and we jump apart, sitting up to find the source of the noise. Justin's bedroom door is wide open, Jacob standing in the middle. He's wearing white boxer briefs and a long yellow cape tied around his neck. He stands tall with his hands balled into fists on his hips and chest poked out.

"What the fuck, Jacob?" Justin yells at him.

"Have no fear," he bellows in an exaggerated deep voice. "Your trusty sidekick is here."

I start laughing hysterically. Jacob wearing white underwear leaves nothing to the imagination. Justin covers my eyes.

"Get the fuck out," Justin yells louder this time.

"Look."

I hear rustling and struggle to remove Justin's hand from my face. Jacob holds up a blue cape fashioned out of the same material his yellow one is in. "I made you one. Took forever for them to dry. And…" He pulls an extra pink one from behind his back. "I made one especially for Lilly."

Justin is utterly baffled. He's speechless as he looks at his grown brother dressed in tighty-whities and a cape. "Jacob," he says, squeezing the bridge of his nose. "Get out of my room before I shove that cape up your ass."

"Meet me downstairs. Clothing optional." He winks at me and skips out of the door right as Justin hurls a shoe at him, missing by a centimeter.

I'm still giggling when I make it into the kitchen, freshly dressed and showered from the long day before, feeling like a day of adventure lies before me. Jacob's excitement might have rubbed off on me.

He's sitting at the kitchen table, scarfing down a plate of scrambled eggs and toast, his cape tied around clothed shoulders this time. He gives me a cheeky smile full of food.

"You don't have to pretend you don't like what you see."

Tess replaces Justin's role and slaps Jacob across the back of the head. "Eat your food. Lilly, there's plenty of breakfast on the stove. Help yourself."

"Thank you."

There is no mention of Justin and me sleeping in his room last night, and I don't chance it by bringing it up. I fix a plate of eggs and breakfast sausage, sitting opposite Jacob.

"What's up with the capes?"

"Other than they're awesome?"

"Yeah, sure."

"That's the explanation...they're awesome."

Justin struts into the kitchen, running his fingers through his wet hair. "Morning." He kisses me, something quick and endearing, moving toward the food on the stove.

It's not until I tear my gaze from Justin that I catch Jacob scrutinizing me. It's the only way I can describe the seriousness of his attention. My stupid, happy grin slips from my face. It's a complete one-eighty from the happy-go-lucky personality he's demonstrated since I've arrived. It's assessing, and it sets me on edge, reminding me too much of Justin.

"What?" I ask self-consciously.

Slowly, his face morphs back to normal. "Nothing." With a grin on his face, he tosses me the pink cape and stands from the kitchen table. "Meet me at the barn in ten minutes."

"No jumping off the roof," Tess states behind her curtain of newspaper.

"We're not, Mom." He slaps the table and points at Justin. "Don't be late." We watch him escape through the back door, his yellow cape flying behind him.

"He's strange," I say to no one in particular.

"That he is," Tess says with an affectionate smile.

We finish our breakfast, and Justin walks me out past the rows of lemon trees. The ground slopes downwards, for irrigation purposes, Justin tells me. That's why the worn barn can't be seen from the house. The red paint on the wood is almost completely marred, closer to sun bleached with red patches here and there. It's small with only two stalls on the inside that are used for storage purposes, not harboring animals. There's a set of stairs, almost rotten through, that leads to the loft.

Justin cups his hands and yells for Jacob.

"Up here."

"Are these stairs safe?"

"I'm up here, aren't I?" He peaks his head into the small opening. "Come on." And he disappears again.

Justin sighs. "Let me lift you over the bottom rungs. They look the worst."

I hold the capes close as Justin easily lifts my body halfway up the flight of stairs, leaping up behind me. The loft opens to the outside. A sliding barn door is open, revealing a small balcony.

"We aren't actually jumping off the roof, are we?"

"Not jumping," Jacob answers, leading us to the railing. "Gliding."

A line of cable runs from the corner of the roof all the way down into the lemon trees. A handle hangs from it. It's a zip line.

"No way." Justin's voice matches Jacob's excitement as he checks out the cable's durability. "You did this?" he asks Jacob.

"Dad and me. It's been up for a while now. Leads to the tree house."

I squint, trying to see past the canopy of trees to find the end of the line. "There's no way I'm doing this."

"Oh, come on," Jacob says, grabbing the handle. "I'll go first and you can see that it's perfectly safe." He climbs onto the wooden boards of the railing, teetering his weight off the edge, hanging on to the handlebars for support.

"Nope," I say, backing away. "Not happening."

Jacob smiles and pushes off. His body soars through the air and glides underneath the lemon trees, out of sight as he yells the entire way.

"Nope," I repeat again.

Justin laughs at my adamant refusal. "The girl who knows how to hotwire a car can't handle heights?"

"What if I can't hold on?"

"You're not a weakling. You can support yourself." He squeezes my upper arms a little. "You can do this."

"My hands are sweaty." I let him feel my palms. "I might slip."

Jacob runs back from the tree house and emerges from the barn, clipping the handlebar back on the cable. "See, nothing to be scared of. I'm still alive and breathing."

"What if you went with me?" Justin says, sitting on the railing and holding a hand out for me.

I'm hesitant.

His eyes meet mine. "You trust me?"

He gives me a soft smile, encouraging me to step forward. With a pounding heart, I place my hand in his and hand Jacob the capes. Shakily, very shakily, I pull myself up onto the railing.

"Okay, now straddle me."

Jacob makes a smartass remark about straddling something, but I fail to hear him over the pounding of my heart. Every one of my extremities is shaking violently. The ground looks like a death sentence from this high up. Its own smoking gun.

"Don't look down," Justin demands, pulling my chin up. "Focus on me." He helps me, pulling my arms around his neck for balance. I squeal and he chuckles, kissing the inside of my wrist. "Now, wrap your legs around me."

Jacob hands Justin the handle as I latch on. "You ready?" Justin asks, letting go of me and placing both hands on the handlebars. "I'm going to count to three. One…Two…"

I squeeze my eyes shut and bury my face into his neck. There is no three, or I didn't hear it, because the next thing I know we're flying through the air. My hair whips against my face, and I pry my eyes open, catching Jacob's smile, and fist pump as we soar farther away. I understand the term zip line now from the sound the handlebars make against the line.

"Hold on," Justin yells over the wind.

If I weren't in a weird state of panic and exhilaration, I would roll my eyes. Like I would just let go? Justin grunts as his feet hit stable material and hoists our bodies over the ledge. The tree house is nothing more than a platform of wood built in the center of three lemon trees. Only one wall has remained standing over time. My legs feel like Jell-O as I unwrap them from Justin's waist. His hands remain on my hips until I find my balance.

"Not as bad as you thought?"

"It was terrifying." But the smile on my face gives away how much I enjoyed it.

He shakes my hips back and forth. "Go again?"

"Fuck no."

He throws his head back, laughing, his chest rising and falling rapidly from leftover adrenaline. With my own endorphins soaring, I can't stop myself from placing an open-mouth kiss to his neck. His laughter dies under the touch of my tongue, and his neck bobs as he swallows, slowly tilting his head toward mine.

"Do you think Jacob will come looking for us?"

He wraps his arms around my shoulders, his chin balanced on top of my head. "Yes. If he's anything, it's intrusive."

The air is chilly, and morning dew clings to the rich green on the trees. The makeshift tree house is nestled right under the surrounding branches, creating a sense of seclusion.

"It's so pretty here."

taking mine

"Yeah," he says, admiring the view with me. "But you should really see it when the trees are in bloom."

"They still smell like lemons even though there's no fruit." My eyes trail to the two remaining sides of the tree house and the writing taking up most of them. "Who wrote the entire lyrics to The Fresh Prince of Bel-Air?"

Justin laughs. "Jacob was so pissed when they pulled the show that he made a memorial in its honor." He trails a finger over the multitude of writing. There are plenty of signatures of friends who've come and gone over the years, and I notice quite a few phone numbers or dates posted next to them. Justin smiles as I run over a Natalie and then an Elise.

"I'd hate to see what the other walls looked like," I say.

"They got knocked down when Dad planted the trees."

There's a sense of melancholy as his eyes take in everything. It's easy to see how much he loves it here, but not enough to put aside his resentment toward his father. Maybe the happy memories mix a little too much with the bad ones.

"Hey!" Jacob's voice breaks us apart for the second time this morning. "Quit humping each other and bring the handle back." We can't see him, but we can hear his footsteps crunch against the leaves as he walks away.

"He's still just as annoying as when we were little."

When I arrive back to the house, Justin's dad is sitting on the porch, rocking in a chair. There's a pitcher of tea and two glasses on the end table in the middle, and he raises a glass in my direction. Unsure as to how to greet him, being a man who has said few words since I've arrived, I smile politely.

"Jacob showed you the zip line?"

"Yes, sir. You'd think he was fifteen."

"Bruce. Call me Bruce. No sirs around here."

"Okay." Getting the idea he'd like to chat, I take up the vacant rocking chair.

"Justin's told you a lot about me."

I guess we're getting straight to the point. "He has."

"All good things, I'm sure." His good humor makes me smile.

Tess brings out a plate of muffins and places it on the table but doesn't say anything, giving Bruce a kiss before disappearing back inside. Bruce offers me one, which I decline, and he takes a bite before continuing.

"I'm not proud of my past, but I can't be ashamed of it anymore. I've spent these last few years trying to make him proud, show him that I'm trying to be a better father—a better husband—but he still won't talk to me."

He rocks softly in his chair, looking out at the field of trees, gathering his thoughts. It's the first time I've seen Justin in him. He's taking time to access what he's going to say.

"I hope you understand that I had to forgive myself." I don't nod or give anything away when he looks at me. After a moment, he looks away. "It's the only way I can be the person I need to be for Tess."

"You seem happy together."

"We are, for the most part. But Justin's presence hangs over us. He doesn't come home because of me. Tess knows it, I know it."

"She blames you."

"There's no more blame to be had. It's up to us to make the most of it. I'd be lying if I said it doesn't anger me that it's taken three years for him to come home. I see Tess's disappointment every time he makes an excuse not to come visit. But he calls, so I guess I can't complain too much."

We rock for a few minutes, and the muffins start to look appealing, so I take one. I peel the parchment paper back and say, "My mom was an alcoholic."

This catches his attention. "Was?"

"Is. I'm not sure. I haven't seen her since I was eleven."

"I'm sorry," he says, his words laden with sadness.

I shrug my shoulders and pretend indifference. "It's not your fault. Like you said, it is what it is."

"What about your dad?"

taking mine

"Died when I was two. My brother raised me. He protected me from most of it, I suppose. I didn't even know how bad my mom was until middle school. When she left, he didn't have to shield me from it anymore. In a way it was probably a relief."

He lets out a deep breath. Again, another characteristic of Justin's. I wonder if he realizes how deep his dad's genes are imbedded in him. "He sounds like a good man."

"He is. The best." I take a bite of the muffin, chewing as I think. "It's ironic, because Justin was that person for Jacob."

"Yes," Bruce says. "Justin did more than his fair share with Jacob, and I did stay, but there was a time when I thought of leaving. Not because I wanted to, but because it might have been easier on them."

"Are you saying it's worse that you didn't leave?"

"I don't know," he says, his eyes forlorn. "You tell me."

Justin and Jacob emerge from the tree line, and Justin is laughing at Jacob's hand motion gliding through the air. Justin smacks his hand down and does his own reenactment, ending with a smack to his brother's forehead.

Jacob runs right up to us and picks up the spare glass, filling it with tea. Sweat is covering every inch of his skin and some parts of his clothing.

"What happened to the cape?"

Justin slows as he approaches the porch. "It caught one of the tree branches on his way down, pulled him straight off the line."

"Landed flat on my back."

Bruce and I both laugh as Jacob describes his thought process through a drop that probably lasted a couple seconds at most. By the time he finishes, Tess has wandered out to the porch and taken up a seat on the arm of Bruce's rocking chair.

"I told you jumping off the roof is about the dumbest thing you can do without some type of harness."

"Yes, Mother," Jacob says, bowing. "You are always right."

"Damn right," Bruce says, smiling.

Justin is the only one who doesn't contribute to the conversation. Everyone can feel his unease. Jacob tries to diffuse it with humor, Tess tries to act like everything is normal, and Bruce shuts his mouth. It's the same method they used last night at dinner. Before, I didn't see it, but now I do. Justin's attitude hangs over them like an approaching thundercloud. He doesn't announce his departure, instead opting to leave without a word. The screen door slams shut behind him.

All eyes turn to me.

"I'm sorry."

"It's okay," Bruce says, giving his wife a shoulder rub. "No need to apologize."

And I've come to the conclusion that I can't hate Bruce. I want to. I do. But the man who sits before me is not the man Justin describes. People change, right? Bruce whispers in Tess's ear, and they excuse themselves to a walk in the orchard.

Jacob takes up their chair and refills his tea. "He feels like if he forgives him then it means it was okay. That everything he put us through is excusable. And it's not. But he's hurting everybody by not letting it go."

"And you've forgiven him?"

Jacob takes a sip before replying. "Sometimes. Most times. Every now and then it'll hit me, and I'll get angry, but then I realize it's useless. Mom's forgiven him. I need to too."

chapter 14

JUSTIN DROPS OUR BAGS on the bottom step of the porch. Tess envelops Justin in a tight hug with tears in her eyes, making him promise to visit again soon. After she releases him, she surprisingly pulls me into a hug as well.

"You're welcome to come back anytime as long as you bring my boy with you."

We laugh at her obvious attempt to barter for Justin. We spent the night before "bonding" as we baked Justin's favorite dessert, peach cobbler. She, in a very roundabout way, apologized for being so standoffish, claiming she only wants the best for her son and his heart. And she also assured me that she could hear straight into his bedroom and that the walls were very thin.

She folds a note into the palm of my hand. "For future reference."

Jacob pushes her out of the way, telling her she's stealing all the action. Always the comedic relief. "I look forward to pissing off my brother some more, so you have to come back."

"Apparently he didn't hit you hard enough."

"Or too hard, depending how you look at it." He winks.

Bruce stands by the door, not daring to venture too close. A tiny gleam of a smile peeks through as I walk up the stairs and embrace him in a hug. "You're good for him," he says.

With my chin on his shoulder, I say, "No, he's good for me."

He gives me one last good squeeze and lets go. "Remember that. Even when life makes you question everything, remember how much good he brings you."

I don't know why his words pack so much punch, but I fight off a lump in my throat as I descend the steps, waving one last goodbye to Tess and Bruce. Justin's eyes stay trained on me as I walk back toward him, a ghost of emotions flitting across his face. He hugs me. I don't know why, but I hug him back, putting all the strength I can into it. There's something he's seeking from me, and I can feel it with every deep breath he takes. Maybe reassurance.

"I'm on your side," I say.

He kisses my forehead and shifts his arm over my shoulder. "Dad," Justin says, focusing in on Bruce. "Maybe next time I'll take you up on that tea." Tess bursts into tears.

It doesn't escape anyone's notice that Bruce's eyes mist over as he nods. "I'd really like that, son."

Jacob's smile is brilliant when he says, "One small step for man, and one giant—ow."

He rubs his shoulder, the one I just backhanded, and everyone laughs. Justin high fives me as Tess instructs Jacob to help pack the rest of our bags. I'm climbing into the passenger seat when I hear Jacob wish Justin good luck through the open hatch.

I look over my shoulder, and Justin's gaze meets mine. "Thanks, I'm going to need it."

They finish saying their goodbyes, and Justin slides into the driver seat, taking one last good look at the land before him. He starts the engine, rolling down the windows as he reverses, and I breathe in the last whiff of pine mixed with lemon. I'll probably never be able to find a smell close to this again without the help of cleaning products.

I wait until the house disappears from sight and we're engulfed in shadows before I say, "I'm proud of you."

"Yeah," he says, looking at me. "Me too."

The drive seems to go by slower on the way back, and we don't bother to unpack once we finally arrive at Justin's apartment. Sliding onto the couch, allowing Justin to take up the better half of it, I fall into a level of comfort that's become addicting. It feels like...home. Instead of this thought freaking me out like I assume it would if I were more coherent, it only drives me further into his warmth. Justin's lips skim the underside of my chin, but I welcome it this time, giggling at his attempt to keep me awake.

"I feel like it's been forever since I heard you laugh," he says.

"What are you talking about? I spent the entire weekend laughing with your family."

"Correction: you spent the entire weekend laughing at my brother."

I turn on my back and look up at him. "Are you seriously jealous of your brother right now?"

He shrugs, but his smile tells me there's an ounce of insecurity there. "Not him, specifically, but his ability to make you happy."

"You make me happy."

He already knew that's what I would say. Intertwining his fingers through mine, he stays focused on them as he runs his thumb back and forth over mine. "I'm torn between wanting to tell you everything going on inside me, to tell you what I'm thinking, when I think it, and how it makes me feel." He pauses to look up at me. "And the other half of me wants to put all those things in a box and make sure it never gets to see the light of day."

It makes sense. Justin has the ability to see himself better than anyone I know. It's his way of staying on neutral ground, a balancing act of some sort, and I've seen that war wage inside of him many times.

"So, Lilly," he says. "Tell me what to do."

He wants me to carry the responsibility of his feelings. If he tells me, I have to face them. I'll be held accountable. The good, the bad, and the ugly. I don't get to choose the snippets I want. Because I want the easy ones, the ones that don't rock us too hard. I want the ones that give me just enough hope to put in my own box and hide away. But something tells me his box is much deeper than mine, and much darker, as well. The thought of not knowing anything at all is almost worse. I need to know that what I'm feeling, what I've been denying and pushing away, he feels too, and that we're in this together.

If there's anything I've learned the past few weeks, it's that the power of touch is real. I've fought the desire to touch Justin, just to feel how real he is, and to feel the comfort of his presence. I've been touched by him in ways that I never knew could be enjoyable. Touch can calm a racing heart, or set one off. It can push someone away, or pull them closer. And it can convey affection and adoration, and the absolute vulnerability it takes to feel those emotions.

I wrap my free hand around his neck, letting my fingers skim the skin there, and pull his face down to mine. "Show me," I say against his lips, almost inaudible to myself beyond the race of my heart.

He holds still, unmoving, as he registers my words, and in a split moment he's carrying me toward his bedroom. It's the same bed I've been in countless times. But this time, when he laces our hands above my head—looking at me like nothing else matters for him—this bed becomes a place I'll always remember when it comes to what it feels like to fall in love.

With every touch, every feel of his lips, and every unspoken feeling...I give in.

JUSTIN'S LIPS WAKE ME and I protest, rolling over and stuffing my face in a pillow.

"Lilly," he says, giving me a little shake. "Wake up. Kaley's here."

I grumble but don't move.

"She said you had plans to go shopping?"

A faint memory of agreeing to go Christmas shopping after I got back from spending time with Justin's family resurfaces, and I immediately begin trying to think of ways to get out of it.

"It's freaking noon. For the love of Christ, get up." Kaley's voice is like nails on a chalkboard.

It's a conspiracy. No one wants me to sleep.

"You let her in," I accuse Justin.

"I didn't have much of a choice. It was either let her in or let the neighbors call in a noise complaint from her incessant door banging."

taking mine

I take note of his pajama bottoms. Apparently facing Kaley isn't his favorite way to wake up either.

"Get up," Kaley repeats, this time trying to rip the blankets away.

Justin clutches it before I can, and I'm eternally grateful. Justin smirks at my lack of clothing.

"You two are so gross," she says, stomping out of the room. "Be dressed in ten minutes or I'm coming back in."

Justin leans over and kisses me sweetly. It's tender and it makes my heart hurt. His eyes hold the same reconciliation he had in them last night. I saw it the first time we had sex, briefly, and last night was the first time I've seen it since. Whatever conclusion he's come to, it's settled in him. But for some reason, it doesn't erase the unease in my gut.

"That better not be kissing I hear!"

"Go," he says as he lifts the blanket away.

I'm petulant as I stand. As I pass by him on my way to the bathroom, he smacks my bare behind, and a resounding sting echoes through the room. I don't bother to retaliate, already knowing I'm on losing ground, and I just rub the pain away.

"Lilly," Kaley's voice says in admonition.

I roll my eyes. "I'm going to make you wait outside in the cold if you keep trying to rush me."

Smartly, she remains quiet. I turn on the shower and begin brushing my teeth, watching Justin remake the bed through the open door. He's moody and it's making me nervous. He shoves the last corner under the mattress and looks up, catching me watching his every move. This weekend took a bigger toll on him than I realized. It takes me closer to twenty minutes to get ready, not hurrying due to my indecision to leave Justin alone with his thoughts.

"I'll stay," I say, right as we're about to leave.

He shakes his head. "No, go. I've been attached to your hip. You need girl time," he says, attempting to lighten the mood.

I ignore Kaley's groan. "Are you sure? Kaley and I can hang whenever."

"I'm sure. I think I'm going to run and check in with Kip."

Knowing he has something to focus his mind on, I concede. "I'll text you on my way home to see if you want any food."

He holds my face between his hands. "You're the best." He gives me a quick peck on the lips and closes the door behind us.

"What's with all the brooding?" Kaley says, giving me a look.

I sigh. "I think seeing his family messed with him."

At least, that's what I keep telling myself. There's no way that arguably the best night of my life has turned him this inside out. I recall our drive home and how melancholy he was when we returned. Yes, that has to be it.

I listen to Kaley drone on and on about how Lance ended things with Ashley, something about a flavor of ice cream being their downfall, as I warm my hands in front of the air vents. One would think that being in a high-speed car chase would make me less afraid of riding in vehicles, but Kaley's driving makes Justin's pale in comparison. I brace myself against the door as she makes a last-minute turn because she was distracted by someone's customized license plate.

"I didn't know bedazzling license plates was legal," she says absentmindedly, not at all concerned about my real fear of dying. "Oh, we should check out the new boutique they just opened." She claps her hands, excited.

"We should keep our hands on the wheel," I say.

"There is no *we* in driving."

Sometimes I question if she's the one who's pre-law. She can argue *herself* under a bus.

I spend the day following Kaley around town as she buys gifts for any and everyone she's met since she was five. Don't believe me? Her neighbor's Shih Tzu is going to be a proud owner of a bowl shaped like a princess crown. But I do find a gift for Kip. It's a t-shirt that says, World's Okayest Brother, across the front. And like tradition, I'll buy him a new set of bandanas since he never finds time to wash his.

It's a gift for Justin that I struggle with. Every store we venture into I leave disappointed. Generic gifts line the shelves, like cologne

taking mine

or watches, which I consider but know they're meaningless. It's when we're passing a toy store that I get an idea. Once I find what I'm looking for, Kaley gives me a look, not understanding the significance, and I don't explain it.

On the way home, I tell Kaley to stop by Toby's so I can say hey to Kip. It's weird for us to go this long without speaking to each other and I kind of miss him. I know he's busy, but even if it's a quick hug, I just feel the need to see his face.

"I'll only be a second."

The front door doesn't give when I pull it, and I try again, the glass reverberating through my hand. I scan the inside, taking note that the lights are off. It's a Monday afternoon, a little past four, so it's not uncommon to close this early. The holidays kind of slow the business down. I round the side of the building and check the garage, and the main entrance's overhead doors are pulled down. The entire shop is closed. I walk around the entire building to the employee parking lot and see that Kip, Taylor, and Clayton's vehicles are all present. A stab of fear shoots through my abdomen.

I'm surprised when I pull on the employee entrance and it opens. I immediately hear voices coming from the shop, but I can't quite make out whose they are. I stand in the middle of the break room, unsure as to what to do. I spin in a circle, hoping to find something, and my eyes land on an industrial-sized crescent wrench in the corner. I stop myself right before I'm about to grab it. A part of me feels like I'm jumping to conclusions. Nothing may be wrong, and I'm in here trying to find a murder weapon.

Better safe than sorry. I don't notice that the wrench is supporting a box of fittings precariously balanced on the break table. I watch in slow motion as metal tubes sprawl across the floor, halting the voices from the shop. I'm paralyzed for a few seconds too long when a man's presence fills the doorway.

It's Lance. I'm mid step when his identity registers. "Hey, what are you doing here?" I get nothing in response, and his hand wraps around my upper arm, the tips of his fingers turning white from the grip. "Lance, what's going on?"

He doesn't look at me when he shakes his head. "You weren't supposed to be here, Lilly."

As he leads me out of the break room and into the shop, any and all questions die on my tongue. In order, Ethan, Taylor, Kip, and Justin are kneeling execution style, hands tied behind their backs. Kip's eyes fill with horror along with Justin's. He cusses, straining against his ties. My eyes jump to Taylor, who looks more indignant than anything.

"Oh God," is the only coherent thing I can come up with. I repeat it over and over in my head.

Lance shoves me onto my knees next to Ethan, who nods his head in the slightest move. Instinctively, I push back and shove my elbow into his gut. I was aiming a little lower, so I try again, and this time he stops me, twisting my arm at an unnatural angle. I can't stop the involuntary scream I let out.

"Stop!" Kip's yell echoes across the room.

I hear the zip of the ties around my wrists. "Be quiet, she's fine." Lance smirks at Kip in passing, lining up with the other men in front of us.

"Don't touch her again." This time it's Justin's voice. I can't see him well enough to make eye contact, but I know he's angry by the red pooling around his neck and ears.

Lance isn't fazed by his threat, his face impassive. The happy, easygoing guy is gone, not a trace to be found. It's at this moment that I recognize the tall man standing in the middle. He's dressed in a tailored black suit, hair smoothed back, highlighting the gray at his temples.

It's Mr. John Monroe, Kaley's dad, standing with his posture relaxed, a welcoming smile gracing his lips. It's the same smile he's always greeted me with.

"Hi, Lilly. It's nice to see you again." Despite the obviously hostile environment, his greeting sounds sincere.

"Mr. Monroe."

taking mine

"Jimmy. That's what everyone here knows me by, anyway."

It clicks.

Holy shit.

Kaley's dad is Jimmy.

Holy *fucking* shit.

"She's got nothing to do with this. Let her go," Kip demands.

"Considering she participated in dismantling my Italia, I'd disagree." He takes a slow, measured pace toward me, shined dress shoes echoing with every step. He drops down to his haunches, stopping at eye level. "I overlooked your participation because you're Kaley's friend, but even my daughter has conditions."

"I had no idea you were the dealer."

"As I was unaware I had unintentionally hired you. With that being said," he says, "I'll clear your debt as long as you keep your mouth shut. Don't speak a word about me, our transactions, or what you've witnessed here, and you'll be free to go. I'll know if you ever open your mouth."

"I'm not going anywhere." I don't know why I decide to be brave all of a sudden, but I don't really believe Kaley's dad will hurt me.

"Lilly, go," Kip says.

"No."

Lance rolls his head, exasperated, and pulls a knife out from his pocket. I catch my breath as he cuts my ties. "Don't make this any more complicated than it already is."

He pulls me to my feet and I step around him, facing Mr. Monroe. "Not until I know what's going on here."

"I have absolved your debt, Lilly. If I give you a detailed description of my future plans, you'll be a liability."

"What debt?" I turn to Kip and Justin, asking for an explanation. Kip's eyes remain hardened as Justin shakes his head. "Is it the money we received for payment?"

Mr. Monroe looks to Kip and shrugs his shoulder in a what-can-you-do gesture. "She's not giving in."

"Double mine. I'll pay off whatever she owes."

"That would be unrealistic. I'd likely never see a profit from you. No, if she wants to be a part of this, then so be it." He pulls two rolling chairs to the middle of the floor. "Please, Lilly, take a seat."

When I don't move, Lance pushes me down. "You asked for this," he says.

"So, I'm aware that Taylor did not inform anyone as to why I acquiesced a service from you."

I nod.

"Once you realized two plus two doesn't make one, you decided to do some investigating." Again, another head nod. "Which led you and Justin," he says, motioning with his head to Justin's position in the lineup. "To strip my car, looking for clues. Which led you to find…"

He trails off and raises his brows at me. "To find guns and cocaine," I finish for him.

"Yes!" He snaps his fingers. "And do you understand the implication of your actions?"

I remain still.

"I'm sure you didn't. But it led to both of my storage containers being retrieved by law enforcement. Or, more accurately, the DEA."

I look to Justin and he looks back at me just as intently. I run my eyes to Taylor, who is staring at me with more hatred than I have ever seen in him before. Pure, unfiltered hatred.

"But why? How?"

"That's still a mystery. I have an informant on the inside who says someone on your side tipped them off."

"I already told you," Taylor says, almost seething. "No one called the cops. We're a fucking chop-shop. That's the stupidest decision we could have made."

"I see your reasoning," Mr. Monroe says, leaning back in his chair. "But my informant is known to be very reliable."

"Jimmy," Kip says in a calming tone, trying to override Taylor's outburst. "You've known me for years. As soon as I understood what was going on, I made a call to you. To you, not anyone else."

"I'd like to believe you, I really would, but you've always been the goody-two-shoes of the bunch, now haven't you? That's why I wanted the okay from you before I moved forward with the deal. And for that, I take the blame for not clarifying this with you alone. I had given Taylor too much credit."

They both give Taylor a matching look of condescension.

"For right now, I have allotted everyone their portion of the money owed to me for three cars, the inventory, and the profit I would have made. Altogether, rounding out at almost a million dollars. Split four ways is two hundred and fifty thousand a piece. That's not including the money owed for rendered services."

"This has to be a joke," I say, my mouth not catching up with my brain.

He's serious as he clasps his hands over his folded knees. "Tell me when things get funny to you, Lilly."

I pause. He said if the money is split four ways. There's someone missing.

As if Mr. Monroe can read my suspicions, he says, "You're wondering about your fifth partner, Dan."

Kip's head drops forward, his chin touching his chest, and I already know. He doesn't have to say it. My eyes fill with tears.

"I gave a twenty-four-hour notice that something bad was going to happen if the person who turned me in didn't fess. The clock ran out."

"He had a family."

"Yes, that's why I thought he'd be a good candidate. All the more reason to spare his life. I was wrong."

Kip's eyes are still glued to the floor when Justin responds. "You didn't give us the full twenty-four hours."

"Twenty-three, twenty-four. Tomato, Tomahto. Same difference."

"There. Is. A. Difference," Kip yells, pulling at his restraints.

Mr. Monroe cocks his head. "It doesn't when you have adamantly said that you don't know who the snitch is. That is, unless you really do." His words shut Kip up. "Well then," he says, standing with renewed vigor. "Maybe right now would be a good time to ask again."

He kneels down beside me, much like before.

"Do you know, Lilly? Do you know who tipped off the police?"

Kip staggers to his feet. "Don't touch her."

The third man to Monroe's trio makes his way over to him and kicks the legs out from under Kip, knocking him back down. Everyone remains silent as I shake my head no.

"Oh, come on. Something tells me you do. Do you know who it is, Lilly?"

I once again shake my head. "No, sir. I don't."

He pats me on the shoulder, grimacing at my noncompliance. He stands, putting his back to me when I feel cold metal press to my temple. I don't need to look to know what it is. My heart stops.

"No!" Kip's voice overlaps with Justin's.

"No, wait. I did it. It was me." It's rushed and panicked, but it puts everyone on hold.

"You?"

Justin pushes up from his knees, standing much more calmly than his eyes give him credit for. "Yes, it was me."

Taylor follows. "You stupid son of a bitch. You fucked everything up."

"Sit down!" The third man in the room has been silent all this time, but his voice is scary enough to knock Taylor back down to his knees.

"Thank you," Mr. Monroe says, standing in front of Justin. "I figured it was you or the kid."

Justin remains steady. "Let Lilly go and I'll tell you everything I know."

"How do I know you know anything?"

"Because I know Lance is your spy," he says, and even I can see that it surprises him that Justin would know that.

He thinks it over, ordering Lance to step back, and I immediately cry in relief. Only to cry for the complete opposite reason when he pulls a gun out from under suit jacket and aims it at Justin's face.

chapter 15

WHEN I LOOK BACK at this moment, I'll probably have more clarity. I'll be able to remember without the rush of endorphins and adrenaline coursing through my body, and without the amount of blood fogging my system.

But right now, all I know is fear.

All I hear is shouting.

All I see is Justin.

I see the moment it happens. Justin pulls a maneuver that I've only ever seen in movies, successfully turning Mr. Monroe's own gun back on him, flipping the tables in an instant.

All the while, swarms and swarms of men dressed head to toe in black enter the building. Multitudes of men, in full tactical gear, rush in from the outside. Both sides of the shop open quicker than magic. They yell orders to one another and I have no idea how they can tell who's talking to who. Others are directing Taylor, Kip, and Ethan onto the ground, face down with hands behind their heads.

But my eyes stay trained on Justin as he pins Mr. Monroe down, placing his knee into his back and slapping a pair of cuffs around his wrists. The entire time he's going through the process, reading off the Miranda Rights by memory, he's watching me. His eyes never leave mine as his lips move to the words he's probably recited so many times that the act has become second nature to him.

Because...

Because Justin is a cop.

chapter 16

I RUN. MY FIGHT OR FLIGHT instinct kicks in and I fly. I know it's pointless. There are too many and I'm too slow. I'm aware this doesn't end well. But I feel like I need to escape. I need to process. Just a few more seconds of freedom before reality sets in.

I hear footsteps following me as I run down the hallway, into the break room, and out of the employee entrance. Tiny pieces of gravel pull my feet out from under me, and I catch myself with my hands, barely losing momentum. A nondescript SUV is parked blocking the exit, so I run toward the fence dividing the alley from the opposite block. I'm surprised by my own strength when I heave the top part of my body over the fence. I struggle to find grip with my shoes and am forced to rely on upper body strength when I feel a hand wrap around my ankle.

I'm pulled off the fence by my feet, and I land face-first, literally. The entire left side of my face throbs against the concrete. Without thinking, I reach to wipe the gravel digging into my eye and am immediately rewarded with a strong yank pinning my arm behind me. I yell as I hear an audible pop in my shoulder. The cop angrily says something about resisting that I don't catch, and he runs his hands over my body and closer to my female anatomy than I'd ever feel comfortable with. The next thing I know, I'm standing as he places me on my feet.

I watch as Taylor is escorted out of the back of Toby's, cuffed and looking like he wants to commit murder against anyone within reaching distance. He's placed against the hood of the vehicle blocking the exit and patted down. Kaley is standing against her car, tears running down her face as an officer questions her. Her eyes lock on mine and widen. I tear my gaze away.

Several SUVs take up the street, blocking oncoming traffic in both directions. People exit their vehicles, standing on the outskirts of the barricade, trying to get a look at what's going on. Kip is being pushed up against a nearby vehicle, his head whipping back and forth, looking for me presumably. His eyes light up when he sees me, but they immediately dim. It's not until I recognize his concern that I feel the blood running down my face.

I mouth to him that I'm okay.

I'm deposited into my own vehicle, my rights are read, and the slam of the door rocks the vehicle. There's not a specific emotion I can pinpoint, but it's too much and I cry. I keep my eyes trained, waiting for a glimpse of Justin. The look on his face when he put Mr. Monroe down keeps playing on a feedback loop. As desperately as I try, I can't convince myself that what I saw is true. There has to be some kind of explanation. But even as I fail to find one, I know what I saw.

The SWAT team has begun dismantling their uniforms. Deputies with bulletproof vests that read DEA across the back congregate together, some smiling at a job well done. Ethan and the third man to Mr. Monroe's entourage exit the building.

It's then when Justin finally makes his appearance. He steps out, holding the front door open for the next two people to walk through. Mr. Monroe is cuffed, escorted by Lance, who says something to Justin on the way by. My gaze jumps to Kaley, and I see the shock on her face as well. Lance departs to deposit a very solemn-looking John Monroe into the backseat of an SUV.

Justin walks to a man dressed in slacks and a button-down, clearly the boss with a clipboard in his hand. They talk for a few moments, heads bowed together. The other deputies occasionally glance in their direction but don't approach. My heart skips a beat when they both look up toward my car. I know he can't see me, the window tint too strong, but I hurriedly wipe away my tears with the sleeve of my shoulder.

He takes a step my way, but the man puts a hand on his chest, stopping his pursuit. Justin's face is tense as he allows his coworker to hold him back. It looks like it takes a moment for Justin to concede, but eventually he nods, letting his guard down. The man pats him on the back and says something as he walks away. Justin stands, hands on his hips, looking at my window. I pull back, slinking in my seat. I know there's no way he can see me, but I feel like there's a direct line from his eyes to mine, and it makes me shiver. He laces his hands behind his neck and turns around and walks away.

THE THING ABOUT SITTING in a holding cell alone is that I have plenty of time to think. Then cry. And then think some more.

I've been alone for hours. I'm not quite sure how long, considering I've had nothing but my own thoughts to keep me entertained, and the better half of it I spent crying. Feeling sorry for myself is up there, along with Kip, and Dan and his family. Once I get tired of crying, I'm angry. So angry that I feel like at any moment I'll spontaneously combust with all the fire roaring inside me. I'm very, very angry.

And I've had nothing but time to add fuel to the fire.

By the time a female police officer opens my cell and tells me we're moving, I don't ask questions. She re-cuffs my hands in front of me, and we trek down an abnormally long hallway. She doesn't speak as we buzz through a series of doors, just simply directs me where to go. We're at the last door when I see him standing on the other side. He's wearing the same clothes he was at Toby's, except now a badge hangs from around his neck.

The door opens and we walk through. My heart grows in size and rhythm the closer I get to him. And I realize I hate him. It's a new development to me. I can't recall a single person that I've felt this much admonishment to, not even my mom. Every ounce of me feels like it's been lit on fire and it's seeping from my pores. This person, this man that I *trusted,* is a liar.

A lying bastard.

I clench my teeth, trying to gain some semblance of control. His eyes wander to my swollen cheek. The entire left side of my face feels like it went through a meat grinder, so I'm sure it looks like hell.

His face contorts. "What happened?" he says, angry. At what, I'm not sure.

He lifts his hand to touch my cheek and I whip my face away from his touch. It's as if I stung him, pain lashing his face, and he doesn't try to hide it. I shake my head at my own stupidity. I'm seeing what I want to see, because despite it all, I still want to believe he cares. The officer un-cuffs me, and right as my wrists are free, I plant my feet like he taught me and I pull my arm back. My knuckles hit my target. He stumbles back, cupping his nose, checking for blood.

That's right, I smirk at him. *I want to piss you off.*

I'm immediately bombarded by officers that seem to emerge from nowhere. My arms are brought behind my back, and I feel the familiar slap of cuffs.

"No, it's okay. It's okay." Justin holds a hand up to stop them.

It's not okay, though. How can he say that anything is even remotely okay? *Nothing* is okay. He's telling everyone that it's okay with the calmest expression on his face, and it's like looking at the face of the devil. Because only the devil can lie like he can.

I spit in his face.

It finally elicits a response, and his face is murderous as he wipes the spit from his eye. His eyes hold mine as he steps into me. "Stop it. They're going to put you in a straitjacket and muzzle you. Do you want that?"

With his face so close to mine, I can't stop myself from glancing at his lips. A memory of them placed on mine from the night before filters through my mind. The way they opened to me, tasted me, wanted me.

And I think I hate myself a little bit, too.

Despite everything, I wish we could go back twelve hours and everything could be as they were. None of this would have happened and I would still be blissfully ignorant. But we can't. I snap my eyes away from him, ashamed.

He straightens back up. "She's good. I'll take her from here."

I yank away from his touch when he grabs my elbow. He lets out an agitated breath through his nose but lets me go. We don't speak as he leads me into a small room, much like my cell, with a table and two metal chairs against the wall.

"Sit."

I remain standing. I hear him leave and shut the door when I refuse to acknowledge him. I pace, my hands still cuffed behind me. My anger is now a dull simmer beneath the surface, and something closer, something scarier threatens to take its place. I'm antsy as I wait. I'm beginning to think I'll be left in this room as long as they left me in the other when a man walks. It's the man with the clipboard. Justin follows.

"Miss Lilly Foster," he greets me. "Timothy Fisher, Assistant Director in charge of the Drug Enforcement Administration of the field division, but you can call me Tim. You already know Justin. He's the special agent on your case. Please, take a seat."

At least now I know it's his real name.

He doesn't wait for my response as he sits with a folder in his hand. Justin raises a brow and mouths for me to sit. Having no reason to argue, I do.

"I know today has been a whirlwind for you, so I'll try to keep this quick and get you out of here, hmm?"

He opens the folder, angling it toward me. It's a detailed list of all the crimes I have committed. It fills the entire sheet of paper. I imagine this is what Justin felt like when Taylor...nope. I cut off my train of thought. Justin's rap sheet is false. He didn't feel anything when Taylor revealed Justin's criminal history, because it was all fabricated.

"Grand theft auto, aiding and abetting arms smuggling and drug trafficking. War crimes." I open my mouth to protest and he cuts me off. "Justin has informed me you had no knowledge of your actions. You were going in blind."

taking mine

"Oh, really? What else did he tell you?"

He taps a pen on the table. "He made me aware of your relationship a few hours ago, if that's what you're insinuating. I must let you know it's not uncommon for field agents to become attached to their projects, especially when they're required to monitor their targets for days, months, sometimes years in advance."

"Wait, monitored? Was I monitored?" I look from Justin to the Assistant-whatever-the-hell-his-title-is and back again.

"Not you, specifically, but yes."

I can feel the blood drain from my face. "For how long?"

"Classified information until the trial."

Justin remains stoic against the wall, his arms folded across his chest and his eyes never leaving me.

It's not until now that I realize how much deep shit I'm in. I've been so caught up in my personal fiasco that I've let Justin's presence deter me. I've felt safe with him even in this situation. I thought there's no way he'll let me go down for this. But he will, and he is.

"I want a lawyer."

The man doesn't say anything as he sits back. "Do you have a lawyer?" He already knows the answer when I shake my head no. "Right, okay," he says, standing. "I'm going to step out and let Justin explain to you why you don't want a public defender. Off record." I'm not given a chance to agree when he hits a switch on the wall on his way out. Justin unfolds his arms and sits in the now vacant chair.

"We're offering you a plea bargain. They'll let you go, walk out today, if you agree to testify against Jimmy Monroe."

It can't be that easy. "What's the catch?"

His lips are thin right before he answers me. "Your testimony will implement your brother as an accomplice."

"No." I shake my head, even as he continues.

"If you don't, you're looking at fifteen years or more. This is your best option. A public defender won't do shit to help your case. You know this. There's too much evidence built up against you."

"Because of you," I hiss, and I momentarily forget about the cuffs, straining against them.

Justin sighs. "If I take them off, will you keep your hands to yourself?"

I think about coming back with a smart retort but refrain. He takes my silence as an omission, reaching into his pocket and producing the keys. Scooting his chair across the floor, he waits for me to turn around. I try not to flinch at his touch when he holds my wrists steady. He's so close I can feel his familiarity. I'm immensely relieved when he finally lets go and I can rub the marks on my wrists.

"I won't testify against my brother."

"He thought you'd say that."

"What? How does Kip know?"

Justin glances at the switch on the wall before returning to me. "We offered him the plea deal first. We agreed that I'd offer it to you."

"Why would he do that?"

"Because he's your brother and it's his job to protect you."

I rub my eyes and lay the good side of my face into my hand. I'm exhausted. Emotionally I'm just done. So done. And it's not uncommon for prosecutors to lie during interrogation. "I want to talk with him before I do anything."

He smiles. "Smart girl." He leaves the room for a moment and comes back. "Let's go."

He makes me walk ahead of him, and I get a few dirty looks from the officers who had to restrain me. We're only a few doors down when Justin instructs me to stop. He opens a door to a room with long rows of visitation tables. It's the kind with the partitions that require communication to be through a telephone.

"He's already booked and charged. The only visitation he's allowed to have until he's transported to a nearby facility is through this. I'm sorry." I swallow multiple times to stop the knot in my throat from hurting. "A guard is going to stand in."

He waits a moment, hesitant to let me be by myself, and I sit down on my side of the nearest partition. Not a second later, I hear the

taking mine

opposite door open and Kip walks in. I immediately burst into tears when I see his orange jumpsuit. His face fills with outrage as he yanks the phone from its hook.

"What happened to your face?" I'm sobbing in front of him and all he's worried about is my face. "Who did that to you?"

I struggle to rein in my tears to speak. "I'm fine. It was an accident."

Finally gathering that my emotional well-being should take precedence over my physical one, he cools his features. "Everything's going to be okay."

"No it's not. You're in jail, Kip. You're going to go to prison."

"Calm down. I can barely understand you."

We both take a minute to let me pull myself together. "Why would you give me the plea deal?"

He takes in a deep breath before answering. "Justin came to me right after we arrived. He said he's working on a plea deal that they were going to offer me. He suggested that I give it to you."

"He suggested it?"

"In a way. I can't actively give someone a plea deal, but I can turn it down. If that were the case, the prosecutors would offer it to the next defendant in line."

"Me."

"You. Justin knew that you were their second option."

"But what about you? How much time are you looking at?"

"Don't worry about that. I'll be fine. I need you to be fine."

The man sitting across from me, the brother who raised me, is worried about me when I'm not the one in chains. He's spent his entire life watching over me and it's gotten him where he is today. "It's all my fault." My words come broken through tears. "I was the one who brought him into our lives."

I don't need to say who; he already knows. "No, Lil. This is my fault. I let things get this far. It was my job to protect you, and I didn't do that."

"Did you know Jimmy was Kaley's dad?"

"No. I had no reason to connect the dots. Justin said they have her in questioning about what she may know."

"Kip, I can't take your plea deal."

"You can, and you will. I've stashed some money away in a savings account. It's not much, but it's enough to keep you grounded for a little while. It's what I was banking on using when you got into graduate school."

School, bills, simply living alone gives a whole new perspective on how I'm going to be alone. Kip's always been my safe haven. Without him I have no one.

His smile is weak when he says, "It's time to figure things out on your own."

I spend the next five minutes trying to pull myself together as Kip gives me directions on things I might need to do while he's gone. Justin steps in and announces that our time is up, and Kip reassures me that I'll get through this. I don't know who can actually hear our conversation on the other side of the phones, but Justin doesn't mention my tear-streaked face as we go back to the original interrogation room.

"You're going to need protection," Tim states as he walks through the door.

He drops a pile of paperwork in front of me. "Protection?"

"John Monroe has enough employees all over the state that it puts you in a precarious position."

"Precarious..."

"You're testifying against someone with a lot of connections. We have reason to believe you might not be safe. We can't guarantee that someone won't come looking for you."

"Are we talking about witness protection?"

"No, nothing that drastic. Monroe is a mediocre fish in a big pond, not a shark. So what we're going to do is assign a patrol to you twenty-four hours a day and until the trial is over. Just to be sure."

"Just to be sure," I repeat, new fear sinking in.

"Lance and Justin have both volunteered to split the shifts. You're in good hands."

taking mine

Justin confirms with a slow head nod. "No," I say, pushing the papers away from me. "No, not them. Anyone but them."

"Lilly," Justin says, moving closer to me.

"No," I cut him off. "How am I supposed to trust you to keep me safe when you betrayed me?"

"It's my job," he says, holding a hand to his chest. "What was I supposed to do?"

"Not fucking me would have been a great start."

"Whoa, whoa, whoa." Tim holds his hands up in both of our directions. "Spare me the details. This lovers' quarrel can be had another time. Right now, Lilly, you need protection, and these are two very dependable agents. You're an asset to this case, and I guarantee neither one of these agents wants to see it go down the drain. So, whatever you're feeling needs to be put on the back burner. Got it?"

Justin recedes to his wall and I fold my arms across my chest. "I'm not under you."

"With all due respect, Miss Foster, you kind of are until this trial is over. If you somehow violate our contract, you'll be back in jail indefinitely."

"Can I refuse protection?"

"Are you seriously telling me you'd risk your life rather than have anything to do with me?" Justin's voice is incredulous, disbelief across his face.

"Yes," I answer blatantly, holding his stare.

I don't say it, but it's there. Him. I've lost him. He doesn't reply as he shifts his attention away from me, finding the wall more interesting to look at.

"It's not your life to protect anyway, Lilly," Tim says, standing. "You currently belong to the federal government. The prosecution will take over the investigation from here." He stops once he reaches the door. "One last thing…Justin and Lance have both made it clear to me that you received no monetary compensation for the work you did for Jimmy. I have no reason to assume otherwise since we've searched your home and found no evidence." He pauses one last time and looks at Justin and back, sighing heavily in the small room. "Don't do anything stupid, okay? Any large purchases in cash are going to look questionable."

I'm flabbergasted. Suddenly the conversation Justin and I had about storing the cash at his apartment holds more clarity. He knew eventually my house would be searched and they'd seize anything that looked like evidence. He'd been preparing me for this.

"Now what?" I ask.

Justin slides the papers I pushed away back to me. "Now you read through these, sign them, and we'll release you." He pulls a pen from his pockets and hands it to me.

So I do. It takes close to an hour to finish all of the paperwork and write a summary of my involvement with John Monroe. In the bottom right-hand corner of the loose leaf, I write the word 'stupid,' because that's what this all amounts to, and I lay my pen down.

"I'm sure you've got questions," Justin says, looking from the ground to me.

He's right, I do. So many inconsistencies and contradictions have run through my mind, most of them pertaining to us.

"Can I go home?" I ask instead.

"Lilly."

"No, I can't right now."

"Can I at least get a word in?" Irritation and a small amount of desperation lace his voice.

"No. I'm tired, I want to go home." My voice cracks on the last word, and it makes my anger spike. I'm the one who's desperate. I'm desperate to get back to a place I know, a place I feel any small amount of comfort, and forget about the last twelve hours. Hell, let's make it twenty-four, so I can forget about last night.

And he can see it. It's written across every part of me, just like every other time he could read me so well. Now I know it's probably because of his training. Maybe it's something he already had a knack for and honed it in throughout however long he's been Special Agent

taking mine

Justin. Either way, he knows he's pushing me from the small amount of thread I'm hanging by.

"Okay," he says, rubbing his hand over his mouth. "I'll give you a ride home."

"I'll take a cab."

"I'm taking first patrol, so I can take you."

"You can follow me."

He pinches the bridge of his nose and releases it. "You're going to have to talk to me eventually."

I don't comment as he leads me out the door and points to a lady who will process me. My eyes are heavy as I'm issued through more locked doors and more paperwork. By the time I see the light at the end of the tunnel, my legs are lead and the ground is a magnet, every step taking more effort than the last.

Light is just breaking over the buildings, and the morning air nips at my skin. A few birds chirp and hop around benches, already searching for food. There's a slight breeze in the air, morning dew resting on every surface. It's freezing. The clothes I wore to go shopping in aren't sufficient.

People are already up and about, milling for work. Dog walkers are already on their first run, and taxis weave in and out of traffic, carrying passengers to their destinations. Meanwhile, I'm standing on the stoop of the jail with the life I once knew in shambles. Not a single person on the outside of this building's walls is waiting for me.

A black SUV pulls up to the curb, and I make out Justin's form behind the wheel. Supposing he's waiting on me, I hail a cab. I keep my mind singularly focused on my mission to get home. There's literally nothing to think about. I'm past the point of exhaustion.

It's a thirty-minute drive from the city, and from my position in the car, I can already sense the unfamiliarity of Kip's absence. We park in front of the house, and the distance seems like it's much too great. I think about lying down across the seat of the cab, asking the taxi driver to just keep the meter running, but Justin pays my fare.

rachel schneider

I'm completely spaced as I walk the small pathway to the front door. The turn of the knob indicates that the door isn't locked, and Justin hovers as I push the door open. All I can do is stare.

The entire living room is torn apart. The couch is overturned, cushions cut wide open with the padding strewn about. The windows are bare, curtains stripped from their brackets, morning light flooding the room. Every piece of furniture is taken apart in one way or another. It doesn't take me long to deduce that there's no way the television is operational, face down on the ground with the back paneling removed. Already knowing what I'm going to see, I check the kitchen to find it in the exact same condition. All the cupboards are hanging open and every item is lying on the floor, mostly broken.

"Lilly." Justin's voice is soft behind me.

There's an ache in my heart. It's deep, resounding through every part of me. It hurts. It simply is such a deep pain that my brain can't keep up. Maybe that's what shock is. I'm in shock. I swallow the buildup in my throat and clench my teeth. I face Justin standing on the doorstep, watching me with weary eyes.

I don't say anything as I walk the few feet to the door and shut it.

chapter 17

I AWAKE WITH A HANGOVER—or what feels like one—and force my eyes open, blinking against the sleep. It's still daylight. The sun is seeping through the sheet I hung over the window before crawling into bed. Sleeping on a mattress that's been stripped open tends to be a bit uncomfortable. I sit, groaning as the springs dig into my back.

I left my phone in Kaley's car and it's impossible to locate a working clock, so I walk to the window and peer outside, trying to determine the amount of daylight left. Discovering the sun is still high in the sky, it can't be much later than noon. Five hours of sleep is manageable. I decide a shower is in order. Sitting in jail doesn't bode well in the sanitary department, and I was too tired to do anything about it when I got home.

My chest constricts. Pulling the window cover back, I spot Justin parked out front, window down and smoking. There's no way he's not exhausted. I watch him even though I tell myself to quit, and it's like he feels my eyes on him as he looks at my window. I drop the sheet back. It's an old school cop-out, but I'd still like to pretend he didn't see me.

So I take a shower, eternally grateful that the team of home assassins left me shampoo and conditioner. The house is in shambles. I've seen pictures of homes after natural disasters, and my house can rival those. I cut the water off and pick up a towel off the floor, using it whether clean or dirty. It's hard to tell and I don't care.

Remarkably, I find a mug shoved into the back of one of the kitchen cabinets. I guess whoever was on kitchen duty figured if there wasn't anything wrong with the first fifteen then the last one stood a chance.

rachel schneider

The coffee maker is broken, so I pour the hottest water I can through a filter with some grounds I scooped off the counter. The saying 'no stone left unturned' comes to mind.

It'll never be the same. We may never have lived lavishly, or even mediocre, but it's home. And I can barely see it through the mountain of destruction. I sip my coffee in the kitchen entryway and scan the home I once knew, trying to force a semblance of energy into my bones. Not an ounce of desire to do a damn thing flows through me, but I can't live like this, and Kip would be upset if he saw it in this condition.

Kip, who's sitting in jail right now, doing God knows what with God knows who, and it's so unfair of me to mope when I still have my freedom. A freedom that I don't deserve when I'm basically the person who put him there.

I start by draping all the windows, either by using salvageable curtains I find on the floor or spare sheets, trying to grant some sense of privacy, even though that went out the door with yesterday's revelations. Then I begin picking up everything that belongs in the trash, placing it in a big pile by the door until I can locate some way to dispose of it.

And I don't stop. It takes me the rest of the day to go through every room and dig through the keep items and the throw-away items. It's not until I've amassed more than half the living room's space that I realize the sun is setting. I've effectively distracted myself for the better half of the day, but the sense of accomplishment that I was looking forward to isn't there.

A sheen of sweat covers every inch of my body despite the draft from the windows, and I stare at the pile. My stomach is hollow, having not bothered to eat due to the lack of groceries, and because there's no more room inside me other than the parsimonious weight of hurt. It takes up every square inch of my capacity. I fall back onto the couch, sinking low into its re-stuffed cushions, unable to stand from the force of my gut. The resounding ache that I've been avoiding all day flares. It's deep and pulsing. It gives little reprieve.

taking mine

The glare of headlights beams through the kitchen window. Lance exits an SUV and walks toward Justin's open driver side window. He leans his arm against the door with his back to me, and I catch Justin shaking his head before rubbing his eyes. They don't convene for long before Justin starts his vehicle and leaves. The pulse in my chest intensifies.

He gets to leave. He gets to check out, forget about the mess my life has become, and go on about his like there has been no collateral damage caused by his hands. But there has.

Oh, there so has.

It's left my heart beating angrily in my chest and it doesn't let up. I *trusted* him. He asked me to, and I skipped into him like the naïve girl that I am. My body, my heart, my future, I handed to him on a silver platter. It's a used and vile feeling.

I let my ache unfurl, letting the suffocation sneak in and take all the air out of my chest. Wetness drips from my face onto the hands that I have braced against the counter as my only support. A sob rips from my throat, but it only makes it worse, and that's the scariest part.

There's a plate within my reach, and I chuck it at the wall like a disc. It shatters against the wall, and it does nothing for the pressure, so I do it again with another. And I keep doing it, over and over, knowing with each broken plate that nothing I do will make me feel better. But I don't want to feel better. I don't deserve to. What I really want is to not feel at all. I run out of plates the second Lance kicks in the door, eyes wide as he searches for the commotion.

There's no point in hiding my tears as I look at him. He's concerned, but I ignore him as I walk to the bathroom. My reflection tells me why. The left side of my face has darkened, yellow branching out from the center, swelling all the way to my temple. If I saw me on the street, I'd call the local hospital and ask them if they had a mental patient escape. I turn on the shower, hoping this pushes Lance back outside, not wanting him to stick around to hear my cries. My back hits the wall and I slowly fall to the floor, letting out everything I've avoided.

These tears are different from the ones from yesterday. Those were born out of anger and frustration. These are born from true, unfiltered pain. It's an anguish I haven't felt before. With Justin I felt worthy, and loved, and capable of so much. Looking back, knowing what I know now, I realize that he never saw any of those things in me. He knew my insecurities and used them in his favor, not caring about the repercussions.

And Dan. For his children, for Melanie, and the life that was taken without warrant. It was callous and cruel and he didn't deserve it. Every night his children will go to sleep fatherless, like Kip and I did, and they'll too never find retribution. His daughter will cry herself to sleep, wondering why she never got a chance to say goodbye, and his son will ask himself what he could have done to change it. Melanie will struggle to make ends meet. They barely made rent as it was.

Footsteps thunder down the hallway and I force myself to stand, wiping my eyes, and trying to clean up whatever snot has escaped. The last thing I want is Lance trying to comfort me. The door opens and whatever tears I stopped come roaring back at the sight of Justin. His eyes are bloodshot and apprehensive.

"No," I say as I back away from him. "Get out."

I must do a poor job of looking intimidating, because he pulls me toward him. I struggle to push away, banging my fists on his chest, and when that proves futile, I start kicking.

"Lilly," he says. "Stop."

I refuse.

He turns me around, wrapping his arms around my shoulders. With nothing left to put my energy into, my sobs return and I can't hear anything but the sound of them.

"Shh," he repeats, falling to the floor with me, never releasing his hold.

And I let him, because I'm weak.

taking mine

I SNAP AWAKE. I'm in Justin's lap, but my eyes are trained on Lance trying to quietly take a step back from the doorway. His eyes lock on mine. Justin's still sleeping, his head braced against the wall with his mouth hanging open. Carefully, I extract myself from his arms. I'm surprised this doesn't wake him, but he's still sound asleep. Fearing that the click of the door closing will wake him, I leave a gap as I follow Lance back to the kitchen.

"Everything okay?" He's sweet enough to pretend he's not really asking me that question directly.

I clear my throat. "Yeah." My voice is hoarse.

He nods. "Okay. Tell him to come get me when he wakes up. Hey, Lilly," he says, stopping once he gets to the door. "Justin is the most stand-up guy I know. Before you write him off completely, listen to what he has to say, okay?"

He leaves and I'm left standing in the same spot I was last night when he found me wreaking havoc on the dinnerware, which brings my attention to the mess I still have to clean up. I tip-toe around the broken shards and grab the broom. Justin comes barreling into the kitchen, trying to blink through the haze of sleep in his eyes. His shoulders fall when he sees me.

He scrubs his hands down his face. "Good morning."

Despite the ugliest storm hanging over us, there's a sense of liberation in the air. Last night did good for us. For me.

I continue sweeping. "Sleep okay," I ask.

He rubs the back of his neck. "Could have been worse."

"Lance is waiting for you outside."

Justin looks in Lance's direction but doesn't move. "We should talk."

"I'm not ready," I say, keeping my eyes trained on the broken pieces of glass.

"Lilly, you have to know that it was real for me."

In the middle of my bathroom meltdown last night with his arms around me, I was reminded of what I already knew...how much his touch spoke to me. He cradled my head to his chest and brushed my hair back as I cried, not letting up until I fell asleep despite his own exhaustion. I needed that. I needed him. He's the calm in my storm. Too bad it's a hurricane and he's the eye.

At some point during his time with me, undercover or whatever you want to call it, I do believe he developed some kind of feelings. Call it protective or a strange attraction, but something happened. But it can't be love, because you don't lie, and deceive, and use the people you love.

That's what makes what I'm about to say all the easier.

"Okay," I say.

He opens his mouth to continue arguing when my words register.

"But it doesn't matter."

His face contorts. "How can you say that?"

I finish sweeping and prop the broom up against the wall. "Because the fact of the matter is, Dan is dead, and my brother's going to prison for a very long time," I say, meeting his eyes. "And you're the one who put him there."

"If you just let me explain."

I hold my hand up. "I told you I'm not ready."

"But—"

"I don't need another revelation to break me like it did last night. Let me live in ignorance for a little bit longer. I just need to feel like I can survive for a few days."

He's frustrated by my refusal to hear him out. "You promise that you'll come to me when you're ready?" he asks, at a loss for what he can do.

"Yes." Accepting my answer, he runs his hands over his hair, trying to figure out what to do next. "Go. I'm sure Lance is tired."

He looks at me, waiting for me to look at him. But I don't. Because as high as Justin can build me up, he can bring me down just as low.

taking mine

SAVING THE HEAVIEST BAG for last was my first mistake. I should have taken it when I first started bringing the trash to the street. Five trips in and I'm starting to think about saving it as a decoration. It would be a great conversation piece. The sound of an engine dying catches my attention and I look through the opening of the front door. Since Lance kicked it in, it doesn't shut all the way. If it weren't for my morning workout trudging garbage, I'd be freezing.

Justin's returned from wherever he went after he left my kitchen this morning. I had expected him and Lance to trade shifts, but instead he drove away. Justin gets out holding a brown bag in one hand and says something to Lance that must be a dismissal, because he starts his own SUV and pulls away. I level myself as I watch Justin walk to the broken door.

He raps his knuckles against the wood, already spotting me through the gap as he pushes it open. "It looks good in here," he says, observing my progress. He lifts the brown bag. "I brought some stuff to fix the door."

"You didn't have to do that."

"Technically, I do. It's a security risk to have a front door that won't lock, let alone shut."

"Just give me the receipt and I'll reimburse you for the materials," I say, grabbing the last trash bag and dragging it toward the door.

"Don't worry about it. I used the company card. Here, let me help," he says, reaching for the bag in my hands.

"No, I got it," I say, pulling it out of his reach.

"Lilly, don't be stubborn."

I don't respond.

"Is this how it's going to be," he says, his face hardening. "You're going to pretend everything between us didn't exist?"

I throw my hands up. "And what would you rather me do, Justin?

Tell me, because I'd love to figure out a way to make our situation suck a little less."

He bends, catching my eyes with his. "You said you're not ready and I'll respect that, but you don't have to shut me out in the meantime."

I sigh, nodding, and it pacifies him enough to let me pass. He's not going anywhere. He'll be in close proximity for however long it's going to take for the case to go to trial. Depending on how long the prosecutor takes to build the case, it could be months, sometimes a year or more. Justin's already nailing a piece of trim over the doorjamb when I return.

I place my hands on my hips. "How old are you?"

He stops, leaning back on his knees to look up at me. He holds my stare as he says, "Twenty-six."

I nod, already expecting his answer to be much older than what he told me before, and I walk away.

"Is that it?"

I don't bother to turn around when I reply, "Yup."

I'm in my bedroom when I finally hear him return to his work, the hammer meeting the wood a little harder than before. If he's insistent on telling me the truth, then it'll be according to my request. I'll ask the questions and I'll do it on my time. I don't owe him anything, and he owes me everything.

About fifteen minutes later, I hear his footfalls making their way down the hall. He grips the trim of the door, leaning slightly inside my personal space without actually stepping over the threshold.

"Your door is fixed. Just make sure you turn the knob completely when opening and closing." We stare at each other in silence. "Have anything else you want to ask me?"

I stare up in thought and then shake my head.

"Nothing at all?" he says, obviously perturbed by my snub.

"Nope."

He bites the inside of his cheek and shoves off the door. "Fine. You know where to find me if you need me."

The front door slams so hard I'm almost positive he broke what he managed to fix. I smile, but it's only momentary before the shame sets in. I force myself to shake it off. He doesn't get to make me feel bad when he screwed me over in the first place.

KALEY'S FACE MORPHS as she begins to cry on my doorstep. Lance, who stands next to her, shoots me a panicked look. I've never seen Kaley cry, and I'm sure he hasn't either. Her two main emotions consist of happy and smartass with little wiggle room between the two, so watching her mid breakdown is basically traumatizing. It sheds a whole new light on being on the consoling side.

"I just don't know what else to do," she says, crying into the palms of her hands.

I guide her to the couch and force her to sit. "I'm sure everything's going to be okay. You've got a lot of jewelry and clothes you can sell."

The judge ordered all of Johns Monroe's assets to be frozen mere hours before his bail was set. A seven-figure bail proves costly when you no longer have access to your bank accounts. The prosecutors do believe that Monroe's wife, Kaley's mother, has been smuggling money into an off-shore bank account in Switzerland, but in that case they're out of luck.

"But what am I going to do when that's all gone?"

Go figure that I'm the person trying to coach Kaley on the hardships of life. "You'll get a job and support yourself. You'll make it just like the rest of the world does when they don't have rich parents."

"Like you did when you were stealing from other people?"

I clench my teeth. "Don't pretend you have any idea what it's like to live on the west bank. You're crying about not living in a six-thousand-square-foot house anymore and I'm over here trying to keep the water on."

This shuts her up, but it doesn't erase the anger shining behind her eyes. "Then why weren't you in class today?"

Her question throws me for a loop. Today was supposed to be the first day back from Thanksgiving, but when I woke up this morning, I didn't feel like getting out of bed, so I didn't. I slept in as late as I physically could before my brain forced me awake, and then I still didn't move until I heard Kaley banging on my door.

"I don't think I'm going to go back."

"How can you not go back?" she exclaims, incredulous.

"I mean," I say, raising a shoulder in indifference. "I'm not going to go back."

She reaches over and pokes a finger into my forehead. "You are the stupidest, stupidest, stupidest person I've ever met."

I swat her hand down. "Excuse me," I say, completely alarmed by how fast the conversation flipped on me.

"You've worked your ass off to get where you are and you're just going to quit? Nuh uh," she says, poking me again. "You're going to wake up Wednesday and get dressed and finish off the rest of the semester."

"No, I'm not," I say. "And I'm finding it bizarre that you're trying to order me to do so."

"Lilly, you're so smart. Giving in now is just stupid. Five years from now you'll regret it."

I scoff. "Says the girl who came here freaking out about what she's going to do in life."

"I'm not like you. I haven't been working for a degree. I don't even have enough credits to graduate in May. Besides, I probably won't have the money to attend next semester."

"Me neither," I say.

"But this semester is paid for. You might as well go. You can switch to somewhere cheaper next year."

A knock on the door turns our attention to Lance as he peeks his head in. "Everything okay in here?"

Kaley rolls her eyes. "Everything's just peachy, Protector of the Weak."

Lance winks at her. "That sounds like the start of a good porno. Want to test it out with some role playing?"

"I've been there and you're not a very good actor."

He makes kissy noises and shuts the door.

"You two hooked up?

"Yeah, but that was before you met." I'm confused and she must see it because she says, "I met Lance last semester."

"When? How?"

"He was at a frat party at the beginning of the summer. We hooked up on and off during the break. I called it off because I thought he was being too clingy, but now I see that it's just because he was trying to milk me for information. Too bad for him that I didn't know anything."

"How ironic," I say.

"We both got fucked by undercover cops. Go us," she says, raising invisible pom-poms.

"So you're not testifying?"

She shakes her head. "I literally know nothing. That's why I don't have my own round-the-clock secret service. At least you have Justin to pass the time."

Something on my face must give me away because her face falls. "What's wrong?"

"Nothing," I say, lying. I pace for a moment. "How are you okay with being used like that?"

"Like what?"

"Finding out that Lance was sleeping with you for information."

Her face screws up in thought. "He's a boy. He's going to sleep with anything within walking distance. Ashley had nothing to do with the investigation, but he slept with her. It's just how it is."

I slouch back down, unmoved by her revelation.

"Besides," she says, placing a hand on my knee. "I didn't love Lance...and he didn't love me."

I fight the burn in my throat and look away.

Sensing my refusal to talk about it, she zips her lips. It takes approximately two seconds for her to break the lock on her mouth. "Do you love him?"

There's an ongoing loop in my head where I ask myself the same questions every day, all day, and I don't need Kaley adding to them.

Gathering that I'm not going to let my walls down, she deftly re-zips and smiles. "I promise to not bug you if you promise you'll be in class on Wednesday. There's only four weeks of school left."

She's right, and I'm angry with myself for needing someone to push me. Just because my heart is trying to kill me and I'm slowly dying of starvation doesn't mean I can't function. School is important.

I sigh. "Fine."

"Good," she says, standing, new cheer in her step. "Don't make me use the sympathy card to get in again. Next time I'll just get Lance to kick the door in."

My mouth is still hanging open when she leaves.

That bitch.

"MUST YOU FOLLOW ME?" I say, careening around to face Justin.

"Yes," he says, stopping when I stop.

I clench my teeth to hold in a growl, swiveling back around on the sidewalk. I hope he doesn't plan on sitting in lecture with me. That's where I draw the line. I need some form of space, and having him chauffeur me around campus is demeaning as it is. Listening to girls giggle in the bathroom about the cute boy waiting on his girlfriend almost did me in. I can't even pee in peace.

At least he can't smoke on campus. I'm sick of seeing smoke billow outside of his car window every time I look outside. I've fantasized about walking out there, crumbling the cigarette pack between my fingers, and shoving them in his face.

I hear his footfalls pick back up with the echo of mine in the hallway. I'm late, no surprise there, but I'm here and that's what counts. At least, that's what I told myself when I pressed snooze three times this

taking mine

morning before forcing myself to get out of bed. Justin reaches for the door handle.

"No, you're not coming in with me."

"I won't have a visual."

"It's not any less than when I'm at home."

He lets his grip fall from the door, taking a step back. "Text me if you need me."

I'm surprised he relents, but I don't question it. I keep my head down and thankfully, unlike Whitticker, my Criminal Rights professor doesn't like to call people out when they're late. The classroom is fairly empty, nobody ready to give up Thanksgiving break. I choose a spot in the last row, happy with the amount of empty seats surrounding me. The back entrance to the classroom opens and I roll my eyes.

Pissed that Justin just couldn't let it go, I don't bother to look up as he takes the seat next to me. "I'd be lying if I said murder hasn't crossed my mind a few times today," I say, annoyance dripping from my voice.

"That's funny, me too," a voice says. Although familiar, it's not Justin's.

I look up and my eyes clash with the guy Justin punched months ago when we went to Blackjack's. It's the guy whose car we broke down, and he works for John Monroe. His eyes are clearer, less cloudy than I remember them. There's no escaping the hostility.

"Get your shit. We're going outside."

It's not that I don't want to move—actually, that's exactly what it is—but it's like I physically can't. Somewhere between the synapses that run from my brain to my legs, there's a communication issue.

"I don't think you heard me, so let me clarify," he says, pulling a knife from his front pocket. He points the tip into my side, right under my ribs. "Stand. Now."

I don't think he'll actually gut me right here in front of everyone, but I don't want to chance it. I slide out of my seat, careful to not let the blade dig in any farther, as he opens the door. Once we're outside, he braces me against the wall, his forearm digging into my throat. My backpack keeps a barrier between the brick and me.

"I think you have a pretty good idea who sent me," he says, his face inches from mine.

The amount of pressure he's pinning me with is laughable, enough so that I can't stop the giggle that escapes my lips.

"What are you laughing at?"

In the last week alone I've had a gun pointed at my head, gone to jail, and been confined to my house. It's the first time in the outside world I've had in five days and I'm being held up by knifepoint by a pretty boy wearing a polo and Axe cologne. My life has become a bad action comedy. Oh, did I mention I've only had peanut butter, bread, and ramen noodles for substance? Yeah, it kind of takes the cake.

"I'm sorry," I say, trying to stifle my smile but failing miserably. "Really. I am."

He steps back, completely baffled by my amusement. "I'm threatening your life and you think it's funny? Are you demented?"

"You're right," I say, straightening my features. "This matter is to be taken seriously. Proceed."

He's put off by my strange behavior but raises his knife anyway, closing the distance between us. Reacting at just the right moment, I grab hold of his arm holding the knife and plant my feet, this time aiming for where Justin taught me to. My fist connects with his throat, catching him off guard, and he staggers backward, dropping the knife. His hand closes around his throat as he chokes, eyes wide from shock.

I run.

The quickest way to Justin is through the classroom and into the lecture hall. It's not ideal, but it's my best option. I don't bother looking around as I sprint down the stairs. The professor yells at me for disrupting the class, but I ignore it. Justin snaps up from the wall when I ground to a halt in front of him.

"Behind the building."

He doesn't ask questions but tells me to stay put, already running toward the exit. I pace, keeping my eyes peeled on both entrances

taking mine

for his return. And really, I have so little patience, and after fifteen minutes I decide I've waited long enough. When I walk outside, a cop car is pulled up against the side of the building. An officer has the perpetrator in cuffs, leading him to the car, as another one talks with Justin. His badge reads Burns, and he looks up at me when I approach, prompting Justin to turn as well. Justin's arms are folded across his chest as he rolls his eyes at my disobedience.

"I told you to wait."

"I never agreed."

Burns doesn't catch the animosity between us, or he chooses to disregard it. "It's fine, ma'am. He's not a threat anymore, although he is a bit mouthy. Mind telling me what happened?"

Justin turns to me, looking me over for any obvious signs of harm. His annoyance slowly dissolves. "You punched him in the throat," he says, with a hint of a proud smile.

It's hard not to revel under his praise, but I manage to keep my smile in check. Justin gives me a deliberate look, but I ignore it as I recall everything that happened. Officer Burns writes everything down in a notebook he keeps in his breast pocket, intermediately asking questions as I go along. Justin grows more and more amused as I speak, his grin overtaking his face by the time I finish.

"You did good, kid," Burns says, giving me a fist bump.

Justin holds out a hand to Burns and does the strange grip, shake thing all men are subject to knowing. "Thanks for getting here so quickly," Justin says.

"Not a problem. We were just having breakfast at that strange café across the street when the dispatch came in. Good job calling it in so quick."

Burns shoots me a wink and struts back to his cop car like he's solved world peace and is looking forward to taking the rest of the day off.

"How'd you catch him?" I ask.

"You must have clocked him hard, because he barely made it to the end of the building. When he saw me, he started running. I got to him right in time." He lifts his arm to get a look at a strip of grazed skin speckled with dots of blood along the underside.

"Are you okay?" I say, turning over his arm to inspect it better.

"I'm fine," he says. "Just a little brush burn."

"You should at least disinfect it. Wash it out in the bathroom."

He smiles at my concern and shakes his head, having never lost the grin that's starting to become contagious. "You did good."

I'm not sure what he's talking about until he makes a swinging motion with his fist. "Oh, it was nothing. He actually kind of walked into it."

"Say what you want," he says, walking backward from me. "But he was still gasping for air when I tackled him."

I jog to catch up. "What's he being charged with?"

Justin turns forward when I reach him. "The knife should be enough to charge him with attempted murder, but the goal is to get him to confess that John Monroe hired him to scare you out of testifying, so they'll probably offer him a plea deal. That's what John Monroe gets for hiring a douche bag to do his dirty work."

"You don't think he'll send someone else, do you?"

Justin pauses. "I can't imagine he has many guys left. Lance was working under him for almost a year and he thinks most of the men fled when everything got raided."

"What exactly did Lance do for him? Sell?"

Justin bites the inside of his cheek. "There's a lot I don't even know, but from what he's told me, I assume it was a little of everything."

"That doesn't explain why he clung to Kaley so much, since he knew she didn't know anything."

"Nothing like that," he says, avoiding the obvious. "Kaley was becoming suspicious of John, and he had mentioned to Lance that he didn't want her getting too close to his work, so Lance volunteered to keep an eye on her for him."

"That's...awful," I say, trying to grasp how I would feel if Kip ordered someone to keep tabs on me.

"Lance didn't tell John much, other than whether or not she was snooping. Lance didn't want Kaley to know about John as much as John didn't. It's what's kept her out of this mess."

"You two skirt the rules a lot. I would say you don't take your jobs very seriously, except you still turned us in."

He stays looking ahead but becomes serious. "Don't accuse me of something you choose to stay ignorant to."

His words bite, and it's equivalent to throwing a bucket of ice water on my head. For a few minutes there, I forgot we're not on the same team. "It's corrupt," I say.

"All law enforcement and government agencies get away with a lot that people don't know about. It's not corrupt," he says. "It's the norm."

We walk back to the parking lot in silence, neither one of us acknowledging the other. I had also forgotten what it's like to receive Justin's cold shoulder, and I have to fight the urge to eradicate it. I hang on to it, focusing on the lies and deceit.

"Justin," I say as we're about to get into our separate vehicles. He's standing on the other side of my Honda, his hand braced against the inside of the SUV's door. "I have a question." He perks up at the prospect that I might want to understand this, him, a little more. "Did you ever actually get arrested for robbing a store?

Just like when he had to confess his real age, it takes him a moment to respond. "My dad was the chief of police. He was able to use a few connections, so I was never charged."

I purse my lips. "Was that before or after he got sober?"

"Before, why?"

I shrug my shoulders. "Just wondering."

I'm starting to gather that for the most part, Justin told the truth, or as close to the truth as possible. I'm struggling to cling to those tidbits of information and focusing on all of the inconsistencies. It's a dangerous thing to want the truth all the while hoping it doesn't make me question my decisions. It's so hard when everything is gray with black and white muddled in the middle. I need the divide between the two so there's no doubt.

I focus on the image of Kip behind the glass partition during visitation, and I hold on to it for my sanity.

I SPOKE WITH MY PROFESSORS, and they agreed to give me the rest of the semester's work via email. This is a blessing and a curse. I no longer have to worry about getting accosted at school, but now I have to learn all the information on my own, and take all my exams on one day. Can't pick and choose, I guess.

Kip met with the judge, and his bail was set higher than we can afford, but we already knew it would be. The good news is that the prosecutors are trying to expedite the process. They don't want a long, drawn-out preliminary meeting, so they're offering deals to the minor violations. John Monroe has turned down every deal they've thrown at him, aiming for as little to no jail time as possible, and the prosecutors want to get him to trial before his attorney can build a case. Not that they have much to worth with—the evidence is really damning. Lance recorded enough audio to not leave anything to question. John Monroe is going to prison. He's just deluding himself. His wife, on the other hand, is missing. Most likely still in Switzerland, hiding.

So they offered Kip a plea deal anyway. His arraignment is today, and I'm waiting to hear whether or not Kip took it and what it'll mean for his future. I'm sitting on a bench outside the courthouse, trying to ignore Justin's smoking habits as I wait to hear a word from Kip's public defender. That was an entirely different argument within itself as Kip refused to spend money on an attorney or allow me to visit him. He doesn't like me to see him incarcerated, but he's going to have to get used to it. There's a good chance he's going away for a long time, and I'm not going that long without seeing him.

But for now, I have to live with Justin's assurances that he knew a decent defender that would do right by Kip, and that's not saying much considering I trust him all of zilch. But for some ridiculous reason, Kip does, and that just rubs me the wrong way.

taking mine

I don't catch his name, but Kip's lawyer exits the courthouse wearing a brown suit that's baggy in all the wrong places. I'm not one to pay close attention to attire, but even I can't miss the atrocity that this man is wearing.

"Miss Foster," he says, reaching a sweaty hand for mine to shake.

I stand. "Yes?"

"Kip asked me to give you a rundown on what he decided and where he's headed from here."

"Okay."

I sit back down and he follows my lead. "The prosecutors offered Kip a very good deal. According to the evidence, he never actually transported the drugs or had them in his physical possession. He was simply an accomplice."

"But he didn't even know that," I say, trying to defend him.

"And that has all been presented to the court and taken into consideration. Same ethics, I'm afraid," he says. "From my understanding, Taylor Moore received a plea deal very similar."

"You still haven't explained what exactly they offered."

He opens his briefcase, pulling out a single piece of paper and passing it to me. "Kip pled guilty to two federal counts of conspiracy to transport fifty kilos of cocaine over state lines. He'll serve eight years in a federal penitentiary. He'll be eligible for parole in four."

It's as if I was standing in the courtroom and the sound of the judge's gavel ricochets through my body as he reads off the indictment. Eight years. He'll be over thirty before he's even considered for early release. But I knew the odds were stacked against him. It could have been worse. The maximum sentence reaches closer to twenty. And with the two counts, he really made out like a bandit. It's just the finality of it that stings.

The lawyer seems to let me process this before he says, "He'll be transported by the end of the day. You can visit him this weekend if you would like."

I blink back my emotions and fold my hands. "He's okay with that?"

The man smiles, and it's the first emotion he's shown since I've met him. "He said he knew you would anyway."

I smile. "He knows me so well."

He stands to leave. "I almost forgot," he says, digging in his suitcase once again. "He wanted me to give you this."

I pull the sheet from his hand. It's a savings account with far more money than I thought Kip possessed. "Wait, what is this? I mean, how?"

"It's an account that was opened by your father right before he died. I don't know the specifics, but everything you need to have to access to it is right there on that paper. You'll have to speak with Kip if you have any more questions."

I'm still staring at the paper in disbelief when I feel Justin sit down next to me, having all but forgotten he was even here.

He whistles. "That's a lot of money."

I nod, at a loss for words.

"What are you going to do with it?"

I shrug.

It's filled with more zeros than I thought my parents ever saw in their lifetime. My parents were poor when my dad died. He was just a mechanic making minimum wage. The only way he would have ever made this much money was if he was doing something illegal. It's extremely fishy that it was opened only a week before he was killed. Maybe Dad wasn't as innocent as we thought. It's still in his name, but Kip and I are down as authorized users.

"Justin," I say, breaking the silence. "What happened to your Jeep?"

He breathes deep before blowing it out through his nose, blindsided by my question, and equally annoyed. "Are you going to keep building your case against me, Lilly? Is that what you're doing? Only asking the questions that you know catch me in a lie?"

"It's a simple question."

"Don't deflect," he says. "You already gathered that it wasn't mine."

taking mine

He shakes his head, turning away from me. "Don't bother speaking to me until you're ready to see the truth, because I'm tired of your games."

"Really novel coming from you," I say to his retreating back.

This really pisses him off and he turns, punctuating every step back toward me. He leans over, using both of his arms to cage me in against the bench. "I never played games, Lilly," he says, his face turning redder by the second. "Everything I said and everything I did was because I was trying to protect you. If you need someone to direct your blame and anger toward, look at yourself."

My head physically snaps back from his words, and he doesn't even flinch. He pushes off the bench, his steely gaze locked on mine as he walks away, leaving me by myself for the first time in weeks. I look around to see if anyone noticed our interaction, but the front stoop of the courthouse is surprisingly vacant.

Good. No one can see the heartache that I'm trying to rope in as I force the lump in my throat down. I give myself five minutes. That's it. I center myself, concentrating on my feet contacting with the ground, and my heartbeat matching the rhythm.

Justin is pacing outside of his SUV, a cigarette between his lips when I approach, but I don't look at him as I pass by.

He says my name.

I ignore it.

He says it again.

I open my door and his hand slams it shut. It's like his words slowly come into focus and I catch the tail end of his sentence.

"...really sorry."

I try to concentrate on his face, but it takes too much effort, and I open my door and get in. He's saying something through the window, but it's muffled. I drive home, and I can't recall how I got here. I walk inside, Justin on my heels, following me as I undress. I climb into bed, and he sits at the foot, everything he says fuzzy around the edges. I fall asleep feeling like my grasp on reality is slipping, my life jumbled into pieces too confusing to put together.

chapter 18

THE CORRECTIONS OFFICER hands me back my ID, too bored and too busy to bother looking up from her paperwork to make sure I match my identity. With the amount of paperwork and background screenings it took to be approved, it's strange that it's so lax to actually get in the facility. The guard points to the rules hanging on the wall and tells me to read over them before I go through the metal detector. After a relatively personal pat down and pocket search, I'm directed through a door and into a room the size of a small cafeteria.

Kip stands from a table in the middle, smiling when he spots me. We hug, only briefly, the rules stating no contact longer than a few seconds, and we sit.

"You look good," I say, pleasantly surprised by his appearance. His hair is cut shorter than I've seen it in years, and he's wearing a uniform similar to scrubs.

"You look like hell," he says. "Have you been sleeping?"

"Yes, Kip."

"Don't roll your eyes at me. You look like you have two black eyes."

I self-consciously run my fingers under the bags I know are there. Personal experience has told me this doesn't work, they don't magically disappear, but I can still wish.

"School is giving me a run for my money." I chuckle, but it doesn't create the effect I was aiming for.

"Justin told me you're finishing off the semester from home because one of Jimmy's pissants attacked you in class."

I'm flabbergasted. "You talked to Justin? Why would you do that?"

taking mine

"Lilly, you won't tell me anything, and he's by your side twelve hours out of the day. If anyone knows what's going on, it's him. And it's on both sides of the equation."

"You have no right."

This triggers something in his calm facade. "Tell me that I don't have a right to know what's going on in your life when I'm the one who raised you," he says, pointing to the table with every word.

Kip's never used the pseudo-father excuse before. I've said it, he's acknowledged it, but he's never incited it himself. He never wanted to overstep our dad's memory or belittle it in some way. But it is what it is, and for Kip to use it now means he's at the end of his rope, so I need to give him some slack.

"Everything's fine. Attacked is an exaggerated term for what actually happened."

"He had a knife, Lilly."

"Yes, I was there," I say. "And why do people only say my name when they're mad at me?"

He sighs. "I don't want to fight. We only get an hour."

"You're absolutely right," I say. "We should talk about you. How's prison treating you?"

He smiles. "The food sucks, the people suck, and there's a perpetual shortage of toilet paper in the commissary."

I laugh. "Like on back order?"

"Purportedly I should be receiving my share sometime after Christmas. Lucky for me, my bunk mate has a thing for junk food, so I was able to trade two candy bars and a bag of chips for a roll."

"Are you bored? Do you need me to bring you some magazines or something?"

"I'm allowed to receive a monthly subscription, so I'm going to do that, and they sell mp3 players. They're supposed to be assigning me a job on Monday, so hopefully it'll give me something to do."

Kip's attempting to put on a brave face for me, and I need to give that to him. If I look like I'm falling apart or that I feel sorry for him, it'll only make things worse. Kip's a doer, and inside prison he can't do much of anything other than fret over all the things he can't change.

"So…were you ever going to tell me about the bank account Dad left?"

He runs his hands through his hair, folding his arms over the table. "I was going to tell you eventually. I didn't even know it existed until I went through all the paperwork I found in the hall closet a few years ago."

"That's a lot of money. Where would he have gotten it from?"

He gives me a look. "I don't know, but I never touched it. I mean, we were surviving without it."

"Barely," I say.

"We survived," he repeats. "But now it's yours."

"I don't know, Kip," I say, scared by the thought of possessing that much money.

He shakes his head, already gearing up to argue. He's probably already mapped out all the bullet points in his head. "No shop is going to hire a female mechanic and that's if you find anyone who will actually take you seriously. Once you get into graduate school, you won't be able to work, and you're going to need money to pay tuition and live on. You can't do that working as a waitress or at an ice cream shop."

"I'll pull out student loans."

He snorts. "That's your best argument? Are you sure law school is right for you?"

I dig the heels of my hands into my eyes. "Fine. But I'm only taking half. The other half is for you."

"Agreed," he says. "I'm going to need you to put money into my account every month if I'm going to keep having to bribe people for toilet paper."

We laugh, it's a little too loud, and a guard warns us to keep it down. "Lilly," he says, growing serious. "I need to tell you something."

"Kip, I really don't think I need any more surprises," I say, only partially joking.

His grimace looks painful when he says, "The raid at Toby's was a setup."

"Yeah...I've kind of gathered that," I say, sarcastic.

"No," he says, shaking his head. "Not in the way you think. Justin, um—" He pauses to clear his throat, and I find myself holding my breath at the sound of Justin's name. "I knew Justin was undercover."

Definitely not breathing. Matter of fact, I might be dead because there's no way in hell this is real life. "What," I mumble.

"Justin came to me after you found the evidence at the shipyard. He met me outside of Toby's the next day, saying he had something he needed to discuss with me. He explained that he was an agent undercover for the DEA and that we had gotten mixed up with a case they've been investigating on John Monroe, a prominent drug trafficker in the area." He pauses, giving me time to digest what he's told me so far. "He proposed a plan. I would set up a meeting with Jimmy to distract him from the DEA confiscating the evidence at the shipyard."

"The weekend Justin took me to meet his family," I clarify.

"Yes," he says. "We didn't want you to be near if it went bad."

"But it did."

He nods, solemn. "When Jimmy found out that his product was confiscated, he retaliated. He held Dan as ransom and demanded that we pay for the merchandise he lost plus interest in twenty-four hours, or he was going to kill him."

"How did Jimmy know who turned him in?"

"He didn't. Lance said we were just suspect."

"And how do we know that Lance wasn't the one that told him?"

"Because Lance tried to warn us that Jimmy was going to jump the gun. We scheduled to meet at Toby's and said we'd bring the money in exchange for Dan. Justin said it would be enough evidence to arrest Jimmy in the act."

"I was never supposed to be there," I say, the pieces falling into place.

"No," he says. "You were never supposed to be implemented in any way. Up to that point, Justin hadn't mentioned your name."

"It was always supposed to be you who got off scot-free with the plea deal," I say, horror slowly seeping into my veins.

Kip's smile is melancholy as he nods slowly. "Neither one of us was going to serve time."

Water pools in my vision and I shakily try to keep them at bay. "This is all my fault."

"No. No, Lilly. You just walked in at the wrong time. That's it. We should have told you what we were planning."

"Why didn't you?" I say. "It's not like I would have disagreed."

"Justin thought that if he went through with it, and everything turned out all right in the end—"

"That I would be able to forgive him for lying to me," I finish.

"He looks like shit, Lilly."

I know. I've seen him. It's an entirely different heartache now. This one is self-fulfilling.

THE SKY IS OVERCAST when I step out of the prison doors, but the glimpses of sunlight through the clouds hurt my sensitive eyes. Visitation ended over an hour ago, but I allotted extra time to refill Kip's account and to cry in the bathroom. I tried to reduce the swelling by splashing cold water on my face, but I double-checked, and I still look neurotic. At this point, I should just get used to it. The wind cuts into my freshly dried cheeks and I duck my face from the sting. The inside of my car is my shield as I start to get in. Justin's engine follows mine, and he exits the parking lot right behind me.

I only drive a few miles before I pull off the interstate and park behind a dingy bar that's closed for the day. I don't bother looking up as I open the passenger door to Justin's SUV when I get in.

"Can you do me a favor?" I ask, finally gaining the courage to meet his eyes. Shame fills me as I find weariness pasted across every inch of him. I've done that to him. I pull a folded note from my pocket and

taking mine

hand it to him. "Can you make sure Dan's wife, Melanie, gets this and the money that I left with you?"

"If that's what you want, of course."

I nod. "It is."

He retrieves his wallet and slides the paper in it, placing it in the middle console for safe keeping. I need to say something, but every quiet second expands in the confined space, and I fight the urge to chicken out. His thumb runs over his bottom lip and it makes me smile.

"What?" he says, a confused smirk kicking up the side of his mouth. "What are you smiling at?"

"Did they not teach you how to hide nervous ticks?"

He pulls his thumb back and looks at it. "I never realize when I do it."

Reaching over the middle, he cautiously runs that same thumb along my cheek. His touch is feather light, almost like he's worried it'll break me. "I'm so sorry," I say.

His lips part as he breathes in my words. His touch stills, and I lean into his hand, all but begging for him not to stop. "I shouldn't have said what I did at the courthouse."

I shake my head to stop his apology. "You were right. I should have heard you out, listened to what you had to stay. Instead, I wanted someone to blame and you let me use you as a target, and for that, I am so, so incredibly sorry."

His eyes soften. "I'll forgive you if you can forgive me."

I'm incapable of stopping my tears. "I already do."

He smiles, and it's more positive than what I feel, but I'm grateful nevertheless. His lips move toward mine, his eyes set on my mouth, and I want it more than I want to live at this very moment. I tell myself to stop it, but another part of me knows that if I walk away from this one point of contact, I'll walk away with one less part of him.

I inhale his breath, needing to take as much as I can, even though I've taken more than I deserve. He presses into me, and I push back, too needy to stop. The ache in me morphs from hurt to desire, and I cling to it. The reprieve is intoxicating, and I chase it over the console and into his lap. I position my legs around him as he pulls me down so I can feel him through the material of his jeans. We rock against each other, seeking more.

I fumble with the button of his jeans, and he slides the seat back, lifting his hips to give me better access. I cuss when I struggle to shake my shorts off, and he helps, leaving them wrapped around one ankle. Almost in the same motion that he slides his jeans down past his hips, he's in me, and we both freeze, absorbing the sensation of each other. Goose bumps break out across my body as I slowly rock back, and his fingers dig into my hips. His eyes are dilated, locked on our point of connection. I physically shake from how good it feels. I lock my hands around his neck, and he pulls my lips down to his, taking his time to enjoy our kiss.

"I love you."

He says it in a momentary break from his mouth on mine and immediately resumes kissing after. There is no opportunity to say it back, but I think it. It repeats when we speed up. It repeats when I cling to him as we finish. And it repeats now, as I drive my car back home, replaying his words in my head and wondering how those three words make everything worse.

chapter 19
four months later

THE WRENCH FALLS FROM MY HAND, and I narrowly avoid it landing on my face. Lying on hot asphalt while trying to change the air condenser in Kip's truck is really making me regret selling my car. But I wanted Kip to have his truck when he gets out, however long it is from now. I should have just paid someone to do it, but I know the outrageous fees a shop would charge for labor, and I couldn't bring myself to do it. Deciding it's time for a break, I slide out from under the truck and am greeted by the blinding smile of the next-door neighbor's grandson. The little twit hangs around like a puppy.

"Need any help, Mrs. Lilly?" he says, bouncing on the balls of his feet.

"No thank you, Cal. I was just about to get something to drink. Want to come inside for a few minutes and cool off?"

"Do you have any of that peach cobbler?" he says, his eyes lighting up.

I smear grease onto the tip of his nose, smiling at his phony attempt to be annoyed. "As long as you don't tell your grandpa. He'll kick my ass if you don't eat your dinner again."

"Don't worry about that, Mrs. Lilly. I learned my lesson on that one." I smile at the memory of Mr. Wilson bringing over Cal's unfinished plate of dinner and insisting that I eat it since I thought a seven-year-old should have dessert instead.

Cal skips inside the kitchen and hops up onto the counter, pulling down two glasses from the cupboard. I pour him a glass of milk and myself a lemonade before scooping us each a plate of sugary goodness. I watch Cal shovel too-large bites into his mouth, and it reminds me of the way Justin always eats—like he's starving.

It took a while, but eventually John Monroe went to trial. My testimony was nothing in comparison to the hours of footage and audio Lance was able to score while working under him, but I did my part nonetheless. He pled no contest, but it didn't stand, and he was found guilty of drug trafficking, arms trading, kidnapping, first-degree murder, and much, much more. The list goes on and on. Sentencing hasn't quite commenced, but there's no doubt he'll go away for an extremely long time.

I'm not quite sure how Kaley's faring since I haven't seen her since the day of the verdict. We stood outside the courtroom doors, trying to prepare ourselves for the onslaught of photographers that were waiting outside. The case blew up in the media, the community shocked by John Monroe's hidden life, and Kaley took the brunt of it. I asked her if she was going to be alright as she chewed a wad of gum between her teeth. She blew a bubble before replying, "Life's a bitch." And then she walked out of the courthouse, head held high and middle finger in the air.

I sold the house. Apparently it's not that hard to forge a name, bribe a notary, and send a few documents to the courthouse to get the deed in my name. The house needed work, and a buyer who was interested in the up-sale of the neighborhood offered cash, which saved a lot of hassle. We closed the day after the trial, making leaving much more efficient. Especially because it was the first day I was bodyguard free, Lance and Justin officially relieved of their duties.

I managed to pack the basics. My bed, books, and the brand new coffee maker I bought after raid-gate. By the time Justin caught me dropping the last box into the back of Kip's truck, everything was packed. He didn't say anything as he walked up the drive and leaned his hip against the tailgate, arms crossed over his chest. Things had been stressed between us since we had awkwardly gotten dressed in the front seat of the SUV. We spent the next few weeks tip-toeing around the issue at hand, and I honestly couldn't even pinpoint what the issue was, but I knew Justin was trying to give me space.

"You're leaving," he said, stating the obvious.

I nodded but avoided his eyes as I braced my arms against the truck. "Yeah."

"You weren't going to at least tell me bye?"

I shrugged. "I didn't know what to say."

This made him angry, and he pushed off the truck, turning away from me. "Kip told me you would run," he said, his voice deep.

"It's just like my brother to still be influencing my life from inside prison. I'm not running," I said in defense. "I'm trying to figure myself out."

"And why can't you do that here?" he said, facing me again. "I get that you feel like you're losing yourself. I get it." He splayed his hand across his chest, emphasizing his point. "But why do you feel the need to do it alone?"

"In order for me to feel like I'm losing myself, I would have had to find it in the first place. Being here," I said, motioning to the house, the neighborhood, the city, him. "Just makes me feel like I'm trapped. I need, for once in my life, to feel like I'm not stuck."

"Lilly, you're stronger than this."

His words hurt, because I knew he honestly believed them, but I knew better. I made my way past him and opened the door to the truck, getting in before he could argue me back out. Because, help me, I wanted him to. I wanted him to tell me he loved me again, and that I'm not the lost person that I saw myself as.

He braced his hands against the door, eyes pleading. "You can't just leave and take my heart with you."

"I'm not," I said, starting the engine and kicking it into gear. "I'm taking mine."

It still seeps in when I'm by myself, wondering how I'm managing to survive without him. For weeks, even though we weren't necessarily together, he was always there, watching over me. I had thought that being away from him would give me the opportunity to move on, to think without his presence clouding my judgment, but in reality it did the exact opposite.

Cal finishes his plate before I do, just like usual, and uses the rest of the time to swing his feet back and forth. "Grandpa said you need a man to fix your truck."

I cough on my bite of cobbler and wash it down with a large drink of lemonade. "Well," I say. "Tell your grandpa if he keeps putting his nose where it doesn't belong, the nosey monster is going to come and rip it off when he's sleeping."

Cal's feet still for a moment. "Nuh uh."

"Don't believe me? Ask him about it," I say, depositing our dishes in the sink.

He thinks about it for a few seconds and shrugs. "It doesn't matter because I told grandpa that you're the prettiest girl there is so it won't be hard for you to find one."

I smile. "You're the sweetest, but it's a little more complicated than that."

"No it's not. Grandpa said all you need to do is be nice and quit cussing."

I roll my eyes and shove him down from the counter. "Your grandpa's nose is in some real danger," I say. "You should run home and tell him to mind his own damn business."

His eyes grow big. "Are you trying to get me in trouble?"

I laugh as I march him outside. "Trust me, he'll be mad at me, not you. I've got to get back to work."

He groans but doesn't argue as he runs to the townhouse next door. It's a one-way street with townhomes lining one side and wooded trees along the other. It's a quiet neighborhood. I'm the last house, and if I had known Mr. Wilson would be such a hardass, I'd probably have looked for something else. Okay, that's not true. As much as Cal is annoying, he's cute, and he keeps me occupied on my bad days. And I can make him weed the flowerbeds out front, so that's a nice bonus.

taking mine

It takes me the rest of the day and a lot of cussing to finish putting the air compressor in. If I were stronger, it might have gone a little more smoothly, but either way I did it. I still have to go into town tomorrow to rent a vacuum to recharge it, but I've had enough for one day.

I pour bubble bath into the water dribbling from the antique faucet into the porcelain tub. The townhouses were all built in the fifties, and most of them still have the original fixtures, or at least mine does. The downside is they're tiny, and every room is subdivided. But it's mine, and mine alone, and that makes me happy. I slide into the water and sigh as the heat seeps into my muscles.

Today was a good day. I accomplished a lot. It's when I'm alone and have nothing to occupy my time when the loneliness creeps in. Living with Kip was never overly chummy, but he was always around. Either cooking or working on something, he stayed busy, making noise. Then living with Justin…

I don't allow my thoughts to go there. Every day I have the same goal—don't think about Justin—and every day I fail.

Sitting in silence is deafening. I've wondered how people born deaf don't go mad. I suppose it's because they're used to it. I hate it because it makes me think, and as much as I thought I needed space to think, it's actually something closer to torture. Guantanamo Bay should just put terrorists in a room by themselves for a few weeks, and then they'll be ready to talk to anybody willing to listen. That's why my only friend is a seven-year-old who likes me because I bake him sweets.

I'm in the bath for so long that the water starts to turn cold and my stomach grumbles, reminding me that I've only eaten dessert today. I get out, brush my hair, get dressed, and head downstairs to fix something to eat. The first couple of months I lived on eating the bare minimum. It was after my thousandth cup of noodles that I committed myself to learning how to cook. I still don't care for it, or the clean-up part, but I love the eating aspect.

Turning on the radio, I rifle through my fridge, pulling the ingredients for a quick skillet recipe. I have to admit, as much as cooking is monotonous, it's therapeutic. It's the quickest way I can garner a proud moment for myself when a new dish comes out just right. Like, hell yes, I made this creamy pesto chicken caprese casserole. It's just a fancy way of saying baked chicken pasta slathered in tomato sauce, but that's beside the point. I can make it, and I'm awesome.

A heavy pounding on my door makes my stomach drop. No doubt Cal opened his big mouth to Mr. Wilson and I'm about to get a verbal spanking. Grudgingly, I trudge to the door, an apology already poised on my lips when I open it. But all speech leaves me at the sight of the woman standing there.

She's just as intimidating as I remember her, and I instinctively take a step back. "Tess."

"Lilly," she says with a mild tone.

Why is she here? "Is everything okay?"

"Everything's fine. Can I come in?"

"Can I say no?" I ask, only half joking.

"No," she says, but this time with a real smile.

She steps in, and I close the door behind her. "The kitchen is to the left," I say, trying to avoid the mountain of laundry piled on the living room couch.

She sits at the tiny kitchen table I found at a resale shop and looks around. Her eyes stop on the only item I have magnetized to the refrigerator, and I want to dive across the room to block her sight of it. Instead, I try my best to act like a sane human being, and continue my work on dinner. I turn down the heat to prevent the butter from burning.

"What are you cooking?" she says, peering over the counter.

"Chicken."

She points to the breasts I have marinating in a bowl. "You should butterfly those so they cook evenly."

My knife freezes mid cut. "Did you come here to give me cooking pointers, or is there something you have to say?"

Her eyes narrow, lashes so thick I can't see her pupils, but I know they're drilling daggers into me. I brace myself, but surprisingly, she relaxes. "I always knew that whenever Justin decided to finally bring a girl home, she'd be the one."

My heart pumps furiously in my chest. Just being within proximity of someone who's a part of his life kicks it into gear. Hearing her say his name is almost too much to bear. Realizing that I'm not able to concentrate, I cut the stove off.

"Look, Tess," I say.

She cuts me off. "I didn't want it to be you," she says. "When he first told me about you, I immediately didn't like you."

"This is going so well," I say, garnering a laugh. "You knew everything before you even met me?"

"Not much. Justin only told me the bare minimum, that you've had a difficult life and that I shouldn't judge you for that."

I huff through a humorless laugh. "I was so nervous about meeting you, about making a good impression, and you'd already made your mind up about me."

"I was wrong, I admit it, but I wouldn't have given you that recipe," she says, pointing to the paper hanging from the refrigerator, "if I didn't absolutely know that my son loved you."

The paper is folded into sixths from when she slipped it to me when Justin and I left after visiting.

Let's get to the point. "What do you want?"

She drops her hands. "I honestly don't even know. All I know is that my son isn't happy, and I want someone to fix it. Do I think you're worthy of his love?" She shakes her head. "But it doesn't matter. Only you matter to him."

"You're right," I say, meeting her eyes. "I'm not good enough for him. How can I live with that every day?"

She sighs, trying to think of a way to explain something. "You know, when Bruce decided to get sober, our relationship struggled more than it did when he wasn't. We fought constantly because he wanted me to leave him." I give her a look and she nods, waving her hand in the air. "I know, I know. Sounds ridiculous. But it was his own personal vendetta against himself, and he thought I deserved better."

"Well," I say. "You did."

She shrugs. "Maybe, but I didn't think so. And I couldn't figure out why he just wouldn't let me love him. That's all I wanted to do."

"But that's kind of self-mutilating on your behalf, right? Why would you want to love someone who constantly hurts you?"

"Because I knew that he had intentions to never let it happen again. I knew that his heart outweighed all of his wrongdoings. And Lilly," she says, making sure she has my attention. "What you did wasn't all that bad. Lashing out was to be expected, and it's obvious it'd be directed at the person you love the most. In fact, Justin blames himself for not trusting you with the truth in the first place. Maybe you two would have been spared all of this mess."

I shake my head. She doesn't understand. "It's so much more than that."

"How so?"

"I've never—" I clear my throat, uncomfortable with what I'm about to reveal. "I don't know how to love someone."

Her eyes soften, and I turn my eyes away from the pity. "That's the wonderful thing about falling in love," she says with a wry smile. "Someone can help you figure it out.

"I'm just trying to find myself," I say, knowing that I sound like a parrot by this point.

"I can guarantee you, you're not going to find how by secluding yourself." She walks to the fridge and takes down the piece of paper. "And I'm taking this back until you gain some sense."

I throw a hand up. "I have it memorized anyway."

She looks at me, dubious. "Did you perfect the caramelized sugar on top?"

I open the fridge and retrieve the bowl. "You tell me."

She peels the film back and breaks a piece of the crust off. "It could be better."

I'm about to tell her she's delusional, that I've made it every week for four months, when there's more knocking on the door.

taking mine

"Were you expecting someone?" she says, eyebrows raised. "It's almost nine o'clock."

I roll my eyes. "No, I was not."

She walks with me to the door, taking the bowl with her. I open the door to find Mr. Wilson wearing an angry mug and holding a plate of brussel sprouts. "Mr. Wilson," I say, not at all feeling the sweet smile on my face.

"Don't you Mr. Wilson me, young lady. After thirty minutes of trying to coerce Cal to eat his vegetables, he confessed that you're feeding him more of your asinine peach cobbler."

I drop my head back. "I told him to keep his mouth shut."

"No, I believe what you specifically told him to do was to tell me—"

Tess shoves the bowl at the old man. "That she wanted you to have the rest." Mr. Wilson is taken back by Tess's interruption. "It's the best cobbler, hands down, and if you hate it, you can keep the bowl.

I give her a look.

Mr. Wilson looks down at the plastic-wrapped container and back to me. "Well...that's awful nice of you."

Tess smiles. "How old is your son?"

"Grandson," he corrects. "He's seven."

"That's the hardest age for picky eaters. If you just throw a little cheese on top of those sprouts, he'll eat them right up. It's the only way I could get my boys to eat them growing up."

"I'll take that into consideration," he says.

"It was nice meeting you, but I've got a long drive home, so I'm going to head out." She looks at me pointedly. "I look forward to seeing you, Lilly." We watch her get into her car and back out of the driveway.

"I'll have Cal return the bowl as soon as we're done."

"No hurry," I say, trying to close the door. "Goodnight, Mr. Wilson." I peek out the eyehole and watch him stand there for a moment, staring at the bowl in his hands. I catch a small smile as he briefly looks up and walks away.

rachel schneider

IT'S BEEN TWO WEEKS since Tess showed up at my house and dropped a colossal wrench in my engine. The thought of Justin being just as miserable as I am makes me giddy. In turn, I'm reaching new levels of shame for finding pleasure in it. What kind of person finds joy in knowing the person they love is miserable? Me. I'm selfish and I admit it.

I'm a mess.

I'm up and down and back and forth and everything in between. Yesterday I had somehow convinced myself that I'll be an awful lawyer, and was set on marching into admissions today to switch my major to something more accomplishable, like accounting or history. Then I woke up this morning and realized I'm just being a wimp, and I need to pull my shit together.

What would I even say if I was confronted with the chance to see Justin again? *I'm sorry for running away like a scared baby? You were right. I should have been stronger than that. I should have stayed and come to grips with everything I felt between us.*

He knew before I did that I loved him, and I have no doubt that he knew it when I left.

All this time I've been trying to remain steadfast in my beliefs, and I can't help but wonder if we've both been miserable for nothing. If I give in now, it would feel like I did it to be frivolous and childish. Maybe I did, but I want to stand on my own two feet. I need to prove that my happiness isn't dependent on someone else, which is redundant because sometimes I feel like I'll never be happy with myself.

And if I'm being truthful, another new goal of mine, a sliver of me is still peeved at the thought that our relationship was based on false grounds. I've tried to shove it down, to be understanding, to see the bigger picture, but it only leaves a bitter residue around my heart. I thought I could let it go. I even left thinking I already had, but I can add liar to my growing list of poor attributes.

taking mine

I re-tuck my hair behind my ear for the millionth time today as I scan the breakfast options available.

"The cream cheese danish." The guy behind the counter points to the pastry all the way to the right. "It's the only one you haven't tried."

His hair is scraggy, blending into the beard hanging from his chin, and a flash of silver dangles from the center of his nose. "I guess I'll have the danish," I say.

Even as miniscule of a decision as it is, I'm marginally relieved. People behind me in line are probably happy as well to move forward. He rings up my order, and I feel a need to thank him for helping me, so I do. There's possibly a smirk behind the forest of hair covering his mouth when he says, "Ah, every day you come in here and stare at the food like it's a do-or-die decision. I figured, why not help you out, take a little stress off your back."

"Well, thank you," I repeat.

I'm crossing the threshold, holding the pastry between both of my hands, when a very important thought occurs. If I am grateful for a stranger making a small decision for me, or leading me toward one, why am I so hell-bent on not allowing Justin to do the same?

I've spent the better half of my life relying on Kip, and I thought since he's gone that I'd need to prove myself. Prove that he did a good job and I'm not some helpless girl who fumbles through life.

Justin inadvertently stepped into the same role. He kept things from me. No matter how noble his intentions were, it only brought those feelings to the surface. I don't want to be a pet project. I want to be wanted. How will I ever know the difference if I can't fend for myself?

But who said I can't stand on my own and lean on someone when I need to?

Oh yeah.

I did.

chapter 20

"CAN I COME?" Cal says, his fingers curling over the top of my driver side window.

"No," Mr. Wilson and I say at the same time.

"But why not? I want to ride the zip line."

Okay, so in my nervousness, I may have blabbed a little to Cal about where I was going. I didn't tell him any specifics about why I was driving six hours, only that it's really cool. It's kind of what I get when my best friend is a seven-year-old.

"Maybe another time," I say, ruffling his hair.

He pouts and drops back to his feet, letting go of the window. "You owe me an extra plate of cobbler when you get back."

I smile. "There's already a plate waiting for you at home. I made it this morning."

His eyes light up marginally, but Mr. Wilson, ever the downer, shuts it down when he says, "You have to each your lunch first."

I wave and they wave back, standing in my front yard and watching me depart for the longest, most thought-provoking drive of my life.

After leaving the coffee shop yesterday, I went straight home and packed a bag, then remembered that I had two assignments due by midnight. So I convinced myself to wait a day. Right before dinner, I received a package addressed from out of state. It was from Kaley, and it contained the Christmas presents I had bought Kip and Justin. There wasn't a note, but a picture she had taken in front of the Eiffel tower, blowing a kiss to the camera.

So here I am, driving six hours to Justin's childhood home and hoping he lives nearby. Tess made it seem like she sees him all the

taking mine

time, so that's what I decided, and I'm sticking to it. I'm tired of myself and my wishy-washy emotions and how they conflict with what my head is telling me. It's exhausting.

As the miles tick down, I get more anxious. I purposefully refuse to think about what I'll say because it'll just cause doubt, and I need all the confidence I can muster. I emailed Kip last night to let him know I'd be gone for a day or two, and he emailed me back to make sure I bring a spare tire. I've been keeping him up to date since he only lets me visit once a month. The good thing about federal prison is the email access. I moved closer to him so that I wouldn't be making a long drive to visit, and now he won't even let me see him. He apparently thinks my life is more interesting than it is, considering my Saturdays are jam packed with reruns of Family Feud, cooking, and procrastinating on doing laundry.

The road leading to Justin's house is longer than I remember, and with every bend my heart grows in size. Every inch I get closer, the higher my heart rate picks up. It's like it knows he's so close. The house comes into view, and I let out a breath as I park, dust flying up around the windows and settling onto the windshield. Jacob appears from behind the screen door, his face masked in shadow until he pushes it open and steps out into the light. There's no smile or welcoming, a mask of indifference clouding his eyes, and it eerily reminds me of Justin.

It does nothing to calm my nerves. We're in a standoff, so I speak first, "Hey, Jacob."

He scrubs his jaw with the palm of his hand, giving me nothing in return.

"Justin wouldn't possibly be here, would he?"

Tess appears in the doorway behind him, a smile lighting up her face, at complete odds with her son's reaction. "Lilly," she says, walking onto the porch. "I was starting to worry that you were dumber than I thought."

I weigh my head. "I feel dumb."

rachel schneider

Her smile grows. "That's good," she says. "Justin's in the orchard with Bruce. They've been working on a down harvester all day, but I can take you on the buggy."

"I'd like that."

"No," Jacob says, taking the steps toward me. "I'll take her."

Intimidating was never an adjective I'd have used when thinking of Jacob, until he walks straight past me with his head down. I give Tess a look and she shrugs, absolutely unrepentant about dumping me with her seemingly peeved son. Gearing myself up, I follow Jacob to the barn, his back to me the entire time. He slides himself into what appears to be an off-road go-kart, and I get in, thinking I'd normally be much more excited about riding if it weren't for the circumstance.

"Are you going to do it again?" Jacob says, looking at me.

"I can't make any promises. I'm a mess, Jake," I say, not wanting to lie to him. "All I can tell you is that the past four months have been the most miserable learning experience of my life."

He lets that sink in for a moment and nods.

I stop his hand from turning the key. "And I love him."

This does a little better of a job convincing him, his smile cracking the hard exterior he's fronted. "You're not very good at words, are you?"

I laugh. "No, I don't think so."

He starts the buggy and we zoom through the line of lemon trees. He takes a left turn, and I'm confused as to how he knows how to navigate where we're going, turning again at a gap in the foliage. The trees change into vines of grapes, going as far as the eye can see, the slope of the land dropping.

"This is the first year we've cultivated them," Jacobs says, his voice raised above the howl of the engine. "That's why Dad and Justin have been busting ass to fix the harvester. If we want to see a profit, we need a good picking." He makes one last turn and they come into view.

A large tractor straddles the row of grapevines. Justin and his father high-five, huge smiles across their faces, proud as the engine kicks into gear. He looks so happy. Tess lied. He's doing perfectly fine. Can I turn around and go home?

taking mine

Jacob's smile is sweet when drops me off, and I'm pretty sure I grimace, making him laugh. The buggy whips up dust as Jacob swings it around, flying in the direction we came from. The sound of the retreating engine must garner their attention, because they look up at the same time.

Justin's smile falls from his face.

He straightens from his position over the machine, his feet balanced on the wheel as he turns around. He's shirtless, and tan, and much leaner than I remember. His face is more defined, with a deeper skin tone that people only get after spending copious amounts of time in the sun.

Bruce says something, and Justin nods a reply before hopping off the massive tire, his body taut as he lands. He wipes his hands on the legs of his jeans as we he walks toward me, stopping within arm's reach.

"You cut your hair."

I don't know what I was expecting him to say, but that wasn't it. Shy, I reach up and pull a strand into view. It took me a while to get used to not being able to put it into a ponytail, and now I've completely forgotten about it.

"Do you like it?"

I can't stop my smile. "No."

A hint of a smile appears before he snuffs it out. His eyes trail up my legs and over my body, quickly but not overtly. "You look good," he says, squinting against the sun.

"You too," I say, sure I sound out of breath.

He wipes his hands again, turning to check on his dad before turning back around. "What are you doing here, Lilly?"

My name is stern on his lips and it guts me. "I don't know."

I need him to read me. I need him to see what I'm feeling so I don't have to voice it. I need him to know how sorry I am. Of all the times I have turned away from his ability to perceive what I'm feeling, I'm begging for it now.

"We can walk to my place from here."

He picks up a water bottle and a t-shirt, tossing the shirt over his shoulders and taking a sip. His eyes stay locked on mine as he swallows, and he holds the bottle out to me in offering. I decline. There's so much between us that it feels empty.

"This is the edge of the property. I live in a studio apartment right down the hill." He points, and I can vaguely make out a small structure on the other side of the fence line.

After a few paces, I speak. "You and your dad look like you're getting along."

"Yeah," he says with an ounce of uncertainty. "As long as we keep things superficial, we're fine. It's the past we can't agree on."

I swallow. "You haven't forgiven him?"

"It's not forgiveness that's the problem," he says, looking at me. "It's like being in remission. It takes time and a few slips before you finally feel like you're standing on steady ground."

We walk the rest of the way in silence, and I mimic Justin as he toes off his shoes at the door of his apartment. Once I'm inside, it's equivalent to being transported to another universe. Where his apartment and childhood bedroom was void of any personality, his apartment is overflowing with it. A bed sits in the far right corner with a headboard covered in books. The kitchenette on the other side has copper pots and pans hanging from the ceiling, the cabinets stained a rustic color, and strange granite covering the counters. Nothing matches, but everything somehow fits. If there's one thing similar to the apartment, it's the flat screen hung up on the opposite wall, able to be viewed from the bed and the threaded couch nestled in the middle of the room.

I walk to his bed, looking over all the paperbacks and textbooks stacked in the shelving outlets. On top, there's a tin box with metal toy soldiers stationed across the lid, all in varying positions. I go to pick one up when Justin stops me.

"They have lead in them," he says, still standing by the door, watching me take in his tiny apartment.

"This is nice," I say, looking around. "Different."

taking mine

"It used to be a storage shed," he says, shrugging. "When I came back from training, the owners let me convert it."

"Training?"

"Yeah. It's similar to basic training that the military go through, except more competitive."

I'm disjointed, being in his surroundings and it looking nothing like the person I thought I knew. He has everything from Stephen King and Dean Koontz novels to a textbook on Modern Art. A gaming station sits under the flat screen with popular football games stacked on top. A pile of dirty clothes litters the floor at the foot of his bed, completely opposite the state of the apartment.

I need something to ground me, to remind me that he's still Justin, and there's only one way I know how. I walk toward him, and his eyes hold mine as I shakily place the tip of my fingers against the fabric of his shirt. Maybe if I just touch him, I can gain traction. He breathes deep as I run my fingers over the expanse of his chest, up to his shoulder, and trailing down. I reach the skin of his bicep and he swallows. Not thinking, I stand on my toes and place a kiss on the arch of his neck. It's a brave move on my part.

Justin pulls away, gripping my hand and trapping it between his fingers. "What are you doing here, Lilly?"

I choke down the hurt from his rejection. "I, um…"

I can't look at him as I try to find words for something I don't even understand myself. I feel more than see the coldness rolling off of him, but he wavers as he watches me struggle. Letting out a breath, he takes a seat on the couch, bracing his forearms against his knees.

"Lilly." He says my name again. "I'm only going to ask you one more time."

"I'm not good with words," I rush out, fear settling in. "If you would just let me show you—"

"What?" he says, derision suffocating his voice. "Like you showed me that day in the car?" It's a slap to the face and he knows it. He looks away. "It took a whole week for you to even acknowledge me after that, and the entire time I was asking myself what I did wrong. I had convinced myself that you just needed time to cope, get used to the idea of being with me on top of everything. But really, you had already decided that you wouldn't."

"No, that's not it at all," I say, scooting closer to him. "I didn't know how I felt, I just knew I felt too much. I was scared. I was terrified that you deserved better and that I would never be someone who could stand next to you. All the while, I was trying to figure out what decision was right for me."

"It's not about what's right for you, Lilly. It's about what you want, and no one can tell you that but you. I probably played my hand a little unfairly, but I never pushed you. You made every decision on your own. You just needed to be confident in them."

I process what he says before replying. "You remember when you told me that I didn't know how to trust myself?"

He looks at me, nodding perceptively.

"I realized you were right, and I hated it. Not that you were right, but that I never gave myself the chance. I think, in a way, I crippled myself trying to better myself. The truth is, I have no idea who I am, but now I know who I don't want to be…and I think that's more important."

Slowly, his face transforms, and he says, "Why are you so fucking—"

"Difficult?"

"Beautiful." He smiles, and if my heart could, it would melt. "And difficult," he adds. I laugh, and he wraps a hand around the back of my neck, drawing my mouth up to his. "And smart." He kisses me. "And sexy." Another kiss. "And in so much trouble with my mom."

I break away, laughing. "I think I can handle her."

"What happened to being intimidated by her?"

I place an open-mouth kiss along his throat and feel his grasp tighten. "I proved that I make a better peach cobbler than her. Did I ever tell you how attractive I think your neck is?"

"What?" He laughs.

"I've probably spent way too much time fantasizing about your neck."

taking mine

He pulls back, looking down at me. "That's so weird," he says. "Of all my amazingness, you think my neck is the best?"

"Of course not," I say, reaching for the button of his pants. "You have decent arms."

He gazes down at me. "God, I missed you."

I don't wait, loving the adoration in his eyes, feeling the need to give the same in return. "I love you. And I know I've got a lot of making up to do, but we'll work on it, together. Like remission."

He swallows. "You can start by repeating that."

"I love you," I say, running my fingers over his jaw.

"I love you, too," he says, placing a feather-light kiss on my forehead.

We kiss slowly, gradually increasing pressure in the process. I sit up, and he peels my shirt off before doing the same to his. Leaning over, he kisses along the curve of my shoulder, down my chest. It's slow, and careful, but it's exactly what we need. He unbuttons my shorts and drags them down my legs, trailing his mouth over my exposed skin. I run my hands through his hair as his mouth lands on the part of me that seemingly needs him most. He gives everything to me, and it reminds me of the night before everything fell apart. This is a do-over, our do-over.

He disposes of his jeans and repositions himself above me, hiking my knee up to his hip as he slowly enters me. We don't speak, our eyes locked on one another as we collectively let out shaky breaths. It's amazing, and I don't need to second-guess whether this is what I want or what I need, but it's just right.

Afterwards we lie on the couch, unmoving, half his body still on top of mine. Neither one of us makes an effort to move, comfortable with every inch of our skin touching.

My words come out raspy when I say, "How are we going to commute?"

He leans up on his forearm. "We won't. I'll move to Brighton."

"How do you know where I live?" He gives me a look. "You're right, dumb question. But what about your job? How does that work?"

His lips thin, and I'm scared of what he's about to say, a trickle of uncertainty. How often does he go on jobs? Who's to say how long he'll be gone?

"I no longer work for the department," he says.

"What, since when?"

"Since I pulled the trigger on the investigation. The case was aiming to get Lance to the higher-ups, who John Monroe was working for, so they could pinpoint when the drugs were entering the country. When Kip's and my plan fell through, and with what happened to Dan, it kind of forced my boss's hand."

"I'm confused. When were you let go?"

"Right after you were released."

I sit up, forcing him to do the same. "Did you know you would be fired?"

"It was insinuated."

"Justin—"

"Lilly." He says my name with a smile. "It's fine. I've got enough savings to get me by, and I'll find a police department near Brighton."

"What about the farm? Jacob said you've been helping your dad harvest."

"We should be done by the end of the month." He pulls me into his embrace, breathing into the crook of my neck. "It'll be just in time for graduation."

I relax. This is what I need, someone to talk me down from the ledge of insanity.

"Can I ask you something?" I say, pulling away. He looks at me expectantly. "Why did you strip in front of the whole class?"

He laughs and pulls a strand of hair out from behind my ear. "First rule of being an undercover cop—do something a cop wouldn't do."

"That makes sense."

"And I may have been showing my ass a little, hoping to get your attention."

"You did a great job."

"Lilly, I was technically never undercover."

"I'm lost."

He sits, dragging my feet into his lap and massaging them. "I was working on the case with Lance, but I wasn't in the field. I just happened to accidentally run into you that day at the café."

"But..."

"You intrigued me." He shrugs with a shy smile. "When we first started surveillance on Kaley, we kept an eye on you. If Kaley knew something, we figured you would too. After a while, Lance came to the conclusion that neither you nor Kaley knew anything, and we were scheduled to stop the detail. That is, until the night you stole the Mustang from Blackjack's."

"I didn't steal it," I say.

"No, you got Dan to steal it. But Lance caught wind of it the next day in John's office. That's when we learned about John's involvement with Toby's and the deal he was making to Taylor."

There's something that's been bothering me, and right now is the perfect time to bring it up. "The Toyota..."

"Bait car," he says, smiling.

I take a second to absorb all this new information. "But how did you know where to put it?"

"Simple. We found the locations with the highest rate of stolen vehicles and followed you to be sure."

"Then what was with the cop?"

"Coincidence."

I lie back down, processing everything. Justin's fingers dig into my instep, and my foot arches at the touch. "So at first you were just into me," I say, staring at the ceiling.

"Yes. And then things got complicated, but at that point I had already made my interest known, so backing off wasn't an option."

"Wow," I say after a moment. "Just wow."

He trades feet. "Remember the day you showed up at my apartment? You were stressed out about school and you just wanted to hang out." He laughs, finding something humorous. "I was so scared to be alone in the same room with you. I remember thinking that there was no way I was going to make it through the night."

"Is that why we went bowling?"

"It was the only thing I could think of that didn't require touching."

chapter 21

THE TAXI PULLS INTO THE DRIVEWAY, and I can't stop the excitement bubbling in my chest. I graduate tomorrow, and he made it here just in time.

"He's super tall," Cal says, standing beside me.

"He only seems tall because you're so short."

Justin doesn't bother to retrieve his luggage as he gets out of the car and envelops me in a hug, spinning me around in the process. It's been three weeks since I returned home, leaving him to finish helping his dad for the season. Finishing the semester is tough as it is with senioritis kicking in, but anticipating Justin's move only added to my excitement.

He sets me on my feet, and Cal takes the opportunity to introduce himself. "Hey, I'm Cal."

Justin's forced to step back, but he takes it in stride, squatting closer to Cal's level. "I'm Justin. Lilly's told me a lot about you."

Cal's parents are no longer in the picture, and Mr. Wilson has been fighting tooth and nail for the state to officially award him custody. Cal's been in a state of limbo, and after watching foster care try to step in a few times, it gave me an idea of where I might like to be in a few years.

"That's because I'm her best friend," Cal says, pointing to his chest with his thumb, an air of arrogance in his posture.

Justin raises an eyebrow. "She told me that. She also told me that you and I might have something in common." Cal waits, a look of indifference crossing his boyish features. "Do you have a craving for some peach cobbler?"

It's like Justin declared war as Cal's face turns numerous shades of pink. "I'm not sharing," he says, all but putting his foot down.

Justin's taken back as he stands from his crouched position. "He's territorial, isn't he?" he says, giving me a look.

I grimace through a smile. "I've never seen him like this."

Mr. Wilson steps out of his front door, calling Cal's name for dinner.

Cal groans, dropping his head back at the same time. "But I'm not hungry."

"You're lucky you even got a chance to visit. You're still punished, young man." Mr. Wilson points at the ground.

Cal doesn't say bye as he drags his little feet home. He looks so sad, and it squeezes my heart. I say his name to get his attention. "We're still on for the zoo next week?"

He smiles. "Heck yes."

Mr. Wilson pulls him inside and gives me a look. "You are a bad influence," he says, shaking his head.

"But you love me," I say.

He doesn't respond as he flips his wrist in the air, neither agreeing nor disagreeing with my statement.

"How does a seven-year-old get in trouble?" I bite my lip, afraid to say it, and Justin grows suspicious in my silence. "Lilly," he says, drawing my name out and wrapping his arms around me.

"He may or may not have been caught stealing other kids' lunch money." His eyes widen. "But it's all circumstantial," I say, trying to reason.

"You really are a bad influence." He laughs.

The taxi honks, completely forgotten about, and Justin jogs over to pay and retrieve his suitcase. He hands me a duffel bag, the same one he brought to the shipyard, and he carries the rest. We drop the bags right by the door as Justin takes in his new residence.

"It's small," I say, feeling a little self-conscious.

He smiles at me, placing the first kiss on my lips since arriving. "It's perfect."

"We can get something bigger after I finish school—"

"Lilly, quit."

I sag in his arms, relieved. "It's just...you came all the way here to move in with me and you might not like it and I just want you to be happy and—"

This time he silences me with a kiss, and he doesn't let up until he's satisfied that I quit rambling. "I brought something for you."

"Like a gift? What for?"

He walks to the duffel on the floor and retrieves something in his hand. It's not until he's closer that I recognize what it is. It's a toy car that's been painted the lightest shades of pink, and it's an exact replica of the car we saw at the charity event. The one that I said resembled a life-sized Hot Wheels car.

Smiling through tears, I clutch it in my fist. Justin's face slowly transforms into concerned boyfriend when he noticed, caught off guard by my reaction.

"Is it okay?"

I laugh. "Yes. Just stay right here." I run up the stairs, retrieving the overnight bag that I never unpacked, and find what I'm looking for. When I make it downstairs, Justin's lounging on the couch with a stupid grin on his face.

"I bought this when I went Christmas shopping with Kaley." I drop the tiny cop car into the palm of his hand.

He stares at it a moment before slowly sitting forward, rotating it in his hand. He makes a fist around it, looking up at me from his position with eyes full of wonder. "If you had any doubt that we're not right for each other, or that maybe me moving in isn't the right decision, this should convince you otherwise."

I smile as I sink onto his lap. "There's no doubt. Matter of fact, I have no doubt that you're going to be on laundry duty until the day you die."

He laughs. "As long as you do the cooking."

"Best decision I've ever made."

We kiss, and I know we'll be okay. Better than that, we'll be happy, because that's what we are for each other. We're just right.

the end

acknowledgements

I SUPPOSE I SHOULD START WITH MY HUSBAND, Marlon, for encouraging me to pursue my dreams, and without even caring whether or not I'm good at it. You inspire me to love without conditions and prove that it is, indeed, possible with every day that you love me.

Alicia, dedicating this book to you should be enough, but we both know it's really, really not. This book wouldn't have happened, our friendship wouldn't be where it is today, and you'd miss out on my awesomeness. So thank you.

Mom, thank you for giving birth to me. I'm not kidding. I wouldn't be where I am, who I am, or as happy as I am without your love.

Myriah, forever and a day ago I begged you for help in your car expertise and coolness. Intentional or not, I found myself using you as inspiration for Lilly, which may weird you out considering there are sex scenes. Get over it.

Murphy, thank God I scored you as my editor/graphic designer because I would have been lost without someone who was willing to put up with my ignorance. Thank you for the encouragement, sacrifice, and patience you bestowed upon me. I'm so sorry.

Book Swapper's, thank you for being the most giving, accepting, smartass group of book friends I could have ever met. Thank you, Sara Ney (last name rhymes with shy) for your help with figuring out my dedication and this acknowledgement, because I still don't know what I'm doing. Christine Kuttnauer, thank you for your awesome voice messages and your ability to pinpoint everything I missed.

Krisitin, I kind of thank you, kind of hate you, kind of love you, kind of don't. You understand.

Elaine, thank you for being the most awesome formatter I could have ever scored.

Marie, thank you for your legal advice and explaining why distributing drugs is the worst idea ever.

Ramzi, thank you for putting up with my technologically challenged self, and for holding back every smartass retort that ran through your mind.

Sara, thank you for editing this last minute and encouraging me online. You're the best.

And thank you to everyone that read this book. Hopefully, most of you loved it, and enjoyed reading Lilly and Justin's story. But let's be real, there's a number of you who hated it. If you're one of those people, raise your hand, because y'all rock, too.

Made in the USA
San Bernardino, CA
26 March 2016